To all those that know me; I owe you something for putting up with me, and I offer this.
I didn't have to write it, and you don't have to read it.
Choice is one of the greatest gifts; I place it firmly in your hands.

Christie Barton

The characters and names in this novel are fictitious; any resemblance to persons living or dead is coincidental.

Self-published by Christine Barton, with CreateSpace.

First printing in 2016.

ISBN-10: 1530365988

ISBN-13: 978-1530365982

Reasonable doubt

by Christie Barton

The prologue, June 2012
Mixology

AT THE FAR END of the beach three dark figures lurked in the shadows. Their faces lit up briefly as a sweet-smelling cigarette passed between them, leaving a haze under the tall palms; too distant from the complex to cause any bother.

Seeping light into the night sky, the hotel stood out from the bay like a twinkling beacon. Oliver checked his watch, and quickly logged out. Hurrying from the internet room, he raced along the smart corridors, crossing the foyer and passing the restrooms on the way to the Piano Bar. Pausing to compose himself at the entrance he adopted a pained expression. Cate was still talking to the Scottish couple. Spotting her husband by the door her eyes indicated that she needed rescuing.

"You've been ages," she hissed when he finally saved her from the enthusiastic Glaswegians. "Are you ok? You're sweating."

"I might need to go again later," said Oliver, smiling weakly and holding his stomach. "I think it must've been the prawns."

"Well, I'm ok. For a moment I thought you sneaked off for another session with your emails."

"What's their cocktail like?" he said, ignoring the suggestion.

"Bloody awful," laughed Cate, discreetly pointing to a brown drink adorned with fruit. "The Cocky Choccy, apparently."

"It looks like the contents of my stomach."

"Tastes like a puddle."

A weekly mixology competition was concocted by the management team of the Pearls Caribbean Hotel to allow guests to get acquainted. Persuading them to stir up drinks was easy, but convincing them to mix with each other proved more of a challenge.

"Ladies and gentlemen," announced the duty manager, "please name your cocktail, so we can begin the judging."

Squeezing Oliver's hand, Cate grinned expectantly.

"I hope we win," she said, gazing around the room at the competition. With pale green and ivory striped walls and polished wooden floors, the charming hotel was occupied mainly by people celebrating special occasions. There were two distinct groups. Spiky-haired men in t-shirts and long patterned shorts tended to be paired with smiling young ladies, sporting firm flesh and cotton frocks. Shaking their pony-tails and glowing with anticipation they represented the newly-weds. Noticeably older, the anniversary couples consisted of men with less hair and more worry lines, and women flaunting big bosoms and expensive clothes. Technically, Cate belonged to this set, but she was glad to be different from most of them.

The judges made their way along the bar; a smooth black counter speckled with tiny silver particles resembling a twinkling night sky. Except now it was more reminiscent of a soggy night in Blackpool, covered with puddles of rum and fruit juice, and small paper parasols. A tall Bajan barman mopped the spills. Winking at Cate he smiled, revealing perfect teeth. He was the one that spent the last ten days padding around her sunbed in worn flip-flops, admiring her ample bosom.

Stopping briefly at each drink, the cocktail connoisseurs sniffed, swilled and quaffed.

"I like this one," said the bar manager. "Banana liqueur in this, and I can taste the rum but it's not overpowering."

Nodding in agreement, the duty manager looked closely at the cocktails, cradling a glass in his broad palm, and holding it up to the light before taking a large swig.

"We should employ some of these guys to come and work for us," he laughed. "It's going to be hard to choose this week."

Sounding slightly tipsy, the bar manager eventually announced the results.

"Third place goes to Punch in the Face."

The crowd cheered as the burly man with a scorched forehead, and his big-boned wife in a yellow sarong, collected a half bottle of rum. Smiling, the man leaned close to his spouse and whispered in her ear. She looked up coyly, fiddling with her dress as if they had just met. Second prize went to the Banana Marma men. The tall blonde patted the shorter man on the back. Beaming with delight, he received a litre of spirit. He walked with a distinctive waddle, thrusting the bottle into the air with one hand like a prized trophy.

"And by unanimous decision the winner is Rumbastic." There was encouraging applause. Rumbastic was Oliver's vibrant creation, warranting a wicker basket loaded with rum, wrapped in yellow cellophane, and tied at the top with a golden ribbon.

Cate sipped pina colada. It was an ideal end to their holiday in Barbados. Her husband possessed a knack for combining alcoholic ingredients, and instinctively knew when the taste, smell and colour were right - a sort of cocktail wizard. Unfortunately, her first marriage turned out to be a beer cocktail; but Ollie was different. After ten years they were still the perfect Bellini. Handsome, intelligent and five years younger than herself, he was an excellent choice for a husband. And he was particularly sexy after a night of cocktails.

Naked in bed with only a sheet covering them, they rested. The ceiling-fan, flicking light around the room from the terrace, hummed in tune with the air-conditioning.

"Do you think the barman really fancies me?" she smiled, pushing up her breasts with both hands, and licking the corner of her mouth provocatively.

"No, he's short-sighted; you remind him of his mother. He's just a boy, and what you need is a *big* man," he mocked, deepening his voice and staring purposefully into her eyes.

"You're right; know where I can get one at this hour?"

"As it happens, I do."

Moving his arm over her body and gripping her left hand, he pushed it into the pillow. Then gently kissing her bottom lip, he nibbled his way down her neck, and back to her mouth for a full-blown French kiss. Her inner thigh twitched. Tangling her fingers in his soft hair she gripped the back of his neck. After a few drinks the outcome was often predictable. There was never a great deal of conversation before or after; either there was nothing left to say or they knew each other too well. Staring wide-eyed at the shadows dancing across the smooth white ceiling, she relaxed as Oliver kissed a path to her breasts. The anticipation was an important part of the ritual. It shouldn't be a formal procedure, but it was obvious what his next move would be. Then a surprise.

"Let's go out on the balcony," he said, suddenly getting up.

A quiver of delight surged through her body. Moving across to the glass doors, Ollie's pale buttocks tensed as he leaned forward to switch off the outside light. Then he extended one arm towards her like a gallant knight helping a lady out of a carriage. Smiling, she offered her hand, sliding over to him on the cool marble floor. He tugged at the doors, releasing a rush of warm air across her skin.

Finger-combing hair from his face he raised one eyebrow in silent invitation, deliberately luring her onto the balcony, nude and vulnerable. She leaned against the rail, peering down at the dark sea quietly lapping the beach like a wet tongue licking at the sand. It was a beautifully erotic moment; the moonlight squeezing through the palm trees illuminated her naked shoulders. The night was still and humid. With his lips pressing softly on her temple and his quads pushing hard on her thigh, her heart raced from the danger of being exposed, and the thrill of being seen.

Slamming his chest against her back, Oliver gripped her stomach with one hand; they were making love outside and it was fiery and passionate. Jiggling and swaying her bare breasts bounced heavily as he pressed against her from behind, his body slapping her bottom in the heat. The balcony joined in, shaking and creaking enthusiastically; someone might appear on the terrace below at any second. It added to the excitement; they hadn't had sex like that in ages. Then Ollie tugged her hair and mumbled something that she couldn't make out.

"What?" she asked abruptly. "The handrail? The handrail's loose?"

Trying to ignore the interruption, he placed one hand on the rail and the other on her shoulder.

"What d'you mean loose? Is it dangerous?" she asked again, pushing back on him. It was certainly wobbling.

"What? No," he said. "It's alright."

"Wait. Wait!"

Stopping suddenly, he placed both hands on the wooden balustrade.

"It's okay," he protested, driving up slowly into her thighs.

"No. I think I'm getting bitten. We better go inside."

"You're not getting bitten, you've got spray on. There aren't any mosquitoes anyway."

"No, I'm getting bitten. I didn't spray everywhere. We'll have to go in."

Wriggling free she ran inside and jumped on the mattress, spreading out her arms and legs like a naughty starfish. The bed was large with crisp white sheets and plump pillows. Oliver stood motionless for a few seconds with a steely gaze and wilting enthusiasm.

Walking over to the mini-bar, he took a small beer from the fridge, opened it and drank from the bottle. Letting out a belch he smiled and knelt at her feet. Slowly, he leaned over and began kissing her legs. Starting with her left ankle, he made his way up, alternating from the inside of one leg to the other. His lips were cool from drinking beer, tickling the soft flesh of her thighs and making her squirm. Gripping her wrists, he forced her to endure the teasing until she cried out for him to stop.

The love-making resumed; with beer-breath his tongue pressed into her mouth. It was unlike their usual sexual exploits; passionate and intense, adventurous even. If only the balcony hadn't turned out to be loose. There was definitely something different about him, though. Something she couldn't quite put her finger on. Unless it was her imagination, he was colder than normal; like a cocktail with too much ice. Perhaps she should pay more attention to him, and spend less time daydreaming about being a TV reporter. For the last three years her focus was fixed firmly on achieving a First in her studies; Ollie could have grown a beard and horns, and she wouldn't have noticed. But things would change from now on. Once her birthday and graduation were over she could settle into a new job, and concentrate on keeping him entertained. A bout of drunken sex was fairly insignificant; if her husband wanted to be spontaneous, it was a good thing. They would be home soon and there was much to do.

The text message

PINA COLADA SEEMED a distant memory back in England. After a few days it was as though she had never been away. Returning to work after holidaying in the Caribbean was like emerging from the cinema into daylight, following a long film. She could scrunch up her eyes and peek at the world through narrow slits, hoping that it would appear more attractive, but reality was blinding; and it wasn't particularly appealing. However, there was always an opportunity to escape; she was having one of those peculiar dreams again. Everyone was in a restaurant on the other side of the river; they were eating, drinking and laughing. No-one seemed to notice that she was stranded on a muddy bank which was rising slowly, allowing her to see down into the glowing room. It was raining heavily, and the river was getting deeper and more torrid with every passing second. Shivering and alone, Cate cried out to the man who was smiling and talking to a woman with her back to the window.

"Oliver!" she shouted, waving frantically. No sound came out, she was screaming into the wind. The alarm beeped and she was awake.

Feeling for her phone, she checked the time and sighed; 5am. Her husband, snoring peacefully beside her, didn't stir as her lips brushed his shoulder. Slipping silently from under the duvet she crept around the bed. Minutes later she was dressed, groomed, and quietly opening the front door. Crossing the threshold at that time was like entering a parallel universe. Yawning, she paused to look up at the dawn peeping out from behind the chimney pots across the street. How abhorrent to go to work so early. But there was one tiny fragment that embraced the morning; less than one per cent, maybe a rogue gene from a prehistoric relative, but it existed. The cool essence of day lingered in the air; inhaling the crispness with one breath she set off towards the supermarket.

Rushmore Drive was peaceful. Each detached home, hugging a brace of cars, slept contentedly with curtains closed. No-one looked out as she strode up the hill, hands in pockets. If they had, they would have seen a blonde with silver highlights; a handsome female, even though she said it herself. Not as slim as she used to be; there was a little more insulation around the pipes, but still, not too heavily lagged. Cate Cooke, nee Bartlett was an elegant woman, with remarkable flexibility in her legs; especially for someone who was about to reach half a century. There were not many positions that her legs couldn't get into, which came in handy sometimes. But the best thing about Mrs Cooke was not her straight nose, pale blue eyes or engaging smile, it was her relentless optimism. Her mother used to say, *'you could fall in a bucket of shit and come out smelling of roses'*. True, but the real trick was to maintain control and avoid the crap altogether; she was pretty good at that.

First light; how fascinating. With the world paused she was the only living creature able to move - apart from cats. They were granted immunity in the curious twilight zone, specifically so they could spring out from behind bushes and from under cars to scare the pants off her. The sleeping population didn't care that she got up at five o'clock every day to pick online food orders. Was anyone worried that she could be attacked by a nocturnal lunatic preying on early-morning shoppers? No – but it was her most pressing concern as she moved away from the houses to cross the small common that joined the estate to the main road.

The seemingly innocuous piece of land was no larger than a tennis court; unfortunately it was enclosed by trees and hidden from view. At that time of the morning it could be a perilous path through the forest of doom for all anyone knew; and approaching it increased her heart rate. Stretching out like a runway through the clearing, a black track divided the rough grass in two. The area was deserted apart from a large clump of bushes to the left, half way across, close to the path. Weaving through the metal railings she jerked her head left and right like a nervous pedestrian. 'NO BALL GAMES' – how many times had she read that faded sign? Cool air swept through her soft hair, lifting it from her shoulders as she bounced along. Everything was quiet, nothing stirred. A plastic carrier-bag stuck out from the bush like a yellow flag, perfectly still, resembling a signal waiting to drop. Sniffing a breath, she quickened her pace, glancing in both directions. The bag twitched, catching her eye. Suddenly she noticed it wasn't trapped on the branches, it was *behind* them. And at the base of the clump, through the leaves there were two white trainers attached to a pair of legs in dark corduroys.

This was it. The moment she dreaded every day for the last twelve months without ever really expecting it to happen. A crazed attacker was hiding in the bushes. Freezing mid step, adrenalin coursed through her veins, making her ears throb as she stood open-mouthed. Gripping the fork in her pocket, she weakened at the thought of using it. The stainless steel table-fork fell out of her jacket on one occasion as she was rushing home after work, prompting a conversation with Stacey the biscuit-shelf filler.

"What's that for?" she asked.

"Protection, in case someone attacks me," said Cate.

"What yer gonna do - fork 'em with it?"

"Of course," she openly admitted. "You might not be keen on assaulting someone if you've got a fork sticking out your head. I like to be equipped."

"Equipped for what? Eating out?"

The bourbon-replenisher was right; all she felt armed for now was a picnic. Biting her top lip, she considered the alternatives. Could she run to the main road without being caught? She glanced ahead. If she was pushed into the ditch at the top of the clearing, she would be completely hidden from any passing cars. Before she could weigh up all the options, a man stepped out from behind the bush onto the path. He was a little taller than her, about five feet six, with a thin body and wild, wiry hair. The first thing she observed was a pair of hairy arms clad in rubber gloves, stretching out towards her. Gasping, she stepped back and almost fell over. The second thing she noticed was that she knew the man. It was her neighbour from across the road, waving the yellow carrier bag as he spoke.

"Alright Cate," he said. "You off to work?"

Idiot. Desperately wanting to scream 'no, I'm picking mushrooms', she gritted her teeth and hissed out a reply.

"Bloody hell Bob, you scared the life outta me."

"Sorry." Grinning sheepishly he shrugged his shoulders.

"Can I ask you to talk quietly? Hamish is trying to go."

Bemused, her eyebrows arched. She couldn't see the enormous Great Dane that walked his master several times a day, and it wasn't easy to miss. Hamish was more like a small horse than a large dog; a shining, golden brown, muscular specimen with black muzzle and huge dark, floppy ears. She looked towards the bush.

"Yes," said Bob, in answer to her enquiring gaze. "He's round the back. He doesn't like me to watch when he's at toilet, it puts him off."

Smiling, she screwed up her nose, and nodded politely.

"I'll go. I know what it's like, Ollie's the same," she said, pretending to tip-toe away.

Sticking out his pointed chin, the man's shoulders lifted as if to laugh; his arms outstretched like a mad surgeon waiting to operate. Then his expression dropped and he stared into space.

"Ollie is?" he frowned. But she was already several paces away and had no intention of explaining. Reaching the metal railings at the other end of the path she ambled confidently to the main road.

Oliver's toilet habits didn't bear too much scrutiny; a bit like the stupid dream. The details were fading already but it was definitely an uncomfortable situation. Ollie was well aware that she was stuck on the other side of the river but didn't want to help her across; he was preoccupied with the woman. Who was the woman? She was vaguely familiar. George was there too, her step-father. He was wearing a fawn overcoat – and he was waving, and walking towards her. And then he strolled straight past her. Apart from ignoring her - what on earth was he doing in the nightmare? Dreams never made sense. She crossed the dual-carriageway without noticing and was close to the supermarket. It wasn't worth wasting time on something she had no control over, especially when her wakeful imagination was more powerful than any night-vision.

Jumping down from the embankment she entered the car park at the far end. There was always an alternative reality; one where she was not just a 49-year-old part-time shopper and journalism student. Invention came naturally. She saw herself with a microphone standing next to the side door, the entrance that everyone used to gain access before the store opened to the public. Others, dressed in blue uniforms, were getting out of their cars and plodding towards the shop like reluctant infants filing into school. They passed without noticing as she delivered her daily report to camera.

> *"It's almost six o'clock and I'm outside Spennimore's supermarket in Wolfinger on this glorious day. The sun peeps over the canopy of the petrol station, marinating everything with an intense orange glow, like it's dipped in free-range egg yolk.*
>
> *And while the town sleeps - a remarkable feat takes place in the bowels of this emporium. Dozens of online shoppers arrive to do their duty for Spennimore's, and indeed, the nation. As the first few shards of light strike the store a small army marches on with a single goal. Shopping selflessly, for those who cannot - or will not - get their own goods, the trolley-dollies sweep the shelves with passion. Bashing barcodes, packing totes, the dawn-raiders of the grocery world leave nothing behind, but burning rubber on supermarket tile.*
>
> *This is Catherine Bartlett, reporting for Newsline, outside Spennimore's. And now back to the studio."*

Squinting into the sunlight Cate smiled, and then turned and walked inside the store. Online shopping could be competently carried out on auto-pilot, which left plenty of time for daydreaming. An elite team, the shoppers were separated from the cashiers, fillers and general assistants by virtue of their 'special' duties. If goods weren't picked, the vans couldn't go out, resulting in financial penalty for late delivery. However, being a member of the illustrious clique wasn't particularly inspiring. It provided enough money to pay the household bills while studying at university, but with graduation looming it was hard to be enthusiastic about work. She was finally closer than ever to achieving her supreme goal – to become a TV reporter.

And if two decades spent buried in the vaults of the Wolfinger Saver's Bank hadn't dulled the desire to stand up and share her thoughts with the world, nothing ever could. Her bank colleagues remained unaware that everything in the branch was broadcast, from the ever changing colour of the assistant manager's hair to the excitement of the ceiling falling in. True to her burgeoning ambition she always found time to exercise her insight and exhume the 'inner-Cate'; a talent developed in childhood. All she needed was a real camera, an actual audience and a degree in journalism. Minor points, and in a few weeks she would have at least one of them.

Even after twenty years it wasn't difficult to wave goodbye to banking and become a full-time student. Her lifestyle wasn't extravagant, and the boys were now men. James was married and ready to start his own family, and Luke was old enough not to live at home. A point he overlooked, irrespective of the numerous hints from his step-father. Cate ignored them both; she hated arguments. Finding solace in her studies, she was an enthusiastic advocate of university life. So much so that Oliver gave up work to become a student of history at the same establishment. An unexpected move not factored in to her financial plan, hence the job at Spennimore's.

The shopping bay was a large, bright room crowded with metal trolleys, each stacked with empty plastic totes. Minutes before 6am the room was packed with employees. Yawning and chatting, they gently rocked their trolleys, like anxious nannies soothing babies in giant prams.

"Good morning team," sung the supervisor. Laura, a stalwart member of management, had more than ten years of service under her efficient retail belt. Always immaculate, her straight, black pony-tail was so thick and glossy it put most thoroughbreds to shame. With her slender figure and broad smile, there was only one minor flaw - her soft brown eyes worked completely independently from one another. It didn't make her less beautiful, but as a result she was self-conscious and shy with men. The male shoppers were a benevolent bunch and never made her uncomfortable, but the drivers were not as considerate.

"How are we all?" asked Laura with her unique talent of appearing to look at everyone at the same time. She took the array of nods, forced smiles and grunts as a positive sign of life. "We've maxed out on hours, so you need to shop your little legs off I'm afraid. Anyone got anything else? No? Off you go then. Run, run, run," she mocked.

Nobody ran. Cate took off at a brisk walk, following the convoy through the warehouse to the shop-floor, where trolleys peeled off in two directions like a supermarket version of an aerial display team. Half went towards the 'chilled' section and the rest made for the ambient food aisles. Within minutes they were spread across the store, pillaging the shelves and weaving around the night-shift workers.

"Aye, aye," said Derek as she swung around the corner and inspected the display for four hundred grams of own label tomato soup with basil. Placing his hand to his chin he stopped replenishing the stuffing section and looked thoughtfully at the shopper.

"You're looking remarkably lovely this morning," he chirped. "If I had to look at you all night, this job would be vaguely interesting."

Derek was an amiable member of the night-shift; some scowled when the shoppers removed items from their freshly stocked shelves. He chatted with everyone and complimented the female staff to see if they would flirt back. There was no hidden agenda. A dumpy, bald man with gold-rimmed spectacles and a red nose, he was perfectly aware that he was about as appealing as a pair of Y-fronts. But Derek was respected by most; the cheerful pensioner worked nights to afford treats for his sick wife.

"Stuffing today, are we Derek?" remarked Cate, looking at the small pile of boxes on the floor.

"I'd like to be," he replied. "Your hair looks nice, are you growing it?"

Playful banter never fazed her.

"Grows all on its own. I don't even need to think about it. Yours looks nice too, have you done something different?" she teased.

Grinning, he picked up a box of sage and onion, and began to fill the shelf.

"Yeah, I polished it last night before I came in."

Shoppers worked against the clock. Putting her weight behind the trolley she pushed on up the aisle, picking and packing with meticulous dexterity. After each 'shop' she returned to the storeroom where Laura stacked totes in lanes, ready for delivery.

"Do you think Ollie would do some overtime this week?" asked the supervisor. "Has he finished university now?"

"Until September, yeah," the shopper replied. "He goes in to do research, but he probably would."

"We need a driver to cover Thursdays and Fridays while Jiffy's off with his hernia. What's he researching?" Jimbo arrived in the loading bay. Cate wiped old delivery information from the empty plastic totes on her next trolley.

"Jack the Ripper," she said, loading carrier bags onto the cart.

"Okay, I'll ring him and ask," Laura called out. Weighing a scruffy-looking bunch of bananas Jimbo scanned the ticket to his hand-held device.

"You can't ring *him*, nobody knows who he is," he interjected.

"Oliver does," smiled Cate as she left.

Fragmented exchange was commonplace due to the pace of the role. A typical sixty item 'shop' took around twenty minutes to complete, including locating, selecting and bagging. Online shoppers were often privy to half-conversations of a personal nature as they circumnavigated the shelves. Frequently eavesdropping from the other side of an aisle, most added helpful comments if the opportunity arose. Jimbo was a routine offender. He had large, inquisitive, green eyes, gelled hair and a small pointed nose, ideal for poking into other people's business. His ability to gossip was more developed than one would normally expect in a thirty-two-year-old male, largely due to the amount of exercise his mouth got.

As ten o'clock approached Cate's stomach rumbled in anticipation of the end of her shift. Rubbing her empty belly, she glanced at her watch. Jimbo was talking to someone in the next aisle.

"His wife's really lovely though."

"I know," a voice replied.

Her stomach gurgled. Pausing, she stared at the tin of beans in her hand, cocking her head on one side to listen to the men.

"At it right under her nose for weeks apparently," said Jimbo. "She couldn't believe it, never thought he'd go off with someone else; not after everything that's happened."

"Yeah but that's the thing," interrupted the other voice, "you've got to work at it." There was no time to wait for the outcome; rounding the corner Cate came face to face with Lawrence. He was caressing a lettuce, and nodding his head.

"It takes effort," he said emphatically.

"You're right Lawrence," replied Jimbo. "You're so right; there's gotta be give and take. Gotta be give and take," he reiterated. They looked at each other and then at their female colleague, as if she had disturbed the international convention for human rights.

"And which one might you be?" she enquired, scanning a jar of mayonnaise, "the giver or the taker?"

"Sorry?" he scoffed, pretending to be hurt. "But I don't recall you being in this private conversation. Isn't it time you went home and cooked breakfast for your husband?"

"Yeah, you know what those drivers are like if they're not fed," added Lawrence, shaking his large, grey head. "All those hungry housewives out there, waiting for deliveries. He'll be getting his scrambled egg on a plate."

"Sauce?" she asked, snatching a bottle of ketchup from the shelf and smiling sweetly at the men. Standing firmly with shoulders back and legs apart she squared up to them, ready for a street-fight with a grocery weapon. Jimbo grimaced, preening his glossy, black hair.

"You'd better go polish your aubergines mate, before she throws something at you."

Feigning a scowl Cate shoved her trolley into the next aisle; it was almost the end of her shop. She stood before the pasta, examining the shelf for orzo but it wasn't leaping out at her.

"What have you lost?" said a voice.

"What?" she replied, staring blankly at the display.

"What are you looking for?" asked Amanda Doyle.

"Oh, orzo."

Leaning forward, Amanda tapped a box. "You were miles away."

"Yeah, pasta reminds me of Venice. Me and Oliver took a gondola to a Duchesses house and had dinner with the Mayor of Venice once."

"Really," smiled Amanda, unimpressed. "I saw him last week in the coffee shop at uni." She hesitated, "Oliver, I mean, not the Mayor of Venice." Cate gave a sideways glance. "He was with the girl with long blonde hair."

"Lucy Watts?"

"Don't know what her name is. I always see them together though. Doesn't that annoy you?" Scanning a kilo of basmati she packed it neatly into a tote.

"No, why should it? They're studying the same subject."

Moving gracefully to the other side of the aisle Amanda selected a small bottle of soy sauce.

"Not sure what they were studying when I saw them," she added quietly, turning the corner.

Engrossed in the Chinese cook-in sauces the comment caught her like a smack in the face with a wok. Ms Doyle wasn't known for spreading malicious rumours. Was she suggesting that Lucy and Oliver were studying each other? He might be good-looking, and an incorrigible flirt, but the idea was absurd. Thoughtfully selecting a jar of Szechuan she started back to the shopping bay. Barbados seemed like a long time ago. To be honest, he was a bit odd while they were away but he was absorbed with his research. In fact, he dashed to the university almost as soon as they landed. Jimbo was an old busy-body. He was always gossiping about someone doing something with somebody or other; but he wasn't talking about Oliver on this occasion. Unfortunately, she hardly saw him at university; the School of Social Sciences was on a separate campus.

Laura was in the storeroom speaking quietly to the new girl.

"...it is still rice, but it's best to ask someone more experienced if you're not sure," she said kindly. Still looking puzzled, the girl trundled into the warehouse. Laura turned to Cate.

"Customer complaint. You know we were out of five hundred gram basmati the other day." The shopper nodded. "Well unfortunately Chloe subbed it for a tin of rice pudding."

"Oh dear, not quite the same with curry, is it."

"No," the supervisor sighed, shuffling some paperwork. "You can't throw it at your daughter's wedding either."

"Probably not. Ten o'clock, I'm off. See you tomorrow." Cate stomped to the staff room, mumbling to herself. She slammed the locker door shut and activated her phone. It beeped twice as she passed the biscuit aisle; three familiar little words from Oliver.

'Get some bread.'

Walking towards the bakery she read his second message. A look of bewilderment crossed her face, followed by confusion. Motionless, she stood with one hand on the crumpets and the other stroking her forehead. Her lips pursed, and her brow crinkled to a frown. What on Earth was he thinking? If he was sending messages to other women she'd kill him; slowly and painfully if necessary. Surely this was a wind up?

"Excuse me, dear," said a sweet little voice, "I'm sorry to bother you but can you tell me if you have any small tins of Kittychunk out the back? Salmon if you've got it."

No response - but the old lady was persistent. She was about four feet tall, with pale eyes and wrinkled skin.

"There are some large tins on the shelf but no small ones," she said looking up hopefully at the online shopper, "could you check for me?"

"They'll be with cat food on aisle twenty-three," she muttered in a distracted and unusually dismissive tone.

"Yes there are some large tins," the old woman repeated, "but I only need a small one since my Oliver passed away."

"What? You called your cat Oliver?" she enquired, suddenly taking an interest.

"Yes, Stanley and Oliver. I had two cats, but poor Ollie died."

"I hope he wasn't poisoned in a jealous rage?" hissed the shop assistant.

"What? Oh no, he got run over, chasing the little fluffy thing next door; little Ginger. One day she sat in the middle of the road licking her paws and a great big lorry came 'round the corner. I didn't see it but a neighbour told me. My Ollie rushed out and pushed little Ginge out the way. Course he didn't make it; got squashed flat, poor thing. Randy little devil, he was in love, see." Wistfully tilting her head on one side the old woman smiled.

"I knew I should've had him done."

Cate looked down at the tiny woman, she seemed so fragile.

"Could you check for me? Salmon if you've got it."

"I'm sorry, we're waiting for a delivery," she lied. There were more pressing things on her mind. The second text was disturbing her concentration, and she wasn't feeling helpful. If Oliver was out chasing fluffy things he was risking more than his Kittychunks.

"Oh, what a nuisance," the woman sighed.

"Isn't it just," muttered Cate, pushing the phone into her pocket and walking out of the store. Her alter ego was waiting by the checkouts.

> *"Police have decided not to press charges following an investigation into the death of a 45-year-old part-time delivery driver from Wolfinger. A Coroner recorded a verdict of accidental poisoning after the man's 49-year-old widow admitted she made an unfortunate mistake.*
>
> *The woman said she hadn't baked a poison pie because her husband was having an affair. Commenting after the inquest she said, "It's easy to mix up mushrooms and toadstools, but I would notice if he was cooking up something with another woman. I wouldn't say that revenge is a dish best served in pastry but mushroom crumble just isn't as effective."*
>
> *This is Catherine Bartlett, reporting for Newsline. Stay with us for more news later, and now back to the studio."*

Samantha

OUTSIDE THE SHOP PEOPLE strolled across the car park, enjoying the sunshine. Some plodded in silence, others chatted; and one wailed for her son to get off the coin-operated giraffe and come into the supermarket.

"I won't tell you again!" the woman said, wagging a finger.

Cate was never naughty as a child; hardly ever, but her mother used the same baffling phrase. If she wasn't going to be told again, she could carry on with what she was doing without being disturbed. But there was always a follow-up scolding.

Walking home there wasn't much else to think about. Except the second text – what did it mean? It was obviously intended for someone else, unless it was some sort of joke. And did he know he sent it to her? She was desperate to find out. A few minutes later, striding down Rushmore Drive, the houses were awake and the street had come to life. Across the road Bob cleaned windows, talking quietly to his enormous dog, as if confiding in an old friend. Standing beside him, Hamish inspected the work. Waving to them both, she marched down the drive and opened the front door. Pausing to kick off her shoes in the hallway she listened briefly before calling out.

"Hallo."

There was a reply from the dining room.

"Did you get the bread?"

Hanging her jacket on the bannister, she mouthed 'oh shit', and then poked her head into the room. It was necessary to look Oliver in the face to judge his reaction.

"No," she said folding her arms and waiting for him to look at her. He stopped tapping on his laptop for a second and gazed up inquiringly. "Got your text though," she added.

"Oh, but you didn't bother to get the bread." He had that look on his face. The - *'I've no idea what I've done, and I'm not going to ask because it's almost certainly something I couldn't care less about'* - one.

She could read him; he was about as hard to decipher as a packet of crisps. Clearly he had no idea she received the second text, elevating her to a position of power. No need to go mushroom-picking straight away. Actually, there was probably a perfectly reasonable explanation, she shouldn't jump to conclusions. If he was up to something surely he would've been far more careful where he sent the message.

"I forgot," she said, staring into the garden, past her unwitting spouse as if an alibi hung in the bushes. "An old lady distracted me, asking for Kittychunks, and then I came home without the bread."

"Yes, you're easily sidetracked, aren't you," he said with a patronising tone.

Maybe, but she would be watching very closely from now on. Smiling sarcastically, she went into the kitchen.

"Do you want tea?"

"Nooo," he replied slowly, like a clockwork toy winding down.

"Laura said she was going to phone you; she needs a driver."

Hastily making a drink and sneaking a biscuit Cate swept away the crumbs and stomped upstairs. It was possible to plot while sipping tea and checking emails. Slipping off her uniform, she pulled on a long, grey t-shirt and black leggings. Next to the master bedroom was a small room that was used as an office; a plain, comfortable space. With a wooden blind filtering the daylight, the pale terracotta walls created a cosy environment; a secret den and safe haven for frustrated journalists. There was an oak desk and a black leather chair for swivelling in. On the walls two financial certificates stood proudly next to a cork pin-board. It was home to a dozen pictures of different sizes, held in place with red drawing pins; Oliver smiled back from every frame.

Slumping in the chair she stared at the photos. Each one told a story; she must've heard them all twenty times. Over the last three years she virtually lived in the office; shaping assignments, editing short films, and constructing radio scripts. And although student life was nearly over she wasn't planning on anything else ending. How empty those little squares on the wall would be without Ollie obscuring the landmarks.

Her reflection frowned in the black computer screen, causing her to stare back sternly. Tapping the space bar forced the monitor to spring into action, ending the standoff. The university results page hadn't changed; classifications weren't due for another whole day. It was unlikely she would be awarded anything less than a First Class degree, but she had to be certain. Confirming the result was paramount, until Ollie's text arrived; now it was getting pushed into second place. What she really needed was to talk things over with Samantha. Sam always put things into perspective and would instinctively know if there was anything to worry about. She was probably at work; a text was the best course of action.

'When are you free for chat? Something I need to show you asap!'

Having a best friend came in handy; they met at high school. Originally, there was a large group of girls, but Samantha was different. Attractive and spirited, as a thirteen-year-old she rode the most amazing black chopper-bike with rear-view mirrors and chrome wheels; a teenage equivalent to a Ford Capri. It didn't take a genius to work out that Sam Stevens would be a great accomplice. Not only did she own the coolest bicycle, she was vivacious and spontaneous, and was certainly going places. At seventeen she learned to drive, and since then all her jobs involved some sort of transport. First it was a bread delivery van, and then came bigger vans and more inspiring goods. After that she drove a taxi, a bus, and a limousine for a government minister. And now she was a train driver.

Essentially, her life was uncluttered, offering the ability to see things with great clarity; focus was her forte – most of the time. Sam had only one tiny imperfection, often rearing its head at the least convenient moment, she was clumsy as an ox when she wasn't steering something.

Things simply came apart in her slippery grip. Countless items were knocked over and a slightly uneven surface was an accident waiting to occur. Shortly after their first ever meeting she kicked the head off her mother's precious china dog; a family heirloom that was now four inches shorter. On another occasion she went missing from a party after falling through the fire-door of a nightclub and finding herself back in the street. But her most famous incident was at Cate's first wedding. Sam looked stunning as a bridesmaid, in a closely fitting dress made of purple taffeta. She signed the Register and was stepping back when she fell down a small stair. Completely off-balance and arms flaying, her ballistic bouquet launched itself into the air, thwacking the vicar on the back of the head before dropping to the floor. Much to the amusement of the congregation, she plunged backwards into the arms of the best man with an involuntary shriek. Best man, handsome Justin, tried to keep her in his grip for several years. But after a long engagement she wriggled free, and despite taking others for a test drive, she never quite found a man she wanted to share a licence with.

Cate's phone 'barked' loudly, signalling a return text from her friend.

'Whats up? On lates meet you at station 12.30'
'Yep, see you at Ellas. What time you starting?'
'1.30'

Meeting arranged. Swivelling in her chair with one eye closed she scrutinised a fly effortlessly resting on the ceiling. Maybe she was overreacting. Ollie was entitled to message his friends; it didn't mean he'd taken a lover for goodness sake. There was no proof the text was about her. Perhaps she wouldn't mention it when they met for coffee, it wasn't that important. Sam didn't exactly see eye to eye with her husband. The whole idea was ridiculous; she would only end up defending him. Oliver did a lot of huffing and puffing but he obviously loved her. They had a great time on holiday, especially on the balcony; he was so sexy that night. After ten years of marriage, they still enjoyed each other physically and emotionally. Not as often as they used to, perhaps, but that was normal in any relationship. She could ask him about the text later, and it would all make sense.

Flopping forward and tapping the space bar again she opened the folder containing the pictures of Barbados. There was one in particular; Oliver leaning against a palm tree with his arms folded. Smiling, her finger traced the outline of his face, partly in the shadow of the spiky leaves. Wearing a pale blue checked shirt, complementing his sultry grey eyes, he looked terrific. His muscular chest bulged through the open neckline and he was smiling in a mischievous and enticing way. A tan really suited him. She went pink in the sun.

Flicking through the photos, she came across the one taken on the day of their anniversary. Ollie had his arm around her. Several attempts using the camera's self-timer produced poor results and the picture was eventually taken by the man with a bandaged head. Apparently, he was with a party of swimmers when a short-sighted turtle bit him on the ear.

Leaning close to the screen she examined the picture carefully. She should make more effort to lose weight; Ollie was right about her stomach. Maybe get her hair styled differently too; it was shorter than usual, which was easier to manage on holiday, but he said it made her look like a 1970s MP. Closing the folder she sipped tea.

There was something going on downstairs. Crossing the landing to the bathroom she could hear her husband talking. However, leaning over the bannister and straining her ears made no difference, he was speaking too quietly. By the time she went back into the office, he was coming upstairs. Grinning, he went into the bedroom. Cate stood in the doorway, leaning against the frame.

"Who was that on the phone? Another bloody call centre." she enquired.

"No," he said pulling his t-shirt off over his head.

"Who was it then?"

"You know who it was."

"No I don't," she protested. "I wouldn't ask if I did, would I?"

"It was Laura; nosey. She wants to know if I can do overtime," he replied, selecting a shirt from the wardrobe.

"Did you say yes?"

"I said I'd go in and see her."

"What for?" she asked. "Why didn't you sort it out over the phone?"

"Suppose I could have, but I can't buy bread over the phone, can I?"

Buttoning his checked shirt he squeezed past her. And then giving her a swift peck on the cheek, he walked into the bathroom and began brushing his teeth. She remained in the doorway for a few seconds. Everything seemed reasonable. The polish was chipped on the fingernails of her left hand, it would need redoing but it could wait until later.

"Oh yeah," she added, walking back into the office, "I'm meeting Sam at lunchtime and I better call in on George on the way home."

With a toothbrush still in his mouth, he grunted an incomprehensible acknowledgement. Moments later, wiping his chin on the dark towel, he left behind a white foaming crust of paste. An act of vandalism that would result in repercussions; the best course of action was to make a quick exit.

"See ya later," he called, trotting down the stairs and picking up the car keys on the way out. The front door slammed. Peering through the wooden slats of the blind Cate watched her husband slide into the car and drive away. Hamish was in the garden across the road, lying outstretched on the lawn with front paws crossing his black muzzle as if playing hide and seek. Bob was nowhere to be seen. Perhaps it was his turn to be 'at toilet' behind a bush and the dog didn't like to intrude; assuming he was a real dog, and not just a man zipped into a Great Dane suit. There was something odd about both man and his best friend but it wasn't fascinating enough to keep her attention for long.

She looked at her phone; there was plenty of time to sift through her inbox for inspiration before leaving for the café. Ella's was a comfortable place to talk, situated within the station grounds. Inexorably smelling of aromatic coffee and freshly baked cakes, it was the ideal setting to talk to friends with a mouthful of blueberry muffin. The seating area was furnished with big-cushioned armchairs. Brown wicker tables with glass tops provided a home for chrome stools, and dishevelled newspapers. Commuters arrived early to sit by the window and watch the world through the steam of cappuccino, and tall glasses of hot chocolate with marshmallows and cream. A large latte came with a small Italian biscuit that tasted of wood, but the coffee was the best in town. Her inbox bulged with unmissable opportunities as usual. The most appealing was an invitation to enter a film-short competition. It would be easy enough to come up with an idea, and there were already several amusing examples on the website. Examining each one carefully, she considered recording a documentary piece on canine communication. Almost time to leave. Another email arrived. The sender's details caught her eye; she could take a quick peek. Amazing! It was the news she was waiting for. Filling her lungs in one large sniff, she leaned back into the chair and exhaled triumphantly. Then springing up, she ran into the bedroom. A hurried glance in the mirror confirmed she should've got ready earlier; the clothes would have to do and there was no time for makeup. She slipped on her grey canvas pumps; heels were not an option, too late for fashion. The back of her neck was damp with sweat when she reached the station, making her hair moist and curly under the straightened top layer. Glimpsing her frumpish reflection in the café window, she spotted her smartly dressed friend inside. Gesticulating wildly with her hands Sam was talking to a short man. He peered up at her through small, round black-rimmed glasses perched on his prominent nose, and wore an untidy grey parka. Entering through the glass door Cate hid behind a spiky pot plant, listening to the conversation.

"I cudda had an injury," the man protested, "flailin' your arms around like a flamin' windmill. What if I had a baby? You cudda had its eye out."

"I'm so sorry," said the apologetic train driver, "I didn't see you there."

"No, cos you weren't looking. I hope you aren't on my train."

"Off duty," she said, "I'm so sorry, have a safe journey."

Muttering to himself, and resembling a mole in a coat pulling a wheeled shopping bag, the man shuffled out the door leading to the platform. Cate leaned into full view, raising her right hand to her chest in an apprehensive wave.

Smiling magnanimously, Sam looked at her watch.

"Hello," she said in an exaggerated tone, "oh, my watch must be fast, it says 12.40."

"Sorry, mine must be slow, it says 12.25. Anyway, just cos I'm late, there's no need to punch the customers."

"I never punched him. It was an accidental tap on the head. How was I to know he was creeping up behind me? I was pointing to where they've moved the clock. Ella can't see it from the counter now."

Ordering large fancy coffees they sat on the red armchairs by the front window, overlooking the street.

"What's up?" she said tasting the froth from her latte with a teaspoon. "What did you want to show me so urgently?"

"I've got an interview, I can't believe it. Newsnetwork want to interview me for the weather presenter job."

"That's brilliant, when?" asked Sam.

"Thursday at half past one. I didn't think I was going to hear anything but I got an email this morning." Gushing with excitement, she bounced around in the chair. "I know it's a junior position, but that's okay. I haven't had time to read all the details but I don't care, I'm gonna do it anyway. I can't believe it."

There was a great deal to plan; the journey to the city, a new blouse, possibly a new suit. Certainly more research was in order, she would need to prepare answers for the interview and go over the job specifications again. They talked nonstop for more than forty minutes, only pausing to take gulps of coffee. Oliver's text hardly seemed relevant. Tomorrow she would receive confirmation of her degree classification, and two days after that it would be her big chance to impress Newsnetwork – oh yes, and her fiftieth birthday.

Another driver was buying food from the counter. Paying for his lunch, he nodded to his female colleague and walked over to her chair.

"You spend more time in here than in your cab," he said, frowning at Sam. His eyelids were heavy, and his face saggy and expressionless. He was the most depressing person, and she was usually adept at avoiding him; hiding behind newspapers, under tables or anything large enough to conceal her slim physique. On one occasion before she took to keeping out of sight he asked her to accompany him to dinner. It was an awful moment, he caught her by surprise and for several nail-biting seconds she couldn't think of a polite excuse. Eventually she told him she didn't go out with men, which wasn't what she meant to say. When his mouth dropped open in shock she added that she was a vegan, which was also a lie but thankfully he walked away.

"You should buy shares in this place," the man grunted, still looking miserable.

"It has been suggested," Sam answered politely.

"Yeah," said Cate, put out by the intervention, "but you wouldn't want to buy an egg sandwich from Sam 'n' Ella's though, would you?"

"No," he snapped. "I wouldn't buy an egg sandwich; poofs eat them. I'm a corned beef man. I like a bit of meat in me bread and I'm not 'aving any rubbish served up from *your* sort."

Sinking into her chair Samantha tried desperately to be absorbed into the cushion. Her hand rubbed her forehead, partly obscuring her face. She squinted at her friend through the open fingers of her left hand.

"Exactly what is my sort?" asked Cate indignantly, wishing she looked less like a fishwife.

"I could tell straight away," he scoffed. "You're one of 'er bloody lot - bloody vegetarian." The man stared at her without blinking his wretched eyes. Then ripping open the packet of sandwiches he took a large deliberate bite, like a wolf tearing a chunk out of its victim, before turning and walking out the door.

"Friend of yours?" she smirked.

"Sort of, we have the perfect relationship; I usually hide before he sees me."

"Good plan."

"I gotta go in a minute," sighed Sam. "Well done about your interview; excellent news. You didn't actually have anything to show me then. I thought there was something wrong when you text me."

Picking up the wide-rimmed cappuccino cup and staring into the froth at the bottom gave her a few seconds to think. Perhaps she could mention the text. There wasn't time to discuss it at length. Sam was ready to start work, so it was probably a safe option.

"Yeah," she said casually, "I got an unusual text from Ollie, and I wanted to know what you think. It's like it was meant for somebody else. Probably an overreaction; I don't really understand. You've got to go, haven't you; do you want me to show you tomorrow?"

"No, you might as well show me now." The blonde driver looked perturbed. She guessed there was something wrong when she received the text; evidently a controversial issue or it would have been mentioned earlier. Anything to do with Oliver was bound to be contentious. Theoretically he had her best friend's interests at heart, but there was an obvious tension; he wasn't completely trustworthy.

Defeated, Cate prepared to surrender the offending communication. A tiny white handbag hung on a long strap diagonally across her body; it was just big enough to hold a phone and her keys. Unzipping the bag, she pulled out her mobile and retrieved the message. Handing it over, she was engulfed by a sense of impending doom. As though she was delivering a contagious disease that would break out from the phone and choke normality to death.

"Hi babe. Sounds perfect she doesn't suspect a thing," her friend read out aloud. "Babe! Who the hell is babe? He never calls you that. Doesn't suspect a thing? She does now. I knew he was an arsehole the first time I saw him. Why didn't you show me this earlier?" she demanded. Pupils narrowing, her pastel green eyes flashed like a cat.

"Well, there's probably a logical explanation. I...I can't even be sure that Ollie sent it. What if he lent his phone to someone?"

"Was he with anyone when the text was sent? Where would he have been at 9.51 this morning?"

"At home, I suppose, he was there when I got in."

"Is he still there?"

"No, he went out to get some bread," she said, leaning forward to rescue her mobile.

"Bread," repeated Samantha as if it was a significant clue. "How did he look, was there anything suspicious about him when he left?" A train was due out in twenty minutes and the café was bustling with travellers filling up on cakes and coffee before their journey.

"Not exactly suspicious - no, he changed his shirt and brushed his teeth," she replied, attempting to ignore the energetic chatter coming from the next table. Three teenage girls eagerly discussed online reviews from men who had unwisely used depilatory cream on their genitals. Even though she was trying to concentrate, it was an amusing conversation.

"Are you kiddin'? He changed his shirt and brushed his teeth to go out and buy bread, and you don't think that's unusual?" exploded Sam. "He's gone to meet somebody. S*he doesn't suspect a thing.* Are you blind?" There was a pause.

"He's probably talking about someone else not suspecting anything," whimpered Cate. "Could be anybody. He changed his shirt to arrange his overtime. He didn't sneak off with anyone." It was all sounding a bit lame, and the panic in her eyes betrayed her.

"Yeah, you might be right," said Sam. She was angry, but hated to see her friend looking so timid and vulnerable. Cautiously getting up from the chair she straightened her uniform. It was time to start work. "Ask him about the text and see what he says. I gotta go. We can talk about it tomorrow." Making her away across the room she glanced back, smiling reassuringly, and narrowly missing a parked pushchair next to the platform door.

Cate winced.

"Yeah, see ya tomorrow."

Raising one hand she signalled goodbye. It was all very well suggesting she asked Oliver; but what if she discovered something she didn't want to know. If he was having an affair; would he leave her, like her father did? She didn't want to face life alone at forty-nine; fifty even. No-one could take Ollie's place. The situation was absurd; she was happy living in blissful ignorance, and didn't want to think about it any longer. There was no point in opening a can of worms; anyway, what would she do with a plateful of invertebrates? Chewing on her bottom lip she looked around the room, hoping for distraction from her dilemma.

Disappointingly, the girls on the next table finished talking about hair removal and were now discussing cake. Cars were stacking up at the red lights as she stared out of the window.

> *"Traffic is at a standstill in Wolfinger following an incident earlier today. Police investigating the strange circumstances surrounding the impulsive purchase of a sliced medium wholemeal, say it was supplied by a local supermarket, now closed for forensic tests.*
>
> *The store manager said staff didn't notice anything suspicious at the time. But on discovering the loaf was bought by a man that changed his shirt before entering the shop, he said he was shocked and*

surprised. He added that in future staff would remain vigilant and if anyone entered wearing clean clothes again, they would be turned away. Other shoppers have been warned not to approach the man who may have fresh breath; although this is unconfirmed.

This is Catherine Bartlett, reporting for Newsline, in the town centre. And now back to the studio."

Rising calmly from the chair, Cate marched out of the door and into the street. It was a twenty minute walk to George's house.

Looking back

GEORGE SPENCER BENNETT MARRIED Elizabeth Bartlett in 1972. At the time he was a thirty-seven-year-old bachelor in love with an incredible woman. It wasn’t inconvenient that she already bore two daughters; a ready-made family meant he didn't have to put up with the discomfort of screaming babies and the expensive attachments needed to use them. Two years doing National Service as a groundsman in the RAF during the 1950s prepared him for most things in life. And although he spent much of his existence successfully avoiding non-adults, he was certain that children were similar to Alsatians. A firm hand and regular meals should do the trick.

He was almost right; Eve was nearly sixteen and spent most of her time reading books and holding hands with her long-haired boyfriend. Mature and polite, she was respectful and well-groomed. It was virtually a pleasure to knock on her bedroom door and remind her that not everyone in the neighbourhood enjoyed pop music played that loud.

His other newly acquired step-daughter, Catherine, was just ten in Earth years, with the smile of an angel and the spirit of a wild stallion. On the outside she was as pretty as she was precocious. But the viscera were completely alien. He gave up trying to work out what was going on behind the innocent facade. No-one else thought it odd that she had a vocabulary far in advance of her age and spent hours glued to the television watching science-fiction. Or that she could survive on a diet of egg and chips; no vegetables, no fruit. No wonder she was insubordinate and argumentative. It was as though she deliberately took the opposing view to everything he said or did, and still managed to make him look unreasonable. She also possessed a cosmic mind-bending power over her mother, one blink of those huge extraterrestrial eyes, and she caved in and conceded his point every time. Impossible child.

However, Elizabeth - more often Betty - was an amazing woman; delicate and beautiful, an orchid on a golden pedestal.

Sometimes he just liked to watch her, baking, dusting or simply ironing his large cotton pants. Every task completed with elegance, like a butterfly hanging out the washing. He remembered her with passion and pleasure; her picture was on the cherry-wood sideboard, next to the clock. She was taken from him on a cool, bright day, twenty-six years ago; the first Sunday in April. They planned to visit the garden-centre by the canal, but never went because Betty got up that morning with backache. It was so severe that it made her screw up her eyes and walk back and forth in the kitchen until eventually he called the doctor. The locum suggested taking painkillers. When they rang again she had been pacing the carpet for two hours; the first in her pink, furry slippers, and the second in her bare feet. Lined with pain her face was grey and distorted; the corners of her mouth trembled and her brow crumpled in distress. The doctor suggested she visit the accident and emergency department of the hospital. When they left the house she was crying; it was serious.

They were on the way in the Vauxhall Chevette when it happened. One minute she was sitting next to him looking out the front screen, and then without warning she leaned over and laid her head on his shoulder. For a second he thought she was only resting, but when she almost slipped into his lap, it was obvious something was very wrong. Stopping suddenly in the middle of the road he cradled her face in his hands. She was pale and limp, and all the vitality and exuberance were missing; evaporated in less than a heartbeat. Her beautiful blue eyes staring ahead blankly into a future she would never see. Wiping away her tears with his fingers, he kissed her softly on the forehead and held her close. Then two young men tapped on the window and opened the door, and all he could do was shake his head and say, 'It's my wife - it's my wife.' Cold tears filling his eyes trickled slowly down his cheeks as he looked up at the man reaching into the car to press Betty's neck. There was no pulse. He didn't care to recall the details after that, the world rushed around him while he moved in slow motion. A ruptured aneurysm drained her life away, and his too for many months; like water spiralling down the plug-hole. If only he could have impeded the flow.

Eventually he joined the 'Fifty-Fifty Club'. Friendship and fun for ladies and gentlemen in the fifty plus age group -

apparently. Or - an eclectic bunch of divorced and widowed oldies. At first he wasn't sure it was for him, he was never big on the social scene – that was more Betty's thing. But he changed his mind after discovering that his new friends all remembered the war, and were delighted to discuss doodle-bugs and rationing for hours; an encouraging result. Nothing like a world conflict for bringing people together and lifting the spirits. Most of them still had jobs to go to, so they met in the evening, every Wednesday at the Sports Pavilion next to the bowling-green. Amazingly, he grew up in the same street as one of the members. Charlie Warner lived three houses away, in the adjoining terrace on Pommel Street; he was two years older and always had a runny nose when they were at school. Now free of nasal congestion but recently divorced, Charlie made it his personal mission to incorporate George into the Fifty-Fifty fold.

"This is Gordon," he would say, "ol' Gawdy. Can you believe it? We grew up in the same street."

George wasn't sure whether he remembered that Gordon was a nickname, derived from Gawd 'n' Bennett but he never corrected him; and consequently he became known as Gawdy again some forty years after he lost the childhood moniker. The other detail he kept to himself was that Charlie used to be called 'Wonky' Warner, on account of having one ear higher than the other. It was even more apparent now that he wore glasses but George politely ignored his asymmetrical view on life. Both ears were useless anyway; he could be called virtually anything without fear of retribution. Wonky Warner had been almost completely deaf since he was a child, after a World War II bomb demolished his house while he sheltered under a table. Surviving the blast elevated him to street-hero for many years; and although he couldn't hear most of the admiration, he became a good lip-reader.

Almost twelve months after losing darling Betty, George met Mrs Grace Braithwaite at the club. She was plump and loud, with a wide gap in her front teeth. It was particularly visible because she spent much of her time laughing and throwing her head back so far it looked as if it would almost roll off her shoulders. The effervescent Jamaican was the merriest widow he ever met, without her ever touching a drop of liquor; she loved life, and her God, and adored 'Gawdy'. Now they were the closest friends, virtually inseparable.

Cate tried to embrace the relationship. She was twenty-three when her mother died. It was good for her step-father to have a companion; he shouldn't be lonely. But the woman was brash, and so unlike her mother that it was impossible to say why he would find her interesting at all. On the other hand, it didn't do to consider the situation in any depth; George and Gracie being intimate made her squirm. Old people engaged in bingo and bowls, not sex.

By the time she arrived at George's house in Blooms Lane it was nearly two o'clock. Ollie's text was puzzling, and she could do without an interrogation into how 'the day had been so far'. Ambling up the path in the bright summer sunshine it was possible to distinguish the outline of two people in the sitting room. Grace was asleep on the brown leather recliner, identifiable by the familiar shape of her hair.

George was in the chair opposite, where he always sat when he wasn't making model aeroplanes, overlooking the road from the front window. Watching his step-daughter sauntering along the street and opening the wrought-iron gate, he settled back in the cushion; preoccupied, as usual, she approached the front door. The knocker clapped twice and then the key turned in the lock.

"That you Catherine?" he called out.

"No it's the Grim Reaper – am I too early?" she replied, poking her head into the room.

"One day you'll come in and find me asleep in the chair, and I'll be dead."

"You won't be asleep then, will you? That's like saying one day you'll wake up dead." Slumping in the doorway she sniggered.

"I will one day," he mumbled.

"Was I asleep? I must have nodded off," said Grace, looking disorientated.

Cate's nostrils twitched; smoked bacon. The crockery on the hearth was from her mother's dinner service, still in use after all these years; the glaze was cracked from being plunged in hot water too many times, and the gold leaf edge was almost faded to extinction. Grace left her crusts again, scattered on the plate.

"How are you today, Catherine? It's nice to see you, how's your day been so far?" she asked with a Caribbean lilt.

"Have you got your results yet?" butted in her step-father, rescuing her from a tedious reply.

"Not yet, classifications are tomorrow, should be ok though. And," she paused, "I've got an interview on Thursday with Newsnetwork."

"Newsnetwork," he repeated, sounding impressed. "Did you hear that Gracie, an interview with Newsnetwork?"
Cate smiled, "I'll put the kettle on, shall I." He had no idea what she was talking about.

"No tea for me," said Grace, pulling herself up from the chair. "I better get back, Collin will want to go out, he'll be wondering where I got to." Her bushy, black hair was flat on one side. Pushing it into shape she liberated her dress from the crevices around her body and waddled out the door. "I see you tomorrow, Gawdy. Bye Catherine. Good luck with your news work people, tell me all about it at the party."

"See you Thursday," she acknowledged, trying to sound enthusiastic. Mrs Braithwaite had to be invited to her birthday celebrations for George's sake, but luckily tickets for the graduation ceremony next month were limited, so she could politely be excluded.

"Is there something wrong?" asked George as she arrived with the tea. "You look tired."

"Not really," she shrugged, digging into the biscuit tin to avoid his gaze. "I didn't sleep well last night, that's all; I had a dream about Ollie. You were in it as well."

"Me? What was I up to?"

"You were walking towards me; we were at a fairground or something. And you were wearing a fawn overcoat."

"Wasn't me then, I haven't got a fawn overcoat."

"You had one in the dream," she sighed, sucking a ginger nut.

"Could be Uncle Jack, he's got a fawn overcoat. Definitely wasn't me, what would I be doing at the fair? In a fawn overcoat, doesn't sound like me."
There was no point in arguing; it was only a diversion tactic anyway.

"No airplanes today?" she said, looking at the table. It was spread expectantly with newspaper and the carefully laid out components of a De Havilland Mosquito. The sitting room led to a dining area lined with shelves from floor to ceiling. Like mahogany runways, the wooden sills were crammed with model aircraft and tiny painted pilots under dusty canopies, patiently waiting for war to break out.

"No flamin' glue, have I. Sure I had another tube somewhere, but d'you think I can find it. Looked everywhere, had all the drawers out, still can't find it."

He was going to rant now; the corners of his mouth turned down and his bristly grey brows knitted together, forming a ridge over his aged blue eyes. Dunking another biscuit, she swept it skilfully into her mouth, nodding with concern in the right places.

"I wouldn't mind if I didn't put things in a safe place," he continued, staring intently at his step-daughter, "turn 'round five minutes later and everything's moved. Expect you'll come across a great pile of things somewhere when I'm gone." He was more than a little obsessed with his untimely demise lately, trying to prompt a wave of sympathy but settling for the usual patronising trickle.

"Mm," she acknowledged, glancing at an uneven stack of boxes in the corner, spewing out spare wings, wheels and pieces of plastic fuselage. He was still rambling. How could she ask Ollie about the text when she got home? Surely there was some mistake; it was hard to imagine him referring to anyone as 'babe'. He never called her darling or sweetheart, or used any terms of endearment; it simply wasn't him. But what if he was seeing someone else? Could he be getting away with it because she trusted him? It really wasn't plausible; he wouldn't risk everything they had together. A tuft of silver hair, sprouting from George's left ear, twitched as he spoke. If Oliver ever developed face-fuzz she would make sure it was well-trimmed. Particularly out his nose, it was unattractive.

"…something'll have to be done, they're a public nuisance," he went on. "I've had the council on, but they say they can't do anything."

"What? What are you talking about?" It was a common hazard – he often changed the subject when she wasn't listening.

"Tweet, tweet, bloody, tweet - every morning, outside my bedroom window. I'm awake at the crack of dawn. No wonder I lose things. We'll see how chirpy they are with a beak full of catapult."

Oh good, a new development; something extra to add to the growing list of irritations in life. She rubbed the bridge of her nose with the thumb and index finger of her left hand in disbelief. Closing her right eye, she peered at him with the other.

"Don't tell me you're shooting poor little innocent birdies off the fence."

"Innocent my arse," he growled. "It's an organised tweet-a-thon!" There was a pause. "I hadn't thought of shootin' 'em…but I could get an air rifle." His eyes lit up.

"Have you been sniffing glue?" she interjected incredulously. "You can't shoot birds out your bedroom window; it's illegal. This is a residential area, not a flippin' rifle-range. Start waving a gun about and you'll have armed police chucking tear gas down your chimney. Please promise me you'll leave the wildlife alone."

She was agitated; an unusual display of emotion. Her normal calm rattled by the realisation that she should pay her step-father more attention instead of dismissing him as just another dependant. A cranky old man he may be, but he was the only person left in the world that could demonstrate any unconditional parental-pride in her achievements. She should keep a better daughterly eye on him, and at the very least, ensure he didn't get arrested for being a sparrow-sniper.

"Haven't got any glue to sniff," he muttered, feeling admonished and looking like a 77-year-old schoolboy.

Perhaps she was a bit harsh.

"Easily sorted, I'll get Luke to pop 'round with some later. Don't want the aviation production line grinding to a halt. Or the glue people becoming insolvent," she quipped. "I'll text him and see where he is."

Finishing up the biscuits together they chatted about the Chinese meal taking place on Thursday. It wasn't a big party – considering it was her fiftieth birthday. Truthfully, graduation was far more important than having dinner at the restaurant, but she couldn't get away with ignoring her half-century celebration. There had to be guests, food, cake and balloons or she would never hear the end of it; if only she could send a clone to grin and whoop, and blow out candles. However, the job interview added a new dimension; it was certainly going to be an eventful day. Scooping up the crockery she walked out of the sitting room.

"Leave the washing-up. I'll do it later Catherine. It keeps me busy."

"I wasn't going to do it anyway," she said cheekily, "I'm not the maid, y'know."

Walking into the kitchen was like passing through a time-tunnel. The beige door was a gateway to the eighties, complete with grey worktops and wooden units. Chintzy curtains wilting at the window contrasted with the starched white netting, like a wedding dress wearing a pinny. A constant aroma of roast dinners was baked into the walls, and ingrained into the old brown carpet that covered the lino. The crockery clinked as she slipped it into the washing-up bowl. Cate glanced at the tea-cosy on the silver tray, next to the kettle and the empty milk jug. Her mother always insisted on smothering the teapot with a red cosy in the shape of a cockerel. Faded and stained with tea, the aged bird was still smiling at her, as it did when she was a child. It looked very much like a weather vane, the sort that sat on church spires. Perhaps it was a sign. George would never remember to watch the Newsnetwork channel. Her mother would've loved it - her daughter on the telly. She stared at the garden through the net curtain; it was neat, like an allotment. The reporter was standing under the apple tree.

> *"Rather an odd day, so far. The ridge of high pressure that's been bringing us this lovely sunny weather was interrupted this morning by something unexpected. Not a hurricane - but it may well be an ill wind. Looking ahead further we see a number of storm clouds building to the west, and a rogue front forcing its way in from the south. It's doing its best to break up the settled weather, and we won't know how it'll turn out for at least another day or so. But there's a good chance that this outbreak could blow*

over without having to pick up an umbrella - or poison anyone acting suspiciously.

This is Catherine Bartlett reporting for Newsline with the short-range forecast. I'll be here again later with more weather but now it's back to the studio."

Her phone wailed, signalling a text from Luke. She replied and then picked up the calendar propped against the tiles behind the tea-tray. Thursday was circled in blue. 'Catherine bday' was scribbled in a space next to the date. Flicking over to the next month, she expected to see her graduation marked in a similar manner.

"Do you want me to write my graduation in, you haven't put it down?" She walked back into the sitting room carrying the calendar.

"Well, that's an interesting point. *Can* you put it in?"

"Yeah - I've booked you a ticket." Tutting quietly, she picked up a pencil from the table. George leaned back in the chair with his hands clasped together in front of his chest. It was when she bent forward to enter a note against the date that she noticed it was on the wrong day. Actually it was the wrong month. She flipped the pages back and forth.

"Where's July? What have you done with it?"

"There wasn't one in it when I bought it."

"No July," she said scornfully. "Whatever possessed you to buy a calendar with a month missing?" He was beyond belief, sometimes.

"I didn't know it was missing, did I? Nor did the other old folk, we all bought calendars last Christmas. Who counts the months? They're all supposed to be there."

She laughed.

"That'll teach you. I told you not to buy cheap stuff from your club." Technically she would be eligible to join the Fifty-Fifties in just a few days, but there had been no new members for years and all the existing ones were well over seventy now.

"You can't trust nobody," he shrugged, shaking his head.

"They rely on people like you, thinking you've got a bargain. Dodgy geezers - quick sale - they're off, and you never see them again."

“Oh I see this dodgy geezer all the time. I’ll see ‘im later if he brings me glue.”
Cate cringed, staring up at the ceiling. Everyone at the club knew that Luke was her son. Maybe he didn’t know July was missing. Or perhaps his dimwit sidekick, Monky, supplied the calendars. That was probably it. He might rip off a few unsuspecting pensioners but he wouldn’t swindle his own grandparent; not knowingly. Hurriedly saying goodbye, she left for home.

Elementary

OLIVER WAS BACK, his sparkling Z4 resting on the drive, clicking and cracking as it cooled in the sun. Cate sighed, a scruffy male was slumped against the front door of the house. He was partly obscured by the car but the long legs, dirty trainers and torn grey jogging pants could only belong to one person.

"Y'alright Mrs C? Waiting for Ell."

"You can come in, y'know. You don't have to wait on the doorstep," she said pulling the keys from her bag.

"Na, yer alright. I don't want to get in the way of yer hoovering and stuff," he said sheepishly. It was the culprit himself, responsible for most of the evil-doing in the world, and likely as not, the downfall of the whole economy. Monky was a gangly youth with greasy black hair, small eyes and a wide mouth. He bore a striking resemblance to an adult chimpanzee, especially as his ears stuck out at right angles from his head, but his nickname owed its origin to being born into the Monk family, apparently. Irrespective of his pedigree, Michael Monk was not popular. It wasn't his fault, but surely Luke could hang out with someone more intelligent than a banana skin.

"I'm not going to hoover," she replied.

"No, yer alright. You might drop some dust, or something, and need to get it out, and then I'll be in the way," he bumbled. "I'll jus' wait 'ere for Ell. We were in town but 'e went to 'is grandad's. Y'know - glue."

"Okay then," she played along, "if you want to wait outside, but if there's a fire you better get out of the way quickly because I don't want you blocking the exit."

"Oh yeah, I definitely won't, definitely," he nodded in earnest. "If I see a fire, I'll bang on the winda and let you know."

"Good," she murmured, closing the door. Monky was the least of her problems. Thrilling news about the interview, but her stomach was trembling at the thought of asking Oliver about the text; it still felt wrong. Sitting at the dining table, hunched over his laptop, he peered at a copy of a crusty old document labelled 'Whitechapel murders.'

"The obvious things always get overlooked," he said as she appeared in the doorway. "But he slipped up here, incriminated himself without even realising."

"Really," she said coolly. Her face was serious for once, chin tucked into her chest, and head cocked to one side. Silence. Biting her top lip she decided the interrogation could wait.

"What's the matter with you?" he asked.

"I've got an interview," she smiled, "with Newsnetwork on Thursday, for the weather presenter." There was no way of containing her excitement. Gripping the back of the chair, she bounced up and down on the spot. "I'm goin' to be on the telly."

Ollie looked up, pushing Jack the Ripper to one side, and closing his laptop.

"Well done," he said, with elevated pitch emphasising his approval. "Thursday though? What about your birthday?" His grey eyes narrowed.

"It's at one thirty; plenty of time. I was thinking, if you take me, and wait for me, I won't have to worry about getting the train. We'll be back ages before we need to get ready and – "

"No I can't," he interrupted suddenly, reaching for the laptop. He looked away, eyes flitting around the room nervously, as if following a fly without moving his head.

Cate stared; what could possibly be more important than her interview with Newsnetwork?

"Why?"

"Because I'm working. I've arranged to cover Jiffy, I can't back out now."

"Of course you can. The best opportunity I've ever had. Ever. And you want to deliver shopping. Anyway it's my birthday, why are you working when you know I've had it booked off for ages. You're seriously not going to make me get a train. Tell Laura you can't do it, she'll understand."

"I can't. I can't let her down."

Disappointment welled in her stomach like a balloon. It was a bad omen.

"But you can let me down," she snapped. "This could be my best chance, just say something's come up and you can't make it. You're incredible sometimes." Tears of anger pricked her eyes; she turned away, concealing her frustration.

"No need to be such a drama queen. I can't drop everything cos you don't want to take a train. I've got stuff to do. You'll be alright. And where am I supposed to wait, there's nowhere to park, it'll cost me a fortune."

Actually, he had a point. It was a nightmare to drive around the city, which was why she didn't want to do it herself. But it would be good to have his support.

"Guess what I just worked out." Getting up he walked over to her, tapping the document.

"Jack the Ripper was a delivery driver?" she scoffed.

"Not quite." Oliver smiled, leaning forward. "Give me a kiss and stop being grumpy."

Closing her eyes and sucking in her lips, she forced him to make do with kissing the tip of her nose.

"Get off," she protested unconvincingly. "I'm researching the weather." Pushing past him, she deliberately brushed her large breasts against his body.

"Do you want to know what I found out?"

"About Jack? No. Jack shit for all I care." Smirking she went into the kitchen.

"You'll be amazed."

"You think?" she called out. "If Abberline couldn't solve it, you've got no chance. You couldn't detect your way out of a paper bag." She had to rescue him from a public phone box once, after an excess of alcohol rendered him incapable of finding the exit. Without her intervention he might still be there pushing the walls.

The kettle was boiling. Gazing into the mirror at the far end of the room, she finger-combed her hair, and then stroked her neck. In fact, she was a much better detective than her husband; if he was up to something he would leave clues. He obviously meant to send the stupid 'babe' text to someone else. If it was an innocent message, there was nothing to worry about. On the other hand, if it was a love note to a covert concubine, he had already made his first fatal mistake. Peering at her reflection, she pretended to smoke a pipe.

"Elementary," she puffed. "The villain was apprehended because he was careless. Only a neophyte would leave such discernible clues."

The front door slammed, interrupting the moment. Pausing, she listened to the voices in the hall.

"Luke? Have you been to Grandad's?"

"Yes," he replied wearily.

"Was he alright? Did you give him the glue?"

"Yeah," he sighed. "Still alive. Still moaning."

Cate walked into the hall carrying a steaming cup of tea.

"Oh was he? Moaning about the calendar was he?"

Glancing furtively at Monky, Luke hesitated for a moment on the staircase, and then continued his plodding ascent.

"Nope, he never mentioned a calendar."

"That was lucky. He seems to have purchased a faulty one from somebody that looked remarkably like you, last Christmas."

"Ah, there could be a lot of people that looked like me last Christmas, mum," he grinned, almost reaching the top stair.

His derision riled her.

"Did you know there was a month missing?" she barked. "What about all the other old people you sold them to? You should've given them their money back."

"How was I to know? I bought them off a bloke in the pub. I didn't find out 'til I sold them all." Stopping, he turned, looked at his mother, and shrugged.

"Did you offer them their money back?"

"Not exactly. Some of them are so old there's every chance they won't make it to July."

She wasn't impressed, frowning as her son brushed blonde curls from his eyes, and scratched his head.

"I think I offered them a refund for any unused months," he added, rubbing his stubble chin with thumb and forefinger. "Didn't I Monk?" Luke glared expectantly at his friend leaning over the bannister.

"Yes," he answered, nodding his head as though it was on a pivot at the back of his neck. "Sold as seen, I think you said Ell."

Inhaling slowly, Cate breathed out in one sharp pant. Rubbing the handrail with one finger, her son turned to walk upstairs.

"Anyway, I don't think he was bothered about the calendar, he's pissed off about some noisy bird, or something."

Glowering at Monky, she desperately wanted to reach up and clip him around the ear, but it was completely unjustifiable.

"Why does Grandad want a gun?"

"Don't take any notice. He thinks the birds are tweeting too loudly," she said dismissively. "And please, for goodness sake, do not get him any sort of gun, under any circumstances."

"Na, don't worry I won't." Reaching the landing, he pulled a face at Monky and pushed him into his bedroom. "He hasn't paid me for the catapult yet," he added under his breath.

Result

THE NEXT MORNING THE sun was up before her again, heralding a new day and more shopping to be done. Groaning quietly, Cate hauled herself out of bed and got ready for work. A cool breeze shook the trees as she crossed the green separating the houses from the main road. Hurrying past the bush she clutched the fork in her pocket. Her eyes darted left and right; no sign of Bob, thank goodness. Minutes later she stood in the online shopping bay. Laura was reading out a management instruction regarding checking dates on perishable foods. Her silky pony-tail flicked and reared as she emphasised the importance of her message. Some members of the team paid attention but Jimbo sniggered and whispered to Ash. They were annoying. Not because they weren't listening, she wasn't either, but because they kept looking across at her. When the sermon was over both men raced to the door, shoving and giggling like teenagers escaping from sex-education class. The other shoppers sauntered into the warehouse but Cate lagged behind, purposefully fiddling with her handset.

"Did Ollie sort out his overtime yesterday," she asked when the room had cleared.

"No."

She looked surprised.

"Oh yes, he did. He came in; all dressed up he was," laughed Laura. "I didn't recognise him at first, out of uniform. Yeah, he's covering Jiffy for me. You're not in after tomorrow, are you, your birthday isn't it?"

Nodding, she loaded carrier bags onto a trolley. "Did he seem normal to you?"

"He never seems normal to me," grinned the supervisor, with one eye on the shopper and the other fixed on something more than ninety degrees away.

"He *is* working Thursday though?"

"This Thursday, yes." Laura smiled, pulling her pupils into parallel vision. "You planning to do any work for us today?"

"S'pose so," she chirped, shoving the empty trolley into the warehouse, and feeling a little more positive.

The morning dragged. After the store opened at seven o'clock, there was a constant stream of customers that couldn't find gooseberry jam, or cornflour, or pudding rice, or anything that required them to actually gaze at the shelf for more than two seconds. They interrupted her daydreaming and slowed her shopping speed.

"What were you sniggering at this morning?" she asked Jimbo while they picked bread.

"Me? Nothing."

"You weren't making fun of Laura were you?"

"No, bless her. Perishable goods are not a laughing matter," he mocked, cocking his spiky, gelled head on one side and staring up at the ceiling. "Not sure about some of the shoppers, mind. Lucky no-one checks their sell by date."

"You're implying that some of us are past it?"

"Course not, I wasn't referring to you Cookie-dough," he smarmed, squeezing a soft brown loaf in his large hands. "There's nothing crusty about you, I meant the customers."

At the end of the aisle Lawrence appeared, carrying a cauliflower.

"Him, now that's a different matter. I've heard his 'best before' date is in roman numerals."

The two men continued to exchange banter as she packed crumpets into the trolley, and made her way back to the shopping bay. Finally the shift came to an end. Collecting her things from the locker room, Cate hurried home.

Bob was washing his car on the drive. Hamish sat motionless at the side of a low hedge looking out across the street, resembling a golden-brown sphinx. A grubby looking bear lay at his front paws, like a grizzly sacrifice; its glassy eyes staring helplessly to heaven. She tried to sneak past, unsuccessfully.

"Alright Cate, you been to work? What's up with your old man? Shot off the drive earlier with his wheels spinning."

"Dunno."

It was very likely he was avoiding someone.

"Poor Hamish was a bit worried, nearly ran over Teddy. I've told him not to leave his toys on the pavement. Mind you Ollie's lucky it wasn't one of his bones, they could wreck a radial."

"Yes. Got to dash, think I can hear the phone ringing."

"Haven't got tinnitus have you? My dad had that."

"No, actually I - need the loo," she smiled, crossing her legs illustratively.

"Yeah, me old mum had a problem with bladder control. You can get that tightened." Hamish turned his head suddenly, as though shocked by the conversation.

"It's quite common Hamish, nothing to be embarrassed about," said Bob, flicking water at the dog playfully, "happens to ladies in their later years."

Cate took the opportunity to escape through the front door. She ran upstairs and into the office.

"Later years, I'll give him later years," she mumbled. "He'll wake up next to Teddy's severed head on his pillow if he's not careful. Then we'll see who's got bladder control."

The black computer screen dissolved as she tapped the space bar. Now she would find out whether the last three years had been worth the pain and effort. Hovering over the keyboard, she stood with finger poised.

> *"Three years ago a woman from Wolfinger embarked on an incredible voyage of adventure. At the time many wondered what compelled her to relinquish a comfortable life in the world of finance in exchange for study at the local university.*
>
> *Some suggesting that banking was no longer fulfilling, others that she was simply at a peculiar age. The truth - it just stopped being fun. And so waving farewell to corporate comfort, campus hoodies and student slang replaced pin-striped skirts and industry jargon. Fine wines and business lunches swapped for soft drinks and curly fries.*
>
> *And now after years of study, and months of employment at little over the minimum wage, the outcome is finally to be revealed. Amongst the piles*

of books and media equipment, a sweet smell of success emerges, coupled with a warm glow of confident accomplishment. Could it be a First Class degree? Or will she just do one - on a two-one?"

Cate logged in to the results page. No turning back now; no amount of imagination could change the actual result. The number '1' was marked next to the word 'classification'. Smiling, she puffed out a sigh of relief.

"It's officially a first! This is Catherine Bartlett, reporting for Newsline from the front bedroom. And now back to the studio; stay with us for more on this story later."

Anything less would have been a shock. She achieved top grades over the last year, and now the result was confirmed. Barking, her phone signalled a text from Sam.

'Do u know yet?'

'Yep, it's a first'

A warm wave of satisfaction washed over her as she slid into the leather chair, leaning back as though she just conquered the world.

'Brilliant, I knew u would. Well done. Want to show u something, shall I come round?'

'Meet me at Georges at 11?'

'11.30 better for me'

George would be pleased, even though he never understood why she gave up a good job in the first place. She rang Oliver. No answer, after several seconds his voicemail suggested she leave a message.

"Hullo, it's me," she said softly. "Where are you? I got my First, by the way, and I'm going to George's in a minute. Ring me back if you want, see you later. Bye."

Stretching out both arms, she yawned, looking up at the ceiling while listening to the silence. No fireworks, no fanfare, and no husband to congratulate her. It didn't matter, nothing could spoil her moment. Her phone beeped.

'Thats good. In quiet zone of library looking up prostitutes'

How typically Ollie.

Father figure

MINUTES LATER, TRANSMOGRIFIED FROM homely shop-assistant to attractive woman, Cate set off for her step-father's house. Approaching the traffic-lights, a man and a young child came out of the dental surgery on the other side of the road. The girl wore a grey school skirt and white blouse, and her father carried a Pink Pony lunch box. Crossing the street, they held hands, laughing and swinging their arms. The man was tall and thin, almost twice the size of his daughter. She looked up at him, nodding and grinning to reveal a large gap in her smile.

Cate chewed her bottom lip; her own father went missing long before her deciduous teeth. He was tall with wavy hair and brown suede shoes. Shortly after her sixth birthday her mother said that he left the family home to become a missionary somewhere in Africa. Apparently, he sent a letter saying he arrived safely and would be in touch, but it was difficult to write from where he was staying. She never questioned the logic at the time. The years rolled by and eventually her mother stopped crying but the subject was never mentioned again. It was as though he never really existed; presenting the perfect opportunity to invent him wrestling crocodiles, fighting pygmies or battling against giant, man-eating pterodactyl. However she imagined him, he always bagged a tiger, and returned home with a pith helmet and a suntan; but never quite made it in reality.

When she was nine there was a flurry of letters in large brown envelopes, and then a divorce, not from Africa but from Swansea. For a while she envisaged great adventures of walking or cycling to Wales, where she would be re-united with her father and live happily ever after. He never replied to her letters. Perhaps he was devoured by a tribe of hungry pygmies from an uncharted area of Snowdonia. 'No accounting for taste' – one of her mother's favourite clichés. She rarely talked about her adulterous husband; but when she

did the phrase always cropped up in conversation, along with other less savoury expressions.
Shortly after the divorce, her mother married George. He was dependable but didn't know anything about children, as though he had never been one. Growing up in the war years didn't help. He was deprived of many things that post-war kids took for granted. Initially, Cate felt sorry for the boy in second hand clothes, who only had *half* an egg with his bread-soldiers. How could anyone have half an egg; even during the blitz chickens must have laid whole ones? Meal times in the new marital home were an instant clash point; she liked the yolk but gagged at the thought of eating the white. It was like consuming a lightly poached eyeball, and her mother didn't mind if she threw it in the bin.
However, according to George it was completely unacceptable; it was wasteful to throw away half the egg, particularly as she ate so many. Her step-father never had the opportunity of a whole egg until after he left school. Naturally, she offered him the white on several occasions - but it only made him angrier. Learning to live harmoniously in parallel was a long process and their paths often collided along the way. As she became increasingly adept at adult manipulation it turned into more of a circus-ring than a battleground. She was the ringmaster, her mother the audience, and George was clearly a clown. And, although he had big feet and frequently exploding trousers, to be fair he was no match for The Bartlett.
It wasn't all bad though. Every evening after dinner George went to the small bathroom with a sloping ceiling. Sometimes she sneaked up behind him, pushing the door open slowly as he filled the sink with steaming water. Often he let the tap trickle into the bowl to give her time to arrive smiling at his right elbow. Then she would climb onto the toilet cistern, leaning forward to pull faces in the mirror. He pretended to be bothered, 'not her again, getting in the way'.
They were her 'war' years. Her father was missing-in-action and George was powdered egg - an instant father substitute. Watching as he lathered his face and scraped away the bristles was fascinating. They floated like iron filings in the creamy water. She was more commentator than reporter in those days. Every shave was a Grand Prix event.

"An amazing crowd gathers around the super basin tonight to witness George - Britain's top razor athlete - attempt to break the world record for removing hair from his chin. The water's in the sink and he's lathering up, wearing a white vest, blue trousers and brown old-man slippers.

And he's off; already leading the others by more than a whisker. Look at the way he handles that blade, up and down the right cheek like a rocket. There goes the left side; I've never seen such skill in a man of his age. Now onto the top lip, but the German contestant is creeping up on him. Can he make it? Only a hair in it as he races across the face and jiggles his razor in the sink. It's going to be close. But he's done it! The crowd goes wild as Bennett takes Gold and pushes the German into second place.

This is Catherine Bartlett reporting for The News at Bathtime, and now back to the studio."

George always protested at the end. 'Do you mind? I'm trying to do me bloomin' ablutions 'ere.' Then he wiped traces of white foam from his chin and winked at the mirror. She could tell, even at that tender age; he might not have actually said he loved her, but equally - he never said that he didn't. They enjoyed a special step-bond.

Ahead, the couple approached the school gates; the man was clean-shaven. He kissed the girl on the forehead. She ran across the playground clutching her lunch-box, with blonde plaits dancing behind her. Waving until she was out of sight, her father put his hands in his pockets and strode off.

Cate continued to George's. He was sitting at the table in the dining room when she arrived, glasses perched on the bridge of his nose. Resting on his elbows, he cradled the fuselage of a model aircraft as though he was about to play a large, grey plastic harmonica.

"You back again," he said without looking up.

"Yep, and I've got my results, it's a First."

"Well done. Is that the top one?"

"Do you know anything that comes before first?"

"Suppose not. Better put the kettle on and celebrate. I can't move - I'm at a critical point."

She made tea and was about to raid the biscuit tin when there was a knock at the front door. Carrying a small black case, Sam entered dressed for work.

"Hello George, how you keeping?" she asked.

"Blimey, you've not come to sell me insurance have you?"

"No, do you want some? I just popped in to see Cate before I start. She did well, didn't she? You don't mind do you?"

Putting the aircraft down, George commenced an inventory of plastic parts; carefully checking each piece against the instructions and running his fingers over the moulded shapes.

"No, have some tea. Have a biscuit - if you're quick enough."

Cate glared, forcing a smile. How rude; she liked biscuits. Samantha congratulated her again, dragging her over towards the front window and indicating with her large green eyes that there was something she didn't want George to overhear.

"I get a better signal over here," she whispered, taking her tablet out of the case. "You gotta see this."

With a few taps on the keypad she logged into her 'Dates2Remember' account. A page of male pictures loaded.

"Wow, he looks fit," sighed Cate, pointing to the photo of a bare-chested man with rippling muscles and gleaming white teeth. "Have you contacted him?"

"Him, yeah he's on all the dating sites. He might've looked like that ten years ago, but he's nothing like that now. Sarah went out with him; he's a fireman, but apparently he's got a short hose."

They exchanged grimaces.

"Anyway, ignore him; look at this one, the one without the picture." Tapping the screen with her French manicure she pointed vehemently.

"Well, what am I looking at?"

"The profile, the profile!"

"Ancient Reg? If I want to see an old man I just look at George," laughed Cate.

Her step-father glanced up. Pushing spectacles up his nose with one finger, he screwed up his eyes to peer at the women.

"What?" he asked. "Am I on the internet?"

"No offence but I hope not, we're looking at dating websites." Sam smiled politely.

"You won't find a decent man on there, young lady; they're all layabouts. If they brought back National Service that might sort 'em out. It'd put our Luke right, I'll wager. He might have a job instead of selling dodgy calendars to old folk."

She raised one eyebrow.

"Not that kind, I'm seventy-six y'know." Hesitating, he asked excitedly, "Can you get air rifles on the internet?"

"No you can't. And you're seventy-seven," intervened Cate.

Sam pretended to look serious.

"Thinking of starting the Home Guard again?" she said, stroking her chin.

"Don't encourage him. He wants to shoot the birds cos they wake him up when he leaves the window open."

"Couldn't you just shut the window?" asked Sam.

"No I flippin' can't," he protested. "That's another thing National Service teaches you. When you've slept with twenty men, you learn to leave it open."

"Yeah, I learned that before I got to twenty," she smirked.

Cate deliberately ignored the innuendo.

"What's so important about this ancient guy?"

"He's not ancient - it's a nickname - from Ancien Regime." A blank face stared back at her. "It's historical. Something to do with the Middle Ages I think; it's code. This is a 'middle-aged' man. Ring any bells?"

"I know lots of middle-aged men. None called Reg though."

"Stop being dense and read the profile."

"Sexy Napoleon looking for French kisses with discreet Josephine. I've got dark hair and smoky blue eyes and I'm a loving, caring male. WLTM student girls - any, but prefer slim and sporty. If you would like to go down in history with me please make contact," read Cate. "Sounds like a weirdo."

"Exactly," said her friend. "And how many middle-aged, weirdo, blue-eyed, dark-haired, history-loving students do you know? This has got to be where he finds his women.

It's Ollie, that's why there's no picture." She was serious now, her face was full of concern and her eyes flecked with anger.
Cate pouted.

"Ollie hasn't got blue eyes, they're grey."

"Actually it says *smoky* blue, which means grey. It's another device to conceal his identity."
There was a long pause. Could Oliver really be deceiving her; it was hard to believe. Looking at Sam, she wanted to laugh; and then almost cried. If he was out looking for younger, thinner women, girls even, what chance did she have? Losing weight might be an option but she was never going to lose the years from her face. They were a team; they were going to grow old together. She didn't want to be alone, and she didn't want anyone else either. He knew everything about her, how she liked to be touched, how she looked without make-up. He understood her odd little foibles, and even put up with the *occasional* flatulent growl in the boudoir department. That was it. The passion was slipping away because they were too familiar; he wanted someone fresher, more exciting.

"I can't see it," she said eventually. "He has got a thing about Napoleon, but I don't think he'd use that on a dating site. He's more obsessed with Jack the Ripper at the moment."

"Yes but that's not likely to attract many girls, is it? The idea of meeting a man and getting chopped up doesn't appeal to most women. I know you're finding this hard to believe, and I can understand why, but if you were on the outside looking in you would see all the signs. Did your mum ever think your dad would run off to Wales with the girl from the butcher's?"
She had a point. Her father didn't even like meat according to her mother. Not that she was a very reliable source when it came to stories about him; only *she* could confuse buying sausages with being a missionary.

"So what are you suggesting? Look in the wardrobe for a French Emperor's outfit? Search his laptop?" Her face was full of disparagement and she avoided eye contact.

"Well at least have a look. I doubt he'll have left any obvious clues though," said her friend, beginning to get more animated. "I might be wrong, but I've got a feeling he's up to something. You really have to start scrutinizing. Pinch his phone and have a look through the messages, check his clothes for girl odour and stray hairs; follow him if you get the chance. If he's not hiding something, he won't have anything to worry about." Sam shook her mane of glossy hair and pushed it back from her face triumphantly.

"Actually, I wish I could follow him on Thursday," whispered Cate, looking over at her step-father. He was filing a grey aircraft wing with an emery board, meticulously removing the small lug where it had been attached to the plastic kit. "He's definitely working, but there's something odd going on. I asked him to take me to my interview but he wriggled out of it. You don't think he's making unscheduled 'deliveries' do you? He's always saying how there's loads of time between drops."

Sam's large pastel eyes opened wide, and her lips pursed in a sort of '*told you so'* expression.

"Who knows? If you want to be certain, get someone else to follow him. Ask *him*," she said, gazing out the front window. "He's your neighbour, isn't he? He could tail Ollie."

Bob walked past the house. Hamish was at his side but his body was obscured by the low hedge. It could have been a large canine head on a stick being dragged along the privet.

"No chance," said Cate, glancing over her shoulder and then looking back at her friend. "That man is omnipresent. If I didn't know better I'd think he was stalking me. Everywhere I go he pops up like a bloody jack-in-a-box." There was renewed strength in her voice, "I don't suppose *you* could…"

"I'd love to - but trains are a bit conspicuous when it comes to surveillance."

"Ask Mr Eyeball to do it," piped up George, still filing. Both women stared at him. It was amazing how he could be deafer than a cardboard box one moment, and have hearing like a bat the next. "He's a private detective."

"Mr Eyeball?" Sam looked at Cate.

"I can't ask him. I hardly know him," she replied to her step-father. "And if he's a private detective, you're a fighter pilot."

"Who's Mr Eyeball?"

"The man next door, he's a community policeman, used to be a milkman. I suppose he might do it, he always says hello to me," Cate smiled archly. She was perfectly aware that George's neighbour, the handsome Iain Ball, was attracted to her. He often invited her to view his collection of classic films. There was a large glass conservatory on the back of his house with the windows completely blacked out. He described it as his home cinema but she always suspected that the lights weren't the only things that went down in there. "I could ask him for some advice, I've seen him sneaking around town like a secret agent." She lowered her voice, "There's something Ollie's not telling me about Thursday; and like you said, if he's not hiding anything, he's got nothing to worry about."

What a dreadful moment. The sudden realisation that her husband might really be having an affair made her feel old and useless. She was still attractive, wasn't she? Other men looked at her sometimes; it was only the outside that was getting a bit flaky. Oliver should know better; he should know that she was a young woman on the inside. Her step-father continued talking but it was too difficult to join in, she wasn't listening.

"He was a member of the Intelligence Service," said George tapping his nose with an index finger. "That was before he was a milkman, of course, but he could deliver anything to your door without you ever knowing," he assured Sam, who was nodding politely as he wittered on.

With heart racing and a lump swelling in her throat Cate chewed on her thumbnail; the room was suddenly hot and uncomfortable. Nothing was proved, but her head was spinning. Her marriage would survive, surely. It wasn't a life that she wanted, microwave dinners-for-one, watching the telly. Not being asked out by couples anymore, while Oliver squeezed the hand of a skinny blonde in the back row of the cinema. And what about all the other bits he was squeezing? Actually, when was the last time they had sex? An unexpected sensation surged through her, like being plugged in to the mains. She had to find out what was going on. What exactly was he up to, and with whom? One thing was for sure, she wouldn't give him up without a fight.

Sam finished her tea.

“Well I’ve got to get off. Lovely to see you again George, I’ve got to go and drive some trains now.”

“Who’d have thought they’d let a little thing like you drive those great big trains…with your track record,” he replied. “Mind how you go.”

Walking out to the kitchen, she grinned, cradling the teacup in her hand, and signalling with a twitch of her head for her friend to follow.

“Shit, the handle’s come off this, you gave me a bloody china cup. Sorry. Don’t tell George please. Chuck it in the bin can you, and don’t let him see it." She laid it gently on the worktop. "Look, this is what I think. Why don’t you talk to the Eyeball man about following Ollie? I’ll write back to Ancien Reg, if that's what he wants to be called, and see if I can get him to take the bait. I’ll make up a profile and we’ll play the bastard at his own game. If he wants to go down in history, let’s give him a date he won’t forget in a hurry.”

"I can't believe this is happening. We were good on holiday, but actually that was the last time we...um...had sex. Why’s he changed? Do you think he's bored? Should I try and spice things up a bit? Entice him in some way."

"Don't know." Shrugging, she made her way to the front door. "Might be a bit late for that. Probably been going on for a while, and you didn't notice cos you didn’t really want to. You could wear some sexy knickers and try waving yourself about a bit to see how interested he is. If he makes an excuse, you'll know he's getting it somewhere else. Look, try not to worry, let's get some evidence first," she said, seeing the anguish in her best friend's face, "then we'll string him up by his balls. Did you ask him about the text?"

“Not exactly. I haven’t really had time,” she said as Sam was leaving.

“Maybe you shouldn’t bother now. Don’t tip him off that we’re on to him. Speak to you later.” A double-decker bus passed as she walked down the path.

Closing the front door, Cate leaned against the frosted glass. The number 12 from Upperfinger wasn't a bad omen on its own, but it was likely to mean that Grace would come wobbling down the path at any minute. She stared at the broken cup in the kitchen. Her phone beeped.

‘At home now. Where are you?’

'Still at George's, back in a while x'

Why did everything have to happen at once? Her stomach was fluttering and there was that sicky feeling again. Oliver's touch was sensual; special, wasn't it? The last time they kissed passionately was in Barbados; the balcony episode. Perhaps she shouldn't have insisted they went back into the bedroom, but there were definitely mosquitoes outside. She had a bite on each cheek to prove it. He seemed to enjoy it at the time. Could he have been thinking of another woman while seducing her? There was so much emotion in his face; it was unbearable to imagine someone else experiencing the lust in his smouldering grey eyes. Time to take action. If the Eyeball was in next-door, she'd enlist him as a spy and then call in at Jemima's on the way home for some sexual inspiration. It was just a blip, most marriages had them. Nothing she couldn't handle, that was for sure.

"Ok, I'd better be off. I'll see you Thursday at the Tun o' Rice," she called out, "and no harassing our feathered friends. I thought you liked eggs."

"Eggs?" George huffed. "What are you on about? Just a minute young lady, don't you go running off. Come back 'ere."

She appeared in the doorway.

"What was all that whispering about? What's Ollie been up to, is he in trouble?" he asked, looking at her over the top of his spectacles.

"Don't know, I haven't decided yet," she smiled wryly. Her step-father frowned. "No, not really; you don't need to worry. There's a competition at work to find the best driver, and they have to be followed secretly to see if their deliveries are up to standard." George looked sceptical. "If he wins we get free groceries for a month," she added. "It's well worth it, but I can't tell him he's been entered…because he'll get disqualified."

"Well you better give him a hint or you won't stand a chance. Last time he delivered here, me buns were squashed and the yogurts were upside down. He's like a bloody racing driver, you'll have to tell 'im something."

"I can't. And you'd better not let on either – loose lips, sink ships," she said holding her nose and puffing out her cheeks. Then she bowed out of the room, wagging her head and bending her knees as if she were disappearing under the waves.

"Talking of which, you can tell Sammy Shipwreck it doesn't matter about the cup," he called after her, "I've got plenty more, unless she's planning on making regular visits." Tugging the door closed, she stepped outside without responding.

One good turn

HOPPING OVER THE LOW dividing wall between the two houses, she tapped on Mr Ball's door. No answer. Brushing her hair from her face with one hand she rang the bell. If he didn't appear soon she would lose her nerve. Still nothing. Cate bit her lip, unsure of what to do next. The door opened suddenly.

"Mr Eyeball," she flustered. "I mean Mr Ball." There was a pause. "Hello."

"Catherine. Hello, what a pleasant surprise," he smiled, seeing her looking up at him from the path. "Come in."

He looked extremely handsome in uniform. Even community police were sexy. In her teens it was firemen but she progressed through the emergency services with age.

"I've come at a bad time, haven't I? You're getting ready to go to work."

"No, no. I was just watching a film, the bell sets off a light in the cinema. Are you okay?"

"Yes, I'm sorry to disturb you. I was hoping you might be able to do me a small favour."

"Of course, come in, come in for a bit. I've always said I'm delighted to help you out in any way. How's your father?" With a wide sweep of his hand, he invited her into his home.

Stepping into the hallway was like entering a vampire cave with a fresh neck. Was he truly enquiring about George, or was it a euphemism for what he wanted to get up to? Whatever – it was an ideal opportunity to use her feminine wiles. Looking down coyly, she brushed imaginary dust from her skirt.

"Well, he's fine actually," she spoke quietly. "It's really not about George, it's something I was hoping you might be able to do for *me*."

"Oh I'd love to," he said almost breathlessly. "Let's have tea in the cinema and you can tell me all about it."

Placing one hand gently on her shoulder, he ushered her towards the back of the house. Her neck twitched as they walked through the kitchen. It was flattering that he was so attentive but she was a little nervous about what he was expecting in return for the favour. If he got his fangs into her, would she be able to resist him? He pulled on the handle of the solid wooden door to the conservatory, allowing the dramatic music from a 1930s film to spill out. Touching his arm with one hand she stopped it from opening fully.

"Some other time perhaps, I don't mean to be rude but I've already had tea with my step-father. Shall I just tell you what it is? It…it's Oliver," she hesitated, looking away, "I need help with Oliver."

The music built to a crescendo, and despite her serious intent it was difficult not to laugh. There they were, close together, the atmosphere was tense and an orchestra was playing in the background. It could easily have been the scene from a black and white movie where the leading lady asks the hero to murder her husband.

"Catherine, I'm intrigued," he said, gazing at her purposefully.

"Cate," she corrected him, staring back. He had big brown eyes, warm and inviting, and exquisite features; well-defined lips and strong cheek-bones. But it was unnerving, the way he looked at her; like a fox entertaining a chicken. Perhaps he had actually been a secret agent once. There was something very 'bodyguard' about the way he was standing, with his legs apart and his powerful arms folded, decorated with dark tattoos. She wasn't sure whether she was going to be protected or interrogated.

"My dear *Cate*, I hope there's nothing wrong between you and your husband. Whatever it is, you've come to the right person. Please sit down."

Moving away from the cinema room and leaving the door ajar, he walked to the table and pulled out a chair for her. The kitchen was white and clinical, almost like an operating theatre. There were no trinkets, cups or appliances visible. The work-surfaces were completely uncluttered apart from one huge red container by the sink. It was difficult to say what it was, but as there was a large farmhouse loaf nearby, she assumed it was a breadbin. Sticking out of the bread, in a manor commensurate with a stabbing frenzy, was a serrated knife. Violin music played sympathetically in the background; it was as though he was choosing it deliberately. He patted the back of the chair.

"You mustn't say anything to George," she said, taking up his offer of a seat at the table.

"Did he see you come in?"

"No, he's glueing a Mosquito. I don't want him worrying. It's probably nothing, but Oliver's acting a bit odd. All I want is some reassurance that he's not up to anything. I'm sure he's not - but if you could follow him and make certain, I'd be very grateful."

"Follow him? That sounds interesting. When would you like me to start?"

"I was hoping you could do it one day this week. I'm sorry, this must sound all rather strange but I want to know what he gets up to while he's working. Is there any chance you could follow him when he leaves Spennimore's on Thursday morning? He's starting at half ten, but I'm not sure when he's finishing, you'll have to stay with him. I'd like to know where he's delivering to – and how long he spends at each address."

"No problem," he said bluntly. "I'm free all day on Thursday. I can get you a full report with photos. I've done this stuff before. Whatever he's up to, you'll have enough evidence to divorce him by Friday."

Not really what she had in mind; it was supposed to confirm Oliver's innocence, not his guilt. Seeing the disappointment in her face, he bent down to crouch beside her, balancing on his toes with his firm buttocks resting on his heels.

"I don't need to know what you think he's been up to," he said softly. "But if he's doing anything to hurt you, he must be crazy. You are the most stunning, most beautiful woman I've ever met. I know we're hardly familiar with each other, but I've watched you visit George since I first moved here. He talks about you all the time; he's very proud of you. You're such a caring person, Cate. I don't like to see you looking unhappy." He stroked her upper arm tenderly with one finger.

Caring? How astonishing; she hadn't noticed that about herself. It might not be completely accurate but he was disarming her with his flattery. His low voice and honeyed tones were almost hypnotic. Such a charming man, so easy to talk to; not quite the monster she imagined.

"I'm not sure Ollie is doing anything wrong, it's all very circumstantial. To be honest, I've never considered that he might be unfaithful, but what if I'm just ignoring the signs? I've no idea what I'll do if I find out that he's…" Looking up at the ceiling, she broke off mid-sentence.

"It's okay," he said, touching her cheek and drawing her eyes back to him. "I know how you feel. My first wife was so amazing, I adored her. There was something very *distinctive* about her. She was pretty and funny, and she had a great figure; everything about her was just…well, perfect. When I lost her I thought my world was going to end. I was so incredibly lonely. Empty, like someone ripped my heart out and there was nothing left inside me. I thought I'd never find anyone as special as her ever again."

His puppy-dog eyes begged her to lean forward and kiss the little crinkles forming on his temples. He looked good for a man in his forties. His hair was dark and soft, although his unshaven chin gave away his age with its patches of grey stubble.

"Your *first* wife," she repeated. "So you married again?"

"No, not yet, I'm still a widower. At the moment."

It sounded odd, as if his second wife was already planned.

"Oh widower, I'm really sorry, I didn't know. I sort of assumed you were divorced, George never mentioned…"

"I don't talk about Miranda much," he interrupted, "it was nearly six years ago now; before I moved here. When I tell people about how she died on the balcony, they jump to conclusions. They're wrong of course; I never hurt her. Just because she was well-off and sixteen years older than me." Glancing at her for reaction, his voice trailed off.

Cate tried not to look shocked. His confession hit her like an iceberg. She was right all along; he was a closet-maniac. He pushed wife number one off a balcony. They were probably having cocktails when he enticed her to look down at the sea crashing below, then he grabbed her legs and tossed her over. She wouldn't have stood a chance. Sex-On-the-Beach one minute, Miranda-on-the-Rocks the next. Bloody hell, sex on the beach! They weren't drinking cocktails, they were having it off when he shoved her over. Ollie was about to do the same thing when they were in Barbados. The handrail wasn't loose, he was just getting a better grip so he could murder her. Then she would be out the way.

There was a horrible silence. The music finished wafting from the cinema and Iain Ball was staring directly into her soul, just inches from her nose. She chewed on her lip again. It was an awful habit, and a complete giveaway.

"People can be so cruel," she whispered, hoping he hadn't noticed she convicted him without a trial, along with her husband.

"Were you on holiday when it happened?"

"Yes, it was our last day. We'd been drinking 'round the pool and then gone up to our room to get ready to go out. I've been over this so many times it replays in my mind like a film. The sun was low in the sky and she went out to the balcony to watch it set. She leaned on the handrail with her back to me, and her hair glowed in the light like someone had drawn 'round it with a golden pencil. I remember looking at her and blowing her one last kiss."

Putting his fingers to his lips, he eerily reconstructed the event. Cate felt his breath on her cheek.

"Then I went into the bathroom to get showered and when I came out it was game over, she'd slipped away." Mr Ball grinned with his mouth closed.

"She fell off the balcony?"

"No, she had a massive heart attack. There was nothing anyone could do."

"Thank God for that," she blurted out. As soon as the words left her mouth she wished she could climb into the enormous red breadbin and disappear. How insensitive. He was so understanding, and so gentle; and clearly he was still suffering from a massive loss himself. His beloved wife died tragically, he poured his heart out, and there she was screaming in his face how glad she was.

"I'm sorry, I didn't mean *thank God she died of a heart attack*, I meant *thank God she hadn't been pushed off the balcony*. Well, not pushed - fell. Of course not pushed, I didn't mean pushed, I meant slipped. You said she - slipped away." She was gesticulating with her hands nervously, and it wasn't helping. Smiling at her embarrassment, he took her right hand in his, holding it still to stop her accidentally poking his eye out.

"You see what I mean," he said. "Don't feel bad about it, most people think the same way. There was an investigation of course. The police thought I was guilty of something. I was thirty-six and she was fifty-two, you see. They were obviously thinking, good-looking guy, one-legged woman; she's loaded, he inherits everything – must be foul play here somewhere. And it was our honeymoon, which made it worse."

Rubbing her nose with her free hand, she attempted to hide the smirk on her face. This was a new twist; his beautiful wife only had one leg? Yes, that might be distinctive. She shouldn't ask but the journalist inside her was desperate to find out.

"Your honeymoon," she sighed. Could she tactfully ask what happened to the lovely Miranda's missing limb?

He saved her the trouble.

"Yes, it was awful. The police wanted to know everything. I had to tell them about her car accident. Well, as much as I knew."

"Car accident?" It was getting worse.

Mr Ball nodded.

"She lost her leg in an accident when she was seventeen."

That was a relief; he would have been twelve months old. He couldn't have caused that; unless he crawled out into the road when he was a baby.

"It never held her back, she had an artificial one. I kept it of course after she died; couldn't bear to get rid of it. It was sort of a part of her, even though it was never really - a part of her."

Was that romantic or disturbing? She couldn't decide but her curiosity wouldn't go away.

"I think I understand. Do you have photos? I'd like to see one."

Winking his right eye cheekily, he stood up.

"I can do much better than that, come and have a look." Holding out one hand, he invited her to join him. The blood drained from her face. Not the leg. Please not the leg.

"Don't worry," he said candidly, "it's not Randa's leg. I've got that upstairs, but I didn't think you'd want to see that just yet; you women are a bit squeamish. I can't think why, it's not as if it's attached to anything. But what I want to show you is something that I've wanted you to see for a long time. You'll really appreciate this. I know you're going to love it."

His enthusiasm was an ominous portent. Tugging gently at her left hand until she stood up, he guided her across the kitchen towards the conservatory. The door was slightly open but she couldn't see in because of the heavy green velvet curtain. Pulling it back with a sweep of one hand he revealed the cinema. It was much bigger than it looked from the garden next-door. Black drapes and blinds covered every glass panel. The house-lights were down but the dim glow from the two enormous antique lanterns lit the room sufficiently for her to see inside. At the far end of the room there was a large screen that took up most of the wall, neatly framed with burgundy curtains and a wide pelmet. The projector was at the opposite end, close to the entrance door, and partly concealed by a partition wall with a small square window. Down either side of the room colourful posters promoted classic movies that were 'coming soon', and the life-size film-star cardboard cut-outs added to the atmosphere. It really was just like a tiny cinema, complete with three rows of four chairs in front of the screen – and an audience. Quaint, but the plastic guests were a little odd.

"What do think?" he asked eagerly.

"Yes, it's very..." she struggled to find the right word. "Authentic," she decided finally.

"I'm glad you like it. Come and meet the team."

Gripping her hand firmly, he marched her towards the screen, and then turned to face the group. There were four 'people' staring back at them.

"I have to admit I got the idea from Miranda. It seemed silly sitting here with just an artificial limb for company, so I thought why not go the whole hog. This is Mr and Mrs Hitchcock, they enjoy sci-fi and thrillers." He pointed at two mannequins seated in the front row, dressed in 1930s style garb.

"Hello," she said apprehensively.

"That's Ernie in the row behind, he'll watch anything, but he likes to be in his favourite seat. And the girl on her own is Leslie. These three joined me when they left the department store in town and Leslie was a gift from an ex-girlfriend. She's named after her. Between you and me she's a bit of a bitch, and she's also got a slow puncture after a slight accident we had at Christmas; so I make her sit on the back row."

Looking around anxiously for an emergency exit, Cate bit on her index finger. He might be handsome but she had come to the conclusion that he was definitely two kernels short of the full popcorn. Leslie was not an ordinary mannequin; she was an inflatable with poseable arms and suspiciously large lips.

"Well, thank you for introducing me. It's fascinating what you've done here." Slipping free of his grasp, she overtly looked at her watch. "I really must be going, I promised a friend that I'd pop in on the way home, she'll be wondering where I've got to."

"Does she know where you are?"

"Oh yes," she lied. "I told her I was coming to your house first. Is there anything else you need to know about Ollie before I go?"

"No, I don't think so but there is one more person you should meet." Walking towards the entrance he went over to one of the life-size cut-outs. It was a petite lady dressed as an usherette, complete with short pleated skirt and a red pillbox hat.

"This is Miranda," he announced proudly. The figure had one hand on her hip and the other held out as if directing someone to a seat.

Smiling approvingly, Cate inspected his cardboard wife; she was very attractive albeit rather stiff. A quick downward glance confirmed there was nothing missing in the leg department. There was, however, a pair of steel handcuffs dangling from the woman's outstretched arm. Suddenly noticing, Mr Ball removed the cuffs and clipped them onto his belt.

"Thank you angel, I'll need those later."

"I'd better let you get on," said Cate, pushing the door open.

"Yes. You can rely on me. If there are any problems I'll ring. What's your mobile number?" He pulled out a small notebook from his trouser pocket. Releasing her details to someone who was clearly bonkers wasn't ideal but she needed his cooperation. A stifled mewing interrupted as she recited the number. It was probably a cat outside the window but it appeared to come from the direction of the breadbin.

"Feed you in a minute, just wait til this lady's gone."

"Your cat?"

"Sort of." Moving swiftly out of the kitchen, he walked down the hall and opened the front door. She followed. What did he mean by sort of? Maybe he didn't own the cat – or perhaps it was only 'sort of' a cat. It wouldn't surprise her if there was a ventriloquist dummy in the breadbin and he was making the noise himself.

"Don't worry about Oliver; he won't even know I'm there. He'll think I'm his shadow."

Extending her arm, she shook his hand warmly.

"Thank you so much. Naturally, I'll pay for your petrol and any other costs you incur."

"That's quite alright," he said quietly, "I'm sure we can come to some arrangement." His eyes were sparkling with that foxy glint again. Leaving him standing on the doorstep, she made her way down the path, not daring to turn around in case he was licking his lips. It was a ten minute walk to her friend's house. Cate always considered that Jemima was one of the strangest people she knew, but it was fair to say that she wasn't a patch on the Eyeball.

A fragrant moment

HOLLY WOODS PARK WAS AN attractive part of town with lush green verges and mature trees stretching across roads and lining the avenues. The dark old houses were built in the early part of the twentieth century. Double-fronted homes with enormous windows and long paths leading to rose-trimmed porches and heavy oak doors. Most of the residents owned expensive cars, displayed on the driveways like great shining trophies. Jemima drove a purple Mini, older than her teenage daughters and far less appealing.

Crunching the gravel under foot, Cate slipped past the battered car and walked up to the arched wrought-iron gate at the side of the garage. It was never locked. The metal hinges squealed as she entered, pushing through the overgrown lilac bushes and making her way to the back of the house. Rapping firmly on the glass doors, she heard a voice from the garden.

"I'm out here in the studio."

Stroking a handful of long feathers in her slim white fingers, Jemima stood in the doorway of the out-building used as a workshop. It was more like a dilapidated shed than anything else, with its warped wooden panels, moss-covered roof and flaking green paint.

"I saw the message about your First, congratulations. Knew you'd do it. I'll just tidy up here, then I'll make us a drink. Making a badger-scarer," she said gleefully, "to stop them getting run over on the corner. I'm pretty sure one is supposed to report a badger collision to the police, but it keeps happening and nothing much gets done."

"Not sure. I've seen a few squashed by the main road but I don't recall any 'police aware' signs," replied Cate, stifling a grin. Peering into the studio, she spotted a woven framework of twigs about the size of a small suitcase. Half of it was covered with feathers and dried grasses, and a tennis ball bobbed up and down on one side, attached by a wire coat-hanger. Considering what Mr Ball kept in his conservatory it hardly seemed odd at all.

Without saying anything further, she strolled to the top of the garden. Minutes later Jemima appeared carrying a tray of tea things. It was a pleasant summer afternoon. The garden was crowded with trees and bushes all bursting with ripening fruit and sweet-smelling blossom. Dreamcatchers and wind-chimes fluttered and jangled in the breeze; it was a noisy place but hypnotic and soothing at the same time.

"What do you recommend to instigate a guaranteed night of passion?" asked Cate, sipping camomile tea beneath the shade of a broad apple tree.

"A night of passion?" Exposing her uneven teeth, Jemima gave a wide grin. "Don't tell me old Ollie is flagging in the bedroom department."

"No…I'm pitching an article for the local free mag; you know, a bit of work experience. It's a topical subject. I mean, it's easy to get complacent isn't it; after you've been together a few years. I thought perhaps you could sort me out some stuff from your kit and I could try it out on Oliver before I write about it. I guess it's best to make sure it has the desired effect before I go recommending anything."

Cocking her head on one side, Jemima smiled naively. They worked together at the bank but she left several years before Cate, 'to get in tune with nature'. She was one of life's eccentrics. Much of her time was spent 'listening' to the planet. Apparently it told her quite a lot; how to live in harmony with the world, where to strategically place her furniture to make it comfortable, and that selling sexy underwear would bring peace and love into the lives of many. Unfortunately it didn't offer advice on making herself more outwardly attractive. She often wore garments quite obviously knitted by a colour-blind dog with one paw in a sling. Her hair was unkempt; a sort of grey ball of string unravelled on her head. But inwardly she was the sweetest, most caring person that anyone could wish to know.

"Well," she sighed after a brief pause, "one has to tailor these things to the person one is aiming to attract. What might work for jolly old Ollie might not tantalise another." Leaning forward she grasped a small lock of Cate's hair between her thumb and forefinger. "It's telling me that it's feeling a little upset," she added, rubbing the tress gently.

"Really?"

In that case Jemima's hair must be screaming for a brush and a good bottle of conditioner.

"Yes, an evening of intimacy will perk it up. I'm sure I can fix it."

After draining the pot of tea, the two women left the garden and went back to the house.

From the patio a set of French doors led into a large, cool dining room. In the centre stood an enormous wooden table covered with dried flowers and small glass jars filled with oils. An ornate crystal chandelier, rather too large for the room, spread insidiously across the ceiling. Cate visited the house many times; it hadn't changed for years. Still the same cream walls partly obscured by spiky plants and triffids; still the same giant mural on the back wall gazing out into the garden. It was a very good likeness, a self-portrait painted by Jemima when she was eight months pregnant. Stark naked, her long chestnut hair cascaded over her plump breasts, and her hands rested affectionately on her swollen belly. Some guests found the eight feet tall mother rather imposing but it certainly proved to be an ice-breaker at dinner parties.

At the time, the artist was extremely proud of her finished work, and greatly satisfied by the ensuing birth just three weeks later. The twins, Moon and Nightingale, were now thirteen years old; apparently, named after the first things their mother experienced following delivery. Luckily, she had either a vivid imagination or too much gas and air, or they might have been called Bedpan and Night-of-pain. Mr Henry Farthing-Thomas, their father, had little influence in choosing names. In fact it was speculated that at sixty-nine years old he had very little influence on the conception. The girls didn't remember much about him. He passed away before their second birthday. And while he may, or may not have bequeathed his genes, he was thoughtful enough to donate his considerable wealth. Cate always wanted to bow as she passed before the portrait; it exuded a superior presence.

"Jem," she said softly, "have you ever contemplated remarrying?"

"What, a man?"

"That was my original thought, yes."

"Good heavens no. I'd have to find one first."

"You must still miss Henry, though. Wouldn't you like a significant other in your life again? I mean apart from the girls."
Jemima was half way up the staircase leading to her workroom.

"Yes, Aitch was a love," she said smiling, "but I haven't really given a thought to replacing him. It's strange, I'm so used to being on my own that I sort of feel more complete without a man. I mean *sharing* your life with someone, that's the thing, isn't it? If you're sharing, you're dividing something, and how can I be 'whole' if I'm divided?"
Pushing open the door she entered a small room. It was stacked with skimpy costumes, odd-looking accessories and homemade candles. Inhaling the heady scent, she closed her eyes briefly.

"If one listens, one can hear and feel everything on this planet. A man, well, a man would just be...noise pollution."
The ladies listened intently. Perceiving her interest, Jemima made a hush gesture with one finger on her lips, her eyes glazing as if her mind had left the room. Cate strained her ears but Mother Nature avoided communication as far as she could tell.

"Why do you ask darling?" said Jem, suddenly waking from her trance.

"Just being nosey, I guess." Picking up a black leather peek-a-boo bra she gaped through the slit in the cup like a voyeur peeping through a keyhole.

"What exactly is it you're aiming to achieve with this night of passion. Are we talking *amour* darling, or just a damn good rodgering?"

"Let's go for rodgering."

"Excellent. And are we thinking of including anything a little more - risqué - shall we say? I've got some handcuffs here." Searching through a drawer she found a pair of pink fluffy cuffs and held them up with one hand.

"No, maybe not the cuffs. I haven't quite recovered from a recent encounter with a community police officer," Cate confessed.

"How intriguing. Okay, how about spanking? Virtually guarantees an intense night of passion, men can't resist it. Well, assuming it's not part of your normal repertoire."

"No, if I'm honest I can't say that it is. Not sure Ollie would go for it though, he doesn't like pain much."
Chuckling, Jemima pulled more items from the drawer.

"Actually, I was thinking about him spanking you, but it can work either way. Look, I'll put in a couple of paddles and one of these little flogging things and you can see how it goes, but I recommend some mutual massage first to get things moving."
She selected a whole range of erotic essentials, sometimes squeezing and listening to them with her head on one side, sometimes holding close them to her nose and breathing deeply. Packing everything neatly into a large jute bag she handed it over with a grin.

"Let me know how you get on. If it turns out really raunchy I'll put it on my website as a triumph, anonymously of course, with a link to your magazine."
Walking home, Cate tried to remember the set of instructions about candles and joss sticks. There were different colours and smells for each part of the evening. Approaching the house she was disappointed that Oliver's car was missing from the drive. Bob was at the corner of the street. Swinging a small knotted plastic bag, he was talking to a neighbour. She acknowledged them both with a smile. Hamish looked up as she passed, Teddy hanging limply in his mouth, drowning in drool.

"Hamish," she nodded politely. He whimpered in return.

"You been shopping Cate? Looks like you got enough to feed an army there. We all invited?" called Bob as she turned onto the drive. The comment didn't warrant a reply.

"I'm not staging a flamin' orgy," she muttered quietly after closing the door.
Welcoming his mother with the usual grunt Luke emerged from the kitchen holding a dinner plate piled with toast. Monky followed close behind with two mugs of tea.

"Alright Mrs C, you been shoppin'?"

"Yes. And no, you're not invited," she snapped, bounding upstairs with the bag clutched tightly to her chest.

Stomping into the bedroom she pushed the jute carrier into the wardrobe. Then regaining her poise she stepped out onto the landing and stared at her son, appearing at the top of the stairs.

"Have you seen Ollie?"

Luke plodded towards his room.

"Yep, tall man, dark hair, grey bits sticking out the side of his head."

"If you don't want to be the blonde kid with an axe sticking out the side of your head, you might be a little more cooperative. Did he tell you where he was going?"

Hoping to become invisible, Monky pressed his body against the wall. Threats of violence disturbed him, and he seemed privy to more than his fair share. Her son was unperturbed.

"Nobody tells me anything," he scoffed, opening the bedroom door with one foot. "But if it helps, he was wearing a white t-shirt and carrying cricket stumps." Turning in the doorway he gave his mother an angelic and disarming look. His pale blue eyes stared back at her innocently. "I'm guessing he went to take part in some sort of sport."

"Prob'ly cricket, Ell," added Monky.

Scowling, she turned and walked into the bedroom.

"Don't eat all my toast," she grumbled.

Cate lit two aromatic candles, placing one either side of the bed before going into the office to prepare for her forthcoming interview. There was a lot to consider and several hours passed before the Z4 growled onto the drive. Pushing the blinds apart she saw Oliver wrestling with a large bouquet of flowers as he climbed out of the car and entered the house.

"I'm up here, in the office."

Seconds later he appeared at the door with the blooms behind his back. Smiling, he presented them like a magician performing a trick. It was an impressive collection of vibrant roses, lilies and carnations, heads bobbing and bowing as they were thrust before her. A sweet aroma cascaded from the petals, filling the room. So why did she smell a rat?

"Thank you, they're lovely. Are you feeling guilty about something?"

"No," he smirked. "I thought you deserved some congratulations, that's all; on your results. Why would I be feeling guilty about anything? I'm going to jump in the shower. You alright?"

"Yeah. I didn't know you were playing today."

"I wasn't, until I got a text; one of those impromptu sessions," he said moving into the bedroom. "Bloody hell, what's that pong?"

She followed him into the room.

"It's not a pong. They're aromatic candles; they're creating a sensual ambience. I think we need some time to relax together, I've got something *planned* for this evening," she said looking up at him provocatively.

"Well you may have to *unplan* it, my shoulder's killing me. And it smells like geranium farts in here, blow those bloody candles out." Disappearing into the en suite he closed the door behind him.

Bowled out in the first over. Perhaps they were the 'after' candles, if only she paid more attention. Taking a deep breath, she stared at the door; and then turned the handle and pushed it open. Ollie stood at the small sink with his shirt off, examining his shoulder in the mirror.

"D'you mind," he complained.

"What have you done? I've got some massage oil, I'll give you a rub. Shit, how did you do that?" Her mouth dropped open. There were three red stripes on his left shoulder. A sudden panic came over her. They were scratches; fingernail scratches.

"What, what the…" she blathered. The words wouldn't come out. Pain seared through her head, and her stomach churned. "How did…who...how did you do that?" Her voice quivered.

Half smiling, he turned to face her.

"It's not what you think," he laughed. "I know what it looks like but I tripped over on the gravel. I was running backwards to catch the ball when a damn dog came from nowhere. I fell arse over tit and skidded along the ground."

Searching for the truth in his eyes, she studied him carefully; his tiny black pupils grew smaller as he spoke.

"Oh," she said quietly, shrinking back into the bedroom. Extinguishing one candle with a sharp puff, she sat down on the bed. Cate looked around the room, speechless and crushed by what she had seen. Her mouth was dry; licking her smooth pink lips she tried hard to swallow.

"What's wrong?" Ollie sat beside her, stretching out a hand to rub the back of her neck. "Are you alright?" he said softly. "You've gone a bit pale." His strong arms reached out, pulling her close. Tenderly, he kissed her forehead, and then her cheek. "Good job no-one had time to get their phone out or I'd be on MyTube by now."

Hugging each other in silence, her head rested close to his chest. His heart was pounding. Those hideous red marks could be the result of sliding along the ground; was she being perceptive or paranoid? Without looking at him, she pulled away and stood up. Blood drained to her feet as if she was flushing away. The other candle was still burning. Trying to move gracefully around the bed she ended up waddling wearily across the room, like a duck in concrete slippers. It took two breaths to blow out the candle. Her world was unravelling in slow motion. Gradually, turning to face him, she watched him remove his track suit bottoms and pants; his firm white buttocks standing out against his tanned torso and legs. Then her confusion lifted and she was able to speak again.

"Was he caught out?"

"Who?" he replied, throwing his dirty clothes at the foot of the door.

"The batsman. Did you catch him out?"

"No, the bloody dog caught the ball and ran off with it. We chased the little bastard for about half a mile."

Surprisingly her mind was quite blank. She experienced the phenomenon before, as a child. Avoiding active thought was a survival technique; it dulled the pain and allowed her to function almost normally.

"I'm going to do some dinner," she announced. "I fancy egg an' chips."

Walking over to the door she stooped to gather the clothes from the floor. Oliver stood naked like a rippling Greek statue about to take part in the Olympics.

"Do you want sausage with it?" he smirked, playfully thrusting his hips forward. Raising one eyebrow she cast a condescending grin.

"Just egg an' chips," she whispered, pushing his kit into the laundry basket on the landing.

As she started down the stairs the taps squeaked and the shower sprang into action in the en suite. From the kitchen she could hear the water drumming intensely on the plastic tray, like an eager accomplice destroying evidence. If he was guilty of anything – if there were any stray hairs or female odours, perfume or otherwise, they would be washed down the plughole without trace. And in the absence of genuine artefacts to examine he would have to be released without charge.

Choosing a large brown potato, she looked sternly at it cowering in her hand. There was no escape; it could protest, but it would end up stripped, chopped and boiled in oil. Versatile, but little sign of intelligence. If Oliver was a vegetable, he'd be a tomato; attractive, firm, ripe – and devious. There was no knowing where one stood with a tomato; one minute a vegetable, the next a fruit. Clearly, they shouldn't be underestimated.

Her egg trauma could be minimised by draining off the white before adding it to the pan; a distinct improvement. She would rather have anal sex than eat egg white; and the odds on either happening were not good. The reporter stepped forward as she closed the refrigerator door.

> *"A local man was injured today while taking part in a cricket match at Wolfinger recreation ground. The accident occurred during the first innings of the extemporised game, when strike bowler Cheesy Dave delivered a short-length ball. Hooked perfectly towards the boundary by top-notch batsman, Cheesy Dave's brother, it looked certain to make a four.*
>
> *However, leading cricketer Oliver Tomato-Cooke sprang into action. Unfortunately while running backwards the slip-fielder was ruthlessly floored by an itinerant canine. Cooke sustained lacerations to his left shoulder, while the dog, thought to be a supporter of the opposing team, ran off with the ball. The wound has been treated with antiseptic cream - and the cricketing shirt was not permanently damaged.*
>
> *This is Catherine Bartlett reporting for Newsline from the kitchen. Stay with us for more on this story later, but now back to the studio."*

The shirt. She stopped slicing potatoes and raced upstairs. Oliver was in the shower. Flipping open the lid to the laundry basket, she pulled out the cricket shirt, trousers and sweaty underwear. His clothes would be covered in grass stains and dirt from sliding along the ground. There might even be blood stains or a tear in the material. Opening out the shirt she laid it on the carpet. Immediate disappointment; there were no obvious marks. Cate kneeled on the floor with the garment in front of her. Bending over she examined the threads. It was uncharacteristically dry for an English summer, and it was possible that the grass on the pitch had worn away. Oliver fell on gravel, perhaps there would only be dust. He was still splashing around in the shower. Searching for stains was turning her cross-eyed. It made no difference if she viewed the shirt close up or from a distance; the marks must have brushed off. His underwear was in her left hand. Sniffing at his pants certainly wouldn't reveal anything worthwhile; that was for sure. Wrinkling her nose, she reluctantly gathered up the clothes and pushed them back into the basket.

What would Sam say? Clean shirt means he's cheating. What would Jem say? Inconclusive; he's hardly likely to let some floozy dig her nails into him when it would be impossible to hide. Stay vigilant, be suspicious, but don't be ridiculous. She didn't notice the bedroom door open, or Monky watching her. He stood at the entrance for a moment and then backed into the room and sat down.

"What's the matter with you?" asked Luke.

"I can't go."

"How old are you, four? Run the tap." He tutted.

"No, I can't go cos your mum's out there, sitting outside the bathroom."

"I doubt she wants to listen to you. She won't hurt ya."

"She hasn't really got an axe, has she?"

"No," he looked up from the game on his laptop. Monky rocked cross-legged on the stool. "It's more of a hatchet," he added gleefully.

"What if she's gone mental with menopause or somethin'?"

"They use it for chopping firewood, you plankton. Never seen her murder anyone with it. Anyway, it's not her style, too messy. She's more likely to poison someone she doesn't like."

"Well she's definitely acting a bit weird. She's praying and sniffing pants."

Luke recoiled. "Not my pants I hope?"

"Don't think so. I don't know all your pants Ell, but I don't think so."

"That's okay then."

Walking to the door he stepped out onto the landing. His mother emerged from the bathroom looking unusually exultant. Clearly, the flushing toilet and the muffled swearing emanating from the en suite were maliciously linked. Watching in silence, he saw her go into the office and come out with the large bouquet.

"I'm doing egg and chips," she said, fingering the flowers and ignoring the stifled profanities. "Do you and Monky want some?" It was an unusually generous offer taking them both by surprise. Luke nodded energetically and then looked at his friend.

"No, you're alright Mrs C. I don't wanna take a chance."

She glanced suspiciously at her son. Shrugging, he backed discreetly into his bedroom.

Her phone barked as she arrived in the kitchen.

'Hi, made up profile and text ancien reg. Did u ask eyeball to follow ollie?'

'Yep, all arranged. bit weird – tell you later. Not sure if im doing the right thing'

'ur not doing anything wrong'

Half-filling the tall crystal vase with water, she began arranging roses and carnations. And then picking up her phone she sent another text without expecting a reply.

'no proof Ollie is'

Enticement

NO-ONE SAT AT THE dining table. Luke took his plate upstairs where the smell of freshly fried potatoes became too much for his friend. Licking his lips, Monky watched the orange yolk drip and congeal over the crisp, salted chips. His mouth watered. Eventually succumbing to temptation, he ate several fries before Luke gently stabbed a fork in the back of his hand.

The Cookes ate in front of the television, watching the news. Most of the reports were about tragedy, misfortune and disaster; the country was in trouble again. But there was an appeal at the end of the broadcast from one of the oldest residents in the region. A man from Upperfinger, soon to celebrate his one hundredth birthday, was being interviewed by a member of the news team.

"Victor, what's your secret?" asked the reporter.

"I don't rightly know," said the man quietly. "But you gotta keep active and do new things all the time to stay young." Smiling towards the camera, his pale leathery tongue moved across his dentures like an old horse licking its lips.

"And there's something special you wanted to ask our audience tonight, isn't there?"

"Yes, I'm looking for a new wife before I reach a hundred," he nodded earnestly. "I been married twice, but I been on me own for six years and it's time to start courting again. So if anyone's interested, I'd like to meet up for friendship and possible romance."

"What sort of person are you hoping will get in touch tonight?"

"Anyone really, I'm not fussy, but ideally I like someone younger. Don't mind foreign food; and a cat's alright cos I still got a flap from last time."

Politely wrapping up the interview the reporter promised to pass on the details of any available ladies that might get in contact.

“That’ll get them queuing up,” said Cate sarcastically. “I wonder if the old lady I met yesterday is watching, she’s got a cat.”

It was a warm evening, a reminder they were in Barbados not so long ago, enjoying cocktails and the exotic delights of the Caribbean. Pouring a second glass of wine Oliver slumped in the armchair and closed his eyes.

“Why is he bothering at his age? He’s already had two wives; you would think he had enough by now,” he said.

“He’s probably lonely.”

“I’m not surprised, he’s got a face like a scrotum. He’s not going to find a woman by going on the telly and asking for one.”

“And where would you find one?” Leaning forward, Cate stroked his thigh, with her eyes fixed firmly on his response.

“Where you find everything, of course; on the internet.”

Glancing sideways, he removed her hand from his leg and took a gulp of wine.

“How’s your shoulder now?” she asked.

“Bit stiff.” He rubbed the joint without looking at her.

“Wasn’t it the shirt you got in Barbados? You’re lucky you didn’t ruin it when you fell over,” she added nonchalantly.

“Yeah.” There was a brief silence. “No, I wasn’t wearing it. I took it off. Topped up my tan while I was fielding; it was scorching this afternoon.” Turning to look at her, his eyes narrowed as if he was trying to work something out. “Oh yeah, who flushed the toilet while I was in the shower?”

“Monky,” she said calmly, leaning forward and picking up the dinner things. “I asked him to wait ‘til you finished but he said he couldn’t.” Cate smirked. “He’s got diarrhoea.” Screwing up her nose she tried to hide her amusement and look convincing.

“Charming,” he muttered as she left the room.

Playing cricket with his shirt off? How alluring; he had a good body. Broad shoulders and, after humping crates of shopping around, his chest was muscular and defined. He even developed a sort of six-pack that looked pretty decent with a tan. She swigged more wine. It would be a shame to waste the stuff upstairs. What if she bent over his firm thighs and pushed out her bottom? Would he pull down her knickers and rub her cheeks with exotic oil? And then slap her slippery buttocks with his strong hands until they were red and smarting. The tiny crispy-edged egg-white slid off the plate and into the bin. It was time to knock him for six.

"Luke! Bring your plate down. I'm putting the dishwasher on."

Her son appeared at the door minutes later, with several plates and cups.

"How long are our ladders, Mum?"

"I don't know. Ladder length, I suppose. Dare I ask why?"

"I'm thinking of being a window-cleaner." Stomping through to the front room he asked his step-father the same question. Oliver was unimpressed; the ladders suddenly became very valuable and Luke could get his own set.

"And another thing," he protested, "tell Monky next time I get the shits I'm going 'round his house to use the toilet."

Sticking out his bottom lip, Luke frowned.

"I'll tell him," he said slowly. "But I'm not sure he'll be happy about it."

Nothing really surprised him; he passed his mother clearing up in the kitchen.

"See ya later." He glanced at her. "And Monk thinks *you're* weird, wait 'til he hears what Ollie's planning."

The front door clicked shut. Taking another bottle of wine from the fridge, Cate dashed upstairs and poured two drinks. Quickly pulling the jute bag from the wardrobe she tipped the contents onto the bed. Incense; something sensual, maybe a little spicy. Sniffing the sticks she found some scented with patchouli, and then she arranged four white candles on the glass plate. With the room suitably dressed and lit, she stared at the crumpled black and pink satin corset. It came complete with matching g-string and silky stockings. Helping herself to more wine she loosened the laces and crammed her body into the lingerie. Now she knew what it was like to be a sausage; it was a tight fit. There was a full-length mirror on the wall by the door. Standing in front of the glass with both eyes squeezed shut, she opened first the right, and then the left. It was a pleasant surprise. The corset accentuated her voluptuous figure, pushing up her pale bosom and trimming her waist. Her legs looked good in black stockings; with some heels and lip-gloss she would be completely irresistible. Sitting carefully on the bed, she smiled and took another sip of wine. An exotic joss stick haze snaked slowly across the room, throwing shadows on the blinds. The atmosphere was perfect for seduction. Adding the finishing touches to her outfit she took a handful of silk rose petals from the bag. Before scattering them down the stair carpet she practised her pout in the mirror and then lay prostrate across the landing. There was one minor detail overlooked, her husband was engrossed in the television and she would have to scream for him to come upstairs.

"Ollie! Oliver! I need you for something, can you come up?"

At first there was no reply, and then the door opened and he appeared in the hallway.

"What are you on about?"

Standing with his head cocked to one side he followed the petal path up to the top step where she rested half over the edge. Her blue eyes sparkled mischievously. But it was the precarious position of her breasts panting over the top of the corset that caught his interest.

"I'm watching the cricket, can you wait until the end of the first innings?" he smiled.

Poking her tongue into her right cheek she raised one eyebrow expectantly; perhaps she should wear white flannels. He walked upstairs slowly with a smouldering grin, staring deliberately at her exposed bosom.

"Suppose I could record it."

When he reached the top he turned, offering her an outstretched hand. She took it gracefully, but before she could get up he pulled her gently across the landing and into the bedroom.

"I didn't know cavemen had Skyplus," she laughed clambering onto the quilt.

"They didn't have cricket either. Just think how bored they must have been."

Dropping onto the duvet he nuzzled close to her ear. One of his fingers traced the line of her sternum until it was softly stroking the cleavage between her breasts.

"So, what's all this for? I thought our anniversary was in Barbados."

"It doesn't have to be a special occasion; just thinking we could have a little cuddle."

Opening her eyes wide she tried to look angelic, confirming she was expecting much more than a hug.

"I told you, I've got some massage oil, it's good for sports injuries. Take your shirt off and I'll give you a rub."

Rolling across the bed she pulled a small bottle of red liquid from a bag. Then unscrewing the top, she held it to her nose and sniffed.

"Better take your trousers off too, don't want them getting all greasy and stinking of lusty lube," she grinned.

Getting up slowly, Ollie pulled his shirt away from his body and then over his head. There was a glass on the wooden cabinet next to him. With beads of condensation trickling down the stem, it was almost full to the top with white wine. Reaching for the drink, he took several large swigs before stripping to his shorts and flopping face down onto the pillow. The marks on his shoulder were paler now and the welts less noticeable. Scratches or grazes? It was difficult to be certain.

Sitting on his bottom, she knelt with one leg either side of his brown body. He murmured approvingly as she dripped oil on his back and began massaging with both hands.

"Mind," he whimpered. "I think it's bruised."

Slathering the lube on his bronzed flesh she worked with her fingers and palms. Her thumbs pushing into his shoulders; moving in small circles like she was polishing his muscular frame. Kneading firmly, she bent forward until her breasts pressed on his back, and then she gently nibbled his right earlobe. He sighed approvingly as her tongue slipped into his ear; tracing the folds and penetrating deep into the auricle, rather like licking out a cream horn.

"Do my legs, can ya. They're a bit achey," he whispered.

Kissing her way meticulously down his spine, she wriggled back to sit at the top of his thighs. Then pressing her teeth into his skin she took tiny bites of flesh just below the ribs. He stiffened to prevent her smooth lips from tickling. Prolonging the torment, she sucked and nipped at him until he let out a groan of pained enjoyment. Cate shuffled forward. His body relaxed and he exhaled with a contented moan. Swinging her right leg across this body she swivelled on his buttocks to face his feet. Oliver supped more wine, draining the glass; he pushed up on his elbows, and then collapsed onto the bed, as though knocked out by a heavy punch.

Pouring oil onto her hands, she rubbed them together and inhaled the sweet musky scent. His legs were slim and athletic. Stretching out and leaning on his thighs, she began caressing his ankles, using her thumbs to massage around the bone and loosen the joint. Next she worked on his calves, lightly chopping with both hands and then stroking upwards in slow sweeps. His breathing became deeper and more rhythmic as she moved towards the top of his legs.

Gradually she came to the soft skin just below his buttocks. Her fingertips teased the flesh, making small circles close to his balls; her body swaying to and fro as she pressed down on him. The air was heavy with exotic joss stick aroma, and the candlelight was warm and romantic. It was almost as good as Barbados, cavorting in the white cotton sheets in the Caribbean heat. Her hand slipped inside his shorts. She had several sex toys but they hadn't dabbled in anything remotely kinky before. Should she ask him about spanking, or just start tapping his bottom with the paddle and see what happened? He'd probably grab it and give her a good smacking; she wriggled in anticipation. Lightly digging her nails into his buttocks she turned to look at him. He was still; the only movement came from his steady breathing, slow and even. Then he let out a low rasping snore. It was an appalling insult; she slapped his backside hard with her bare hand.

"Oliver! You're asleep," she screamed.

"What? No I'm not. I'm just resting my eyes. Carry on."

"This is supposed to be arousing, sexually exciting; it's not supposed to send you to bloody sleep. You don't think I got all trussed up like a frilly sausage just so you could dream about someone else, do you? Wake up you bastard."

"I will. I wasn't asleep. I'm just a bit tired. Let me rest for a minute." His voice trailed off, "I like sausages."

The breathing became deeper and noisier. Biting her lip, she stared at him, exhaling with a disappointed pant. What was she thinking? She could lie naked across the bonnet of his car and he wouldn't notice. And he'd rather be whacked with a cricket bat than spank her until she squealed. Sliding off his body she sat next to him on the quilt. He snored loudly in defiance of her efforts. Reaching down into the bag at the side of the bed she pulled out one of the paddles, a heart-shaped black leather implement with a four-inch tasselled handle. Squeezing the grip she tapped the palm of her hand. His bottom presented an appealing target. Calmly raising her arm above her head, she paused briefly and then brought the paddle down as hard as she could on his slumbering buttocks. There was a sharp crack, like the sound of leather and cork meeting willow on an open pitch; something he was particularly fond of. Jerking violently, Oliver shrieked in pain.

"That bloody hurt. Are you mad woman?"

"Mad? I'm bloody furious," she snapped. It was unusual to lose her composure.

Burying his head in the pillow, her husband shuffled his shoulders until he was settled. Cate fumed at his side. He fell asleep, ignoring her outburst. It wasn't just the initial disappointment. Why couldn't he stay awake and show some interest? Maybe he was already shagged out. Fighting back the urge to cry, she took a deep breath and loosened her corset. She sat on the edge of the bed, flopping forward to rest her elbows on her knees, and her chin on one hand. There was some wine left; filling the glass with the pale Sauvignon she admired it shimmering in the candlelight before taking a large mouthful. And then frowning, she glanced at the TV in the corner of the room. The reporter was in the studio, sitting behind a large desk.

> *"A man from Wolfinger was discovered snoring in bed earlier this evening. The 45-year-old part-time delivery driver was taking part in a sensual massage experience when he dozed off, mid-rub. When questioned about his state of unconsciousness, he confirmed that he was 'resting his eyes' and was not asleep. His wife dismissed this as nonsense, as he was unresponsive and showed no signs of arousal,*

despite attempts to seduce him. Dressed enticingly in stockings and pink satin, she was about to execute the coup d'état when she made an unexpectedly limp discovery.

She said the deliberate breathing and rhythmic snorting were a complete giveaway to his condition, and that she had tried to wake him several times. The man was later pronounced asleep at the scene.

This is Catherine Bartlett with Newsline. Stay awake for more on this story later."

Flowers

THE NIGHT WAS STILL and silent apart from the occasional bouts of Oliver snoring. Each time Cate opened her eyes it was brighter outside the window. The glow of the new day squeezed past the blinds, reaching further and further into the room, like icy fingers of light piercing the darkness. It was like she hadn't slept at all. She kept clearing her mind but the floodgate opened the moment she relaxed, and those niggling doubts came sweeping in. The unexpected flowers, the marks on his back, the absence of marks on his shirt, the text, the excuses; the list went on and on. But most of all, the thing that really hurt was the complete disinterest he showed in making love to her. After all the trouble she went to, to fall asleep just as she was about to do something exciting was highly inappropriate.

The alarm beeped. As usual, her husband didn't stir as she leaned over; hesitating for a moment she kissed him softly. His back was towards her, revealing the scratches on his shoulder but they were even fainter this morning. She poked him gently with one finger. No response. Why did 5am have to be so early in the morning? Couldn't people get out of bed and do their own shopping? Reluctantly sliding from under the duvet she got ready for work. Cate opened the front door and stepped outside; the new day swirled around her in a warm breeze. It was as though the morning was waiting to greet her; like puppy-fur brushing against her legs. She shivered.

No change; the same bright sky and sleepy street she usually encountered at this time. The world was completely ordinary. Things had to be kept in perspective; everything always turned out okay in the end. No need to be melodramatic. Stuffing her hands into her pockets she set off. Hamish was sitting on the pavement across the road. Wagging his bottom he swept the path with his thick tail when he saw her. There was no sign of Bob.

"Alright boy," she said quietly. "What are you doing out here on your own?"

"Morning Cate," came a reply from behind the low hedge. "You off to work?"

She should have known he would be lurking about in the bushes somewhere. A fuzzy shape came into view. His dark, grey locks looking more untamed than usual, like a scouring pad exploded on his head. Surely he hadn't been sleeping in the hedge. Actually, it was unlikely that he ever slept, he probably just plugged himself in and recharged.

"Morning. Yes, off to work again," she replied quietly, trying not to sound too flippant. Where else could she be going dressed in a Spennimore's uniform at the crack of dawn? At least Hamish had the intelligence not to ask. Ambling through the estate to the common, she raced across the clearing with her usual apprehension, arriving out of breath at the dual-carriageway. By the time she reached the car park, employees were converging on the supermarket from all directions. Wednesdays were always busy; there was a crowd collecting in the storeroom, yawning and shuffling about.

"Good morning shoppers," sang Laura; her black pony-tail swishing around as she viewed her colleagues with wide-angle vision. "How are we all?"

"Well, I'm glad you asked, I've got a bit of a sniffle," replied Jimbo teasingly. "Should I go home?"

"Rhetorical question Mr Langley. I don't really want to know, especially in your case. Still breathing - still shopping, as far as I'm concerned." Grinning, the supervisor raised her arms and flicked her fingers in a shooing gesture. "Off you go my lovelies, shopping doesn't pick itself. "

Cate functioned on autopilot for most of the morning. The interview was only one day away. Would Newsnetwork like her? They didn't know she was fifty. Was she too old to begin a new career? A First Class degree should count for something. What if they were all really young? She was a good presenter and a talented writer. They would be judging her ability, not her age. And after all, she had been reporting all her life, unofficially.

It was close to ten o' clock before she noticed the store was open. She scanned a tin of chicken Topcatz but her handset kept rejecting it. It didn't matter how many times the task was repeated, the barcode refused to cooperate. Eventually, she was forced to admit it was the wrong item. Selecting the correct tin, she stuffed it into a carrier and leaned on the trolley. The cat food aisle was packed with customers carefully choosing pet cuisine. One person in particular caught her eye; it was the Kittychunk lady standing by the stuffed toy mice.

"Hello," said Cate, moving next to the old woman. "Aren't you the lady that was looking for Kittychunks the other day? We've got some small tins now."

"Kittychunks?" she repeated. "Oh yes, I managed to get some but I had to walk all the way to Price-co for it. That fussy cat'll be the death of me one day, I'm sure." Her pale eyes smiled. "But he's such good company since my Bill passed away. Fifty-one years we were married you know. We had our ups and downs, but he was a lovely man. Thick black hair he had; a great mop of it, just like my little Stanley; daft cat. It's our wedding anniversary next week - mine and Bill's. I always had a big bouquet every year you know."

Clasping her wrinkled hands to her chest she revealed a thin gold ring on her wedding finger. She rubbed it while she spoke.

"Never stop missing them do you. Are you married?"

The online shopper nodded.

"Take care of him," the woman went on, "be good to each other, love each other, and always have trust. You'll last forever if you have trust, you know."

"I better get on."

"Oh yes, you were so helpful to me the other day, I don't want to get you into trouble."

The old lady was lonely. Shopping was her only opportunity for conversation apart from talking to the cat, which wore a wig by the sound of it. She was comparing flea collars with enthusiasm, fingering each one carefully and shaking her small grey head.

Glancing at her watch Cate gave her trolley a hard shove. In retrospect, she could have been a little more obliging at their first encounter, but the old woman didn't seem unhappy, even though she walked to Price-co.

Jimbo hugged a pack of toilet rolls in the next aisle. His large eyes bulged, and his head jerked forward in a pecking motion as he spoke, exacerbated by his pointy nose.

"Walks in, bold as brass, dressed in his wife's clothes," he said as she came around the corner.

Lawrence leaned against the toilet tissue with his arms folded.

"Never," he interjected with a tone of disbelief.

"Yep, short skirt, stocking tops, tight jumper, the lot."

"What? High heels?"

"I'm not sure about the shoes. He's got bigger feet than her, wide fitting by the look of the boots he wore at the Christmas party. But he was wearing *her* fur jacket. *I paid for it*, he says, *so I'm bloody wearing it.*" Both men laughed. "Watch out, watch out" he added, "Mrs Cooke's about."

Cate hovered by the value-pack loo rolls.

"You look knackered, what you been up to?" he enquired with a grin.

Rubbing her left eye, she suddenly felt vulnerable at being caught eavesdropping.

"Oliver kept me awake most of last night," she yawned.

"Did he indeed? I'm not sure I want to know what you two Cookies get up to in bed." Jimbo grimaced.

"Could be a lot of crumbs involved," suggested Lawrence.

"He was snoring actually. Not that it's any of your business." She wasn't in the mood for levity. "You're like a couple of old women, you two."

There were several items left to pick according to her handset; scanning a packet of moist wipes she pretended to be engrossed in her shopping.

"Touched a nerve," whispered Jimbo. "Handbags at dawn."

Clutching imaginary bags to their chests the men playfully pushed and slapped each other. Ignoring them both, Cate selected a family pack of toilet tissue from a low shelf to reveal the reporter sitting cross-legged in the display cavity.

> *"An online shopper and a grocery assistant were rescued earlier today from the soft tissue aisle of Spennimore's in what was described as a freak*

accident. The male workers were discovered dazed and bruised under a large pile of luxury toilet rolls.

Unconfirmed reports suggest there was an explosion brought about by an accumulation of gas. Eyewitnesses say the two men were laughing and talking for some time when suddenly there was a loud crack, resembling the static from nylon underpants igniting a flammable gas. Onlookers were shocked to see the two employees propelled into the air and become tangled in a mass of toilet tissue that burst free from packs nearby.

One bystander said, 'It was incredible; like an enormous plate of spaghetti exploding and getting its own back by strangling the people eating it. You don't expect your loo roll to fight back.'

It's unknown at this stage which gas was involved or where it leaked from; although the men were previously warned that their constant gossiping could become a hazard.

This is Catherine Bartlett reporting for Newsline from the bathroom aisle of Spennimore's. Stay with us for more news as it happens, but now back to the studio."

When her shop was complete she scooted back to the storeroom. Ten o'clock was tea-break time for those who hadn't finished their shift, and everyone seemed to arrive and clutter up the shopping bay at the same time. Muscling her way in, she manoeuvred the trolley through obstacles with remarkable precision. The room was noisy with chatter and people stacking totes, but there was a noticeable hush when she hung up her handset and turned to leave. She only just stepped into the warehouse when Laura called her back.

"Excuse me Mrs Cooke, before you go disappearing I want a word with you."

Several members of the online team milled about, trying not to look suspicious.

"What? I'm in a bit of a hurry," said Cate.

"You don't get away that easy," called the supervisor, producing a large bouquet of flowers and an envelope from behind a trolley. "Happy birthday. A little bird told us it's a bit of a special one, so this is from all of us, for tomorrow."

The shoppers gave a cheer and added their congratulations. Covering her face with her hands, Cate peeked through her fingers at her colleagues. Several of the team broke into a verse of '*Happy Birthday to you'*, adding to her embarrassment. Curtseying ostentatiously to her audience she took the flowers. They were beautiful; a special arrangement of brightly coloured dahlias, delphiniums and gladioli from the greengrocery department. Beaming with delight she thanked her colleagues and then made her way to the locker room.

Outside the store the sun roasted the roofs of parked cars; the breeze dropped and a clear blue sky framed the busy landscape. She squinted into the sunlight. Customers pushing empty shopping trolleys rushed towards her in their skimpy clothes. Smiling and nodding, they instinctively knew the flowers marked a special event. How thoughtful of the team to buy her a gift. Weaving her way through the traffic, she headed for home across the car park. Unexpected gestures always made her especially happy. Passing the plastic giraffe and the rows of trolleys, she was nearing the exit when something made her stop suddenly. A black cab pulled away from the taxi stand, and sitting on the bench in the waiting area was the Kittychunk lady. On the seat beside her a half-empty shopping bag. Deep in thought, neatly poised, with her flat, navy-blue court shoes pushed together, her hands rested in her lap. Cate crossed the forecourt, walking apprehensively towards the woman.

"Hello," she said with a smile, "caught you waiting for a taxi."

"Yes. Well no. I sit here and watch the world go by for a while before I catch the bus. Taxis are so expensive, I don't bother with them."

"I suppose they are." Fiddling with the change in her pocket confirmed there was hardly enough to get to the end of the street. The old lady should have the flowers.

"These are for you," said the online shopper awkwardly. Cradling the bouquet like a sleeping baby she stooped forward and presented it to the woman.

"For me?" The sun bounced off the blooms, reflecting in her wrinkled countenance and illuminating her face like a buttercup under the chin. "They're very lovely, but they can't be for me."

"Yes they are; really. A present from Spennimore's. Once a month we choose a customer, and today we picked you. Congratulations, and thank you for shopping with us."

"Well I never. Whatever will they think of next?" Reaching out, the woman took the flowers, delicately touching and stroking the petals.

"We thought you deserved a treat with your anniversary coming up, you did say you always had a bouquet. It would be a shame for you to miss out."

Tears of delight welled in the old lady's faded blue eyes. Seeing her enjoyment and gratitude brought a lump the size of a pickled onion to Cate's throat. She hadn't expected that a minor selfless act would have such an effect. The idea of giving the flowers away was partly conceived because she had to carry them home, and had already filled her only vase with the suspicious bunch received from Oliver. But the gift forged so much happiness, it made her feel worthy that she could be magnanimous in the face of floral adversity.

"Will you be able to get them home alright?"

"That won't be a problem. As long as the bus driver doesn't charge me for them," laughed the old girl. "They'll brighten up my front room no end; it'll be like living in a new house. Thank you. And I shall write and personally thank Mr Spennimore."

"There's really no need, as long as you like them, that's reward enough for us."

It might be a nuisance if either the customer or the online team found out the truth, but she would invent a fib to cover it up if necessary. She left the old woman enjoying nods and winks from passers-by. They assumed she was celebrating a special event and that someone cared enough to buy her flowers.

Bouncing along with a smile on her face Cate strolled home. Wednesday was a day for relaxation; George was at the Fifty-fifty club and she had prepared for the interview already. Approaching the house, she looked around; no sign of Bob, the Z4 gleamed on the drive.

There was also a peculiar contraption on the front lawn. Something resembling a coffin on wheels; a shabby brown box about six feet in length, tapered at one end, and daubed with red tribal markings. The largest part of the wooden container was fixed to the rusty chassis of an old pram and a caravan jockey wheel was clamped at the thinner end. Peering inquisitively at the metal arms protruding from the top of the strange cart, she tried to work out what it was for. Luke appeared at the side of the garage before she had time to decide. Looking first at the carriage, and then at her son, it suddenly became clear that the two were inextricably linked.

"What the hell is that?" she asked.

"It's my window-cleaning cart. I'm using it to transport ladders until I can afford a van. What do you think? I bought it from Uncle Pat for a tenner."

"I think you're not leaving that in my front garden. And I know I'm going to regret mentioning this but you don't have an Uncle Pat."

"No, I don't. Pat's Monky's uncle."

Cate nodded expressively.

"You paid ten quid for a coffin on wheels from a Monky's uncle. That says it all. Where are the ladders?"

Emerging from behind the garage, Monky came into view. He carried a bucket in one hand and a chamois in the other.

"Don't actually have them yet. We're gonna concentrate on bungalows to start with; Uncle Pat got rid of the ladders cos of his vertigo. As soon as I've saved up enough I'll get some off iBuy. Unless you can persuade Ollie to give me the key; he's padlocked your ladders to the shelf in the garage," said Luke with a vague air of hope.

Rubbing her ear with one hand Cate walked to the front door.

"Keep it out of my sight. I know I said you should find some work but I don't even want to think about the consequences at the moment."

"Y'alright Mrs C? Shall I give ya bottoms a quick leather while me water's still warm? You could pull the curtains if ya like, so ya can't see me," said Monky.

"A tempting offer," she sighed, "but I'll hold on until I can have the tops done at the same time thank you."

"No charge Mum," added Luke cheekily.

"Go away," she smiled, entering the house.

The dining table was covered with open books and scraps of paper, and Oliver was tapping energetically on his laptop. Looking up for a second as she stood in the doorway he peered at her over the top of his glasses.

"Major breakthrough," he said, raising his hands from the keyboard. Holding them a foot apart, palms facing, he pointed them at the computer as if indicating that he landed a large fish. "I got an email earlier suggesting a massive trail of references - websites, books; this guy is really onto something. I've spent the whole morning collating, and when I've finished analysing it I'm pretty sure I'll have all the proof I need to nail him. The actual Ripper."

"Wow," she said, trying to sound impressed. "Do you want some tea?"

"No, coffee. My dissertation is going to be award-winning. I might write a book; I'll probably get a prize for my contribution."

Muttering inanely, Oliver engrossed himself in his study. He made notes on his laptop, examining a map of London with great interest. If he inspected her erogenous zones with half as much enthusiasm he'd definitely get a prize for his contribution. She made hot drinks, helping herself to several custard creams while the kettle boiled. Taking her tea upstairs she changed from her supermarket uniform into a loose white t-shirt. It was one of her favourite 'thinking' outfits. Long and cool, it was almost like a short dress with a large grey seagull printed on the front. The pattern was unusual for someone who was scared of birds. However, if there was a choice of life after death she would almost certainly consider coming back as one. The downside would be eating out of bins and picking at raw fish; but being able to soar into the wind and squawk with a high-pitched whistle was very attractive. Not to mention the happy compensation of nicking pasties from tourists and target-dumping on their heads from a great height.

The bedroom window was open; something was going on in the street. Hearing the fracas, she looked outside to see Monky lying on his back in the road. Wailing loudly, one of his trainers was missing, revealing a dingy sock with holes in the heel and toe. Luke was laughing, and pushing the odd-looking handcart, while Bob called Hamish from the other side of the road. The Great Dane had a shoe in his mouth and was endeavouring to bark without dropping it.

At least the coffin was off the front lawn. Lowering the blind, she flopped onto the bed and closed her eyes. Fifty minutes passed before she opened them again, and the tea was cold.

Massaging her forehead with her fingers she drew both hands firmly down over her nose and cheeks until they rested on her chin; and then she stared at the ceiling. Was Ollie up to something or not? The suspense gnawed away at her. She should be savouring the last hours of being forty-something instead of dressing up as a siren and employing spies. Reaching across to the cabinet she retrieved her mobile phone and tapped out a text.

'Any reply from ancient reg?'

Sam was probably working. Getting up from the bed she went into the office and checked her notes for the next day. There would be an initial interview, then a sample script, and finally a screen test. Her stomach fluttered. Moving out onto the landing she heard her husband's voice. She leaned over the bannister, cocking her head on one side to eavesdrop. Whoever he was talking to, he sounded happy; flirty maybe, but that wasn't unusual. She had to get closer. Creeping quietly down the stairs she made her way along the hall and stood silently outside the dining room. He was quiet, listening to the other person on the phone, and adding low expressions of agreement in response. Cate's phone barked. Squeezing it tightly in her hand she tried to muffle the sound. Hopeless, it had already given her away.

"Yeah, yeah, hang on a minute." Oliver got up from the table, closing the lid of his laptop. She breezed past him before he could turn around. Casually collapsing on the settee she picked up a magazine from the coffee table and flicked through the pages.

"Well, it's hard to say at the moment but I'm pretty sure you're right," he said, glancing over at her as he marched through the French doors and into the garden.

Slowly edging back to the dining room she watched him pacing around the bushes with the phone pressed to his ear. He was smiling and kicking at the grass with his bare feet. His behaviour wasn't out of character; she just never questioned it before. She was so complacent; he could have been having an affair for a couple of years without her noticing. Rubbing the lid of the shiny silver laptop with two fingers she monitored his progress around the flowering shrubs. He was engaged in conversation and didn't look as if he would finish any minute soon.

Biting her lip, she gently lifted the lid of the computer, fixing her eyes firmly on his movements. As expected, he would be ages yet. She looked at the screen; a four digit password was required. Any normal person might select a birthday. But Oliver would choose - Waterloo, 1815; right first time. A long document appeared; pages of stuff about the elusive Jack. It was unlikely to reveal anything significant. She minimized it. Snooping was such an unthinkable invasion of privacy, it made her heart race. It would be devastating for him to discover that she was spying on him. He was logged into his email account. Nothing interesting in the inbox, or any of the folders as far as she could make out. Cautiously peering outside she watched her husband lean against the tree with his back towards her. If only she had the remotest idea what to look for. Re-opening the Ripper document she scrolled through the pages; perhaps he hadn't left any clues but she could find out what he was up to. The telephone conversation couldn't go on much longer; her nerves were fraying. She scanned the notes, running one finger loosely over the screen, and glancing furtively into the garden every few seconds. The work consisted of extracts and quotes, copied and pasted into one disjointed item. Mixed within the passages were comments and observations, added presumably by her husband, playing detective. Two paragraphs were highlighted and 'remember date' appeared at the top of one section in bold. Bloody hell, Sam's Dates2Remember account; the browser was launched and he hadn't cleared the history. Clicking on the tab would give her a list of all the sites he visited. Several of the web addresses contained the word 'date' but her brain struggled to process the information. Discreetly checking his whereabouts, Cate flew into a state of panic; he was advancing down the path towards her at an alarming rate. Her fingers suddenly became boneless; slithering across the keyboard like jelly. Tapping on the Ripper document she accidentally closed it.

'Do you want to save the changes to "Diss notes1"?' No, of course not. She hadn't meant to change anything. Ollie was half way between the bushes and the patio. Leaping across the room she virtually threw herself at the settee, picking up the magazine as she landed on the cushion. Exhaling with a sigh, she craned her neck forward to see how far he was from the

house. The laptop! It was still open. Bouncing off the seat and flinging 'History Today' to the floor, she ran to the French doors with her back to the table.

"A bee. Watch out," she shrieked, spotting her husband just feet away. Flapping frantically with one hand she managed reach behind her and shut the laptop with the other.

"What?" He stopped, spinning around to see a butterfly dance across the lawn. "If that's a bee it's wearing a very cunning disguise."

"No, not that. There was a bee, but it flew off. Who were you talking to?"

"A mate from uni. I thought you'd be getting ready for your interview," he replied, changing the subject.

There was something very alluring about the way he looked at her, with his crooked smile and steely gaze. Few women could resist his strikingly beautiful eyes; they were soft and grey with a charcoal outline, and simply made for staring into. Standing close to her with his hands in his pockets he was confident and powerful, like a bird of prey waiting to swoop down and rip the head off something small and furry. The collar of his striped rugby shirt turned up on one side. She could reach out and straighten it, and then kneel down in front of him, tear off his shorts and bury her head in his crotch; digging her nails into his taut buttocks while he ran his fingers through her hair.

"Everything's in place for tomorrow. Don't worry," she answered wryly.

"Get out the way then," he said softly, shattering the moment. Brushing past her, Oliver resumed his seat at the table and opened his laptop. It was her cue to retreat to the front room. Pulling her phone from a pocket she finally viewed the text that spoiled her covert operation earlier.

'Nope, not yet'

There were grunts and sighs coming from the dining room. Ignoring her husband's obvious signs of frustration Cate picked up the magazine and pretended to read.

"What's the matter?" she asked innocently, as his swearing became more profuse.

"Can't find my bloody notes. They're gone. Don't say I closed the file when I went outside."

"They'll still be there somewhere. Look in the folder they were saved in."

"No! Shit. I didn't save it." His voice was strained and raised by at least an octave. "Basil sent me the document in an email. I was working off it - I put all those bastard notes on it - but I forgot to save. Must've shut it down when I was on the phone, and now all I've got is the email with the original points he sent me."

Placing his hands over his face and leaning with both elbows on the table, Oliver let out a groan of anguish.

"Hours I spent on that this morning. Bloody hours sorting through those papers."

Covering her mouth with one hand to avoid openly saying 'oops', she fidgeted uncomfortably. It *would* have to be his dissertation. The most important assignment of all time, and she just wiped out a crucial set of notes. How awful; as if raiding his personal data wasn't bad enough. Getting up from the settee and going into the dining room, Cate draped herself over his shoulders and pressed her head next to his, looking hopefully at the screen.

"You must be able to recover it from somewhere."

"Not if I clicked 'no to changes' and it was still in the email, it just reverts back. I don't remember doing it, but I wasn't paying attention."

"Distracted by your mate from uni," she interjected. It wasn't the right moment to push him to reveal the identity of the mystery caller. Gut reaction told her it was a woman, possibly a friend, but definitely a female. Maybe she shouldn't feel guilty for destroying his work. If he wasn't flirting on the phone he wouldn't have made a mistake and lost the dissertation notes. Not that he did lose them of course, but he didn't know that. In which case, the other person was guilty by association and deserved to be a scapegoat. Kissing his cheek lightly, she went into the kitchen.

"Never mind, you've got ages yet before you have to hand it in. You'll just have to do it again." Her phone beeped.

'Commencing operation bloodhound tomorrow. Tracking target from 10.30 hours. Message ends'

Her new friend Mr Eyeball, the oddball. If her husband was making unscheduled deliveries she would find out very soon. Deleting the message with a sigh, she slipped the phone into her pocket. He wasn't callous enough to go behind her back and meet someone else; not on her birthday.

Tapping slowly with one finger on the keyboard, Oliver frowned and then stopped abruptly.

"You didn't touch anything, did you?" he asked slowly.

"Me? Don't try and blame me, women multi-task," she smiled defensively. "Not my fault men can only concentrate on one thing at a time. Shame about losing your notes but that's probably what happens if you wander off when you should be keeping an eye on what's in front of you."

Staring after her, he raised one eyebrow, and then turned back to his laptop without saying a word.

Crossing tracks

ON THURSDAY MORNING THE 10:52 fast service from Wolfinger Central was still in the station at 11.05, allowing time to examine the other passengers travelling to the city in the same carriage. It was difficult to ignore the middle-aged commentator seated toward the top end of coach C. Speaking loudly and energetically, in an unfamiliar language, he continued a conversation that everyone could hear without understanding a single word. He talked vigorously, looking out of the window as though describing something outside that made him angry. Cate peered at the platform, expecting to see a gang of youths kicking a dog, or thugs bullying a pensioner. The grey concrete concourse gaped back at her vacantly, blatantly indifferent to the hundreds of commuters that stamped across it every day.

Two large mackintoshes with fat ladies escaping from the neck, arms and hem, sat close to the railway narrator. Nodding and staring at him they whispered to each other. Like flies trapped in amber, the ancient women were partially preserved in raincoats from a forgotten time; the gaberdine era. Clearly, they weren't impressed by the vociferous stranger who wore a karakul hat resembling a giant blackcurrant pastille squashed on his head. Opposite the big macs was an empty strip of seats. An old man with white hair sat two rows away, by the doors. Clutching the handles of a small plaid shopping bag, his freckled hands were white at the knuckles, as if he gripped some dastardly device. He looked straight ahead, through a pair of gold-rimmed glasses perched on his over-sized ears. The only other person in the carriage, apart from herself, was a woman in dreadful trousers. There was no justification for brown nylon, under any circumstance. It should be outlawed, along with men in slouch beanie hats and drop crotch jeans worn at half-mast.

Pushing her earphones into place, Cate settled into the seat clutching her phone. A news bulletin from the reporter interrupted the music.

"A local woman was arrested and charged earlier today for displaying offensive dress in a public place. The woman, in her mid forties, was forcibly removed from an off-peak train by the Wolfinger Fashion Police, after attempting to leave town wearing brown nylon.

On behalf of the enforcement agency a spokesman said that it was an outrageous and wilful breach of decency that would not be tolerated. He added that the negligent use of nylon was a punishable offence.

Several passengers in the same carriage were treated for shock. Rail operators across the country warned commuters not to approach travellers dressed in man-made garments. The recommended action for sitting next to someone wearing loud trousers is not to attempt to remove them under any circumstance. Industry experts suggest that passengers should move away and exit at the next stop without raising suspicion.

Stay with us for more news as it happens. This is Catherine Bartlett reporting for Radio Newsline."

It was a pity she couldn't see what was going on outside Spennimore's. The Eyeball was probably in disguise. He sent her a text as Ollie was getting ready to go out.

'Bloodhound in place. Tally-ho'

Perhaps he was dressed as a dog? Sniffing lampposts and cocking a leg every time he made a stop. No, he wouldn't be able to follow the van like that. The last time she spotted him sneaking around the town he was wearing black leggings and a t-shirt, with a checked scarf and dark glasses. A sort of cross between a terrorist and a mime.

Having Ollie followed was simply for reassurance. He couldn't possibly be conducting a clandestine relationship while delivering groceries; it wasn't him at all. But there must be a reason for not cancelling his overtime. He wished her a happy birthday before going to work without placing a kiss on her cheek.

"Good luck," he added, pulling a blue Spennimore's shirt over his head. "Text me and let me know how it goes. See you later."

Then grabbing his high-viz jacket, he winked, and disappeared out the door. Ollie had a killer wink; cheeky and sly, almost imperceptible unless staring into his gorgeous grey eyes, with a power reaching far beyond its action. One quick blink was enough to send a shiver from just below her ribs to somewhere between her legs. A connection that meant they shared a secret. It was both sexy and disturbing, like a wolf disarming a doe before consuming the quarry without ruffling its fur.

Her bottom wriggled in the seat. Straightening her striped blouse with the plain collar she glanced at each person in turn but no-one was looking; busy with their own lives, or too apprehensive to meet her eye. Perhaps they thought she was a high-powered female executive. Director of a chain of lingerie stores or online cake shops; in her tailored charcoal skirt-suit, with black leather court shoes and matching designer bag. She was so sharp and confident, with her perfect make-up and glossy hair, it was surprising that she wasn't sipping Earl Grey in First Class. Not that it mattered where she was sitting - the train hadn't left the platform. Maybe she should have bought cakes from Ella's. She could have handed them around the carriage and conducted a sing-song. Interrupting her boredom, an announcement drifted from the speakers overhead.

"Midwestern Rail would like to apologise for the late departure of this 10.52 service to Canchester."

Melodically expressing regret the conductor rattled off an excuse about the driver being *unexpectedly* detained, followed by a tuneful rendition of stops for the whole journey. Seconds later an alarm beeped and the doors squeezed together, locking the occupants in universal transit. Finally she was on the way; one short journey from her dream job. Smiling enigmatically at the reflection in the large window, Cate rested her hands in her lap, with fingers interlocked as if she was about to say a prayer. Being fifty didn't matter. It was the least important event of the day.

Humming with enormous electrical effort the train heaved itself away from the station, picking up speed as it saw the open track ahead. A successful interview was crucial. Half a century of ambition focused into a two hour slot; an opportunity to concentrate three years of study into one hundred and twenty minutes. The adrenalin was good, pumping excitement through her veins. A state of alertness that meant she wasn't old. She could tackle anything and come out smelling of roses, just as her mother said.

Rows of houses flashed past. Narrow terraces with blank, brick faces and paved courtyards; gas storage tanks, obsolete and stained with rust; factories and flats; supermarkets and shops. Then came fields; strips of green and yellow, some with sheep, some without. Trees and hedges; hedges and trees that quickly turned into stately suburbia littered with large houses and long gardens. Enormous glassy-eyed windows looking out over posh patios, blinking in the sunlight; opulent homes for the beautiful people. She might live in one someday if everything fell into place.

Approaching the first stop, coach C slowed noisily and came to rest opposite a large billboard depicting a handsome man gazing at an attractive woman. The huge, side-profile faces illustrated how satisfying they found their loving relationship. *Phish Net and Stockings* was the latest ninety minute rom-com.

Discussing the film, and the trouser benefits of watching the leading man in 3D, two female students burst into the carriage at Horsecross Station. Both had northern accents and handbags big enough to inhabit for a long weekend. They continued a conversation despite intermittent texts and phone calls, taking their seats in the row behind Cate. Her own mobile was in silent mode. A quick glance revealed a text from Sam.

'Happy birthday! Guess what?'

'Cheers. What?'

'Got him. Reg wants to meet u!'

'No shit, when?'

'Don't know yet. Talk later - going into meeting. Good luck with your int'

'Ok, see you at the tun tonight'

Removing her headphones with a tug, she slipped the phone into her bag and pulled out the interview notes. She stared at the pages for ten minutes without reading a word. Ollie couldn't be Reg. He wouldn't be logging into a dating website while he was at work; Mr Eyeball was on a wild goose chase. Never mind, he was probably enjoying it.

The train stopped again; two male passengers boarded at Easton Moor. One opted for the row behind the giggling girls, while the other chose to place himself in a space opposite Cate. Smiling pleasantly as she looked up, the man folded his arms and leaned back in the seat. His features were tanned and well-worn, as if they were chiselled out of wood, and weathered smooth over the years; all the sharp edges were removed but the devastation of the storm remained. With thin blonde hair and pale blue eyes he was extremely striking and vaguely familiar, but she couldn't recall why. He was from Spennimore's maybe. It seemed unlikely, so far from Wolfinger but he grinned as if he knew her too. Finally, after several instances of raised brows and incidental eye-contact, the man spoke.

"How's it going?"

There was no escape; caught in the headlights like a wild rabbit she patted her paperwork and smiled at the stranger.

"Good, thanks," she smirked, racking her brain for an answer. Who was the charismatic man in the expensive shirt and casual suit? A manager. Yes, of course; one of the Regional Managers, he was the one that asked her some questions about barcodes the other week. "How are you? Not working today?" she added, relaxing a little.

"I will be if we ever get there. Damn trains never run on time."

Pretending there was something interesting in her bag she routed around and discreetly tucked the notes into the pocket. Hopefully, he wouldn't ask where she was going. They were still twenty minutes from Canchester.

"Have you been in the industry long?" he asked.

"About a year." There was an uncomfortable silence. "I was in banking for quite a while previously."

"Brave move. And what area are you currently working in?" Leaning forward the man rested his arms on his knees, showing no sign of abatement.

"Online. Don't tend to stick to one particular area, but I seem to spend most of my time on cereals at the moment."

"Exciting stuff."

"Well, it's better than cat food," she smiled. Was he for real? He obviously never worked in the online shopping department. Over enthusiastic managers were such a pain in the arse. Braking hard, the train caused the forward-facing passengers to bow their heads in an involuntary lurch. Cate steadied herself. The last thing she wanted was to end up on a Regional Manager's lap. Looking slightly bewildered he leaned back into the seat.

"Most things are better than cat food, aren't they? Unless you're a cat, I guess. Have you done much on soaps?"

"Not really, I'm allergic to quite a few of them," she replied, grinning to hide her irritation. They stopped in a tunnel.

"Now what? We're already twenty minutes late." Taking a phone from the inside pocket of his jacket, the man tapped the screen and attempted to send a text.

A slight shudder was followed by silence; the train motor shut down. Everyone paused, hoping for a further development, and then the brown-trousered woman got up from her seat, stepping sideways along the aisle as if she was walking an invisible tightrope. Reaching out for the headrests she balanced herself as she made the treacherous journey to the other end of the carriage. Her stomach brushed against Cate's arm as she passed.

"Excuse me," she whispered, "do you know if I can use the toilet?"

It was tempting to give a facetious reply but years of working with the public resulted in a calm immunity to stupid questions.

"I believe so," said Cate. "But you're going the wrong way." Pointing to the sign above the window she looked up at the woman and smiled. The woman tutted loudly, eyes pointing up to the ceiling. Lugging her paunch, she shuffled off in the opposite direction pushing past the passengers as she wobbled along.

"Typical; no phone signal," said the weathered man. "I hope we won't be here too long."

Fingering her watch Cate exhaled with a sigh. Newsnetwork was only a short walk from the station but it would be awful to be late for the interview. Her stomach fluttered, she couldn't even ring and let them know what was happening. A female voice boomed from the public address system, interrupting her mild panic.

"Ladies and gentlemen, this is the conductor. We are experiencing a disruption; I don't have any further information for you at this time as I've been unable to contact the driver. As soon as I receive an explanation as to why we've stopped I will let you know. Thank you for your patience and for travelling with Midwestern Rail."

There was an immediate kerfuffle. Assuming the announcement was made with the intention of placating its audience, it had the opposite effect. Swaying indignantly with heads wagging, the fat ladies oozed from their mackintoshes; the man in the karakul hat muttered loudly, and the two girls jumped up and peered out the window into darkness.

How inconvenient. Not only was she incommunicado, she was stuck in a tunnel with a supermarket fanatic and a clueless conductor. Another broadcast; a male voice this time, with more than a hint of sarcasm.

"Ladies and gentlemen this is your driver. I'd like to apologise for the unscheduled delay and the lack of knowledge of the crew. We are being held by a red light without radio contact, which, as your conductor knows full-well, means I have to detrain in order to use the signal-post telephone. By way of explanation, it appears that dozy cows are the order of the day, and there is also one on the line ahead. Unfortunately we cannot continue our passage until this obstruction has been removed. Thank you for travelling Midwestern Rail."

Gazing around the carriage the travellers exchanged puzzled glances, smirking and shaking their heads in disbelief.

"Ladies and gentlemen, this is your conductor – again," said the female voice with slow deliberation. "I thank the driver for enhancing my life with useful information and I'd also like to reassure all passengers that being a lying, cheating, pot-bellied, bald-headed pig in no way affects his ability to deliver this train to its destination. Thank you once again for travelling Midwestern Rail."

The confused silence in coach C was broken by a cheer from the university students. Kneeling on the seats to face the other commuters they peered through the headrests and then spontaneously burst into a song about suffragettes. After two verses they couldn't agree on the words and collapsed in a heap, swearing and laughing.

Chewing on her bottom lip Cate stared at the ceiling; the carriage was uncomfortably hot. Could it get much worse? The girls appeared in the aisle next to her, facing the weathered man. It was worse.

"Scuse me," ventured the blonde. "Herp yer don't mind but we just noticed it were you. Could we get yer autograph?"

His autograph? Glimpsing sideways without turning her head, Cate saw the girl wore an extremely short skirt, striped, knee-length socks and Ugg boots. Although uncharacteristically dressed for the time of year, she was remarkably pretty, with smooth skin and long, dark eye-lashes.

"Of course," smiled the man, pulling out a pen from his jacket, "…what would you like me to..?"

Cheekily, the girl turned around and bent over, presenting her bottom to the man. Without flinching he signed her pink pants with a flourish, as though buttocks were an occupational hazard.

Cate's face reddened. Possibly not the Regional Manager after all. Rubbing her forehead, she peered at the man through her open fingers.

"Thanks Mike," said the brunette, laughing and crouching to view the signature. "It's really good of yer."

"Lucky you spotted me today," he smiled, putting away his pen.

"Lucky she's werrin knickers today," replied the girl, tugging gently at her friend's arm as they returned to the back of the coach, hardly able to contain their joy.

Glowering in gaberdine the two old ladies looked on in horror, sucking in their cheeks and wobbling their heads. They didn't recognise the man. He was a retired cricketer…and sports correspondent for Newsnetwork. That's where she knew him from. It all came flooding back; how embarrassing. Mike Pick was one of Ollie's heroes. An Ashes superstar from yesteryear; and inconveniently - a reporter from the television channel she was trying so hard to secure a job with. Another breadbin moment but there was never one around to swallow her up before she made a complete twat of herself. No wonder he was confused about cat food.

The old man with the plaid bag took an interest in the autograph signing. Dropping a paper napkin in the aisle, he retrieved it unconvincingly, twisting back in his seat to face away from the commotion. A welcome distraction, she watched as he let down the seat-back table and proceeded to lay out his lunch with great precision. Mr Pick stared at her, scorching the side of her head while she gawped at the old man's ears twitching as he ate a sandwich.

"Bit cheeky," said Mike, trying to draw her attention. She nodded without meeting his gaze; her face flushing. "Those two young girls," he persisted, "quite flattering really; happens occasionally. What time's your interview?"

"What?" Stunned by his question Cate looked up.

"The logo on your notes. Sorry I wasn't spying – just saw our invitation and put two and two together. Sounds like you've got some interesting experience to bring to the role. I hope we're not kept hanging around here for too long; be dreadful to be late for your appointment. Still I'm sure they'll understand. I'll speak to Rich if we don't get there on time. It is Richard you're seeing, isn't it?"

"Richard. Yes," she repeated reservedly, as though accidentally swallowing a fly.

An odd sensation was developing; a ball of heat unravelling in her stomach, rolling up the torso, and pushing down into both legs. Engulfing the whole body in seconds, it was like a hot water-bottle bursting in her belly and trying to get out through her skin. It was an unusual wave of warmth, completely unlike any external roasting; this was something she couldn't escape from. Puffing out both cheeks she exhaled noisily, waving one hand in front of her face with a fanning motion. Bloody hell, a hot flush; fifty for less than a day and suddenly she was hurtling towards the menopause. How could her body be so cruel? She hadn't finished with it yet.

Tipping his head on one side like a confused cocker spaniel, Mike frowned.

"Are you okay?"

"I get claustrophobia in tunnels," she lied. "Could you open a window?"

"Don't think I can, they're all air-conditioned these trains. Not going to pass out, are you?" Standing up he looked around the carriage, spotting a carton of juice on the old man's table.

"Sorry but I need this," he said, snatching the drink.

"Oi, that's mine," the pensioner remonstrated. "Just cos you've batted a century and signed a bum, don't mean you can do what yer like, y'know."

"It's an emergency." Thrusting the carton towards Cate he inadvertently squirted juice out the straw and straight into her face.

"Thanks," she spluttered, spitting and wiping her nose.

"Good grief, I do apologise. Let me," he said mopping her with a handkerchief, and simultaneously removing her make-up. Catastrophe; her bare face peeked through a hole in the foundation smudged across her chin, cheeks and brow. It wasn't something he felt up to confessing.

"There, that's better – didn't get any on your suit, nothing to worry about." Mr Pick smiled, flashing his pale eyes convincingly.

Maybe it wasn't such a bad thing. A random juicing might be an unconventional method of menopause management but it cooled her down; more importantly she had an ally at Newsnetwork.

"What time did you say you have to be at the studio?" he asked.

"My interview's at one-thirty. I wonder how much longer we're going to be stuck here."

The grey door at one end of coach C swung open revealing the woman in brown trousers. Entering cautiously she made her way along the carriage, negotiating the headrests like a set of monkey bars. She plopped herself down, one row in front of the old man as the conductor appeared from the rear of the train.

"All tickets and passes for inspection please, all tickets and passes."

Looking as if she would burst into tears at any moment the young railway employee made her way swiftly along the aisle, circling the date on each ticket with a black pen.

"Hello. We were wondering if you've been able to establish what's going on yet?" asked Mr Pick as the conductor extended her hand towards him. Fixing her eyes on the floor she gave a sigh.

"I can't be certain but I think he's having an affair with one of the drivers; one of the lady drivers that is."

"Oh dear, we did notice a bit of a disagreement," he said, offering his ticket. "I'm so sorry I hope you're able to sort it out, but I actually meant what's going on with the train."

"What this train?"

Answering with a hopeful nod he leaned back in his seat.

"Cow expired on the line apparently. A male cow."

"Expired?" he laughed, attempting to lighten the mood. "Sounds like it ran out of date."

"Ran out of breath. It was crossing the tracks and had a coronary when it saw the train coming. Not ours, the one in front of us. Luckily it was going slow cos another driver reported livestock. We had five sheep on the line last week, but that's not a major incident."

"Hardly at all," he said, humouring her.

"Has to be six for an emergency."

"Indeed. And barring the emergence of the rest of the herd would you possibly have an idea how long it might take to remove the poor beast from our path?"

"I'm not sure," replied the conductor. "I could ask the driver but I'm not talking to him unless he apologizes."

Pushing the ticket back into his hand she sniffed and moved on to the woman in brown trousers.

"Well my dear…I'm sorry I don't know your name," Mr Pick said extending his hand.

"Cate," she replied, reciprocating.

"Well Cate, it looks like we're at the mercy of the expired cow removal team. Should be a bit of an ice-breaker at the interview. I know it's a nuisance but Richie's a good guy; known him for a few years. And he's *very* keen on online stuff. It's a medium that's really taken off for us, good experience to have behind you."

Accepting the situation was beyond her control she relaxed into the cushioned seat. Mike Pick was an interesting man, and he was getting more attractive by the minute. No harm in flirting with her interviewer's best friend. He might be slightly deluded about her background but she could fix that later. The best course of action was to make the most of the opportunity. It certainly wasn't her fault he had the wrong end of the stick, he shouldn't go around impersonating Regional Managers.

The following

THE SHORT CUL-DE-SAC OPPOSITE Spennimore's rear entrance was an ideal place for Mr Ball to conceal himself while waiting for his target to emerge from the loading-bay. Arriving early, he parked his motorcycle carefully and performed a reconnaissance operation, jotting down vehicle registration numbers, and discretely snapping shots with his mobile phone.

"There's a guy outside in a black leather onesie casing our joint," said Lee, placing his clipboard on the table next to Laura. "D'you reckon he's a Regional Manager sussing us out? Or d'you think he's planning a break-in? Looks like the sort of bloke who'd shove a leg of lamb down his pants; he keeps walking past the gate and looking in at our yard."

"Done your vehicle-check?" replied the supervisor gently pushing him to one side. Standing on tiptoe at the back door she tried to peer past the vans and into the road. "Can't see anyone. Probably an online-spotter, it's the latest craze, they've moved on from trains and heavy goods vehicles."

Shrugging his shoulders, the young driver wheeled a stack of totes down the ramp. Mr Ball crossed the street slowly, lurking in the leafy shade of a horse-chestnut. Lee loaded the van, slamming the door and disposing of his hi-viz jacket on the passenger seat before speeding away.

Mr Cooke was never late. Eyeball watched venomously, crouching behind his motorbike, and stroking the front tyre. Oliver strolled across the loading area with a clipboard in his hand and Laura two inches from his elbow, laughing and wagging her pony-tail. Whatever they were discussing, she was clearly enjoying his company. Completing the van-check the couple stood closely together in the yard whispering for a moment before disappearing into the shopping room. Every movement was carefully captured from across the road. Still chatting, they appeared again several minutes later, pushing trolleys piled high with red plastic totes. Oliver loaded them four at a time and then climbed into the cab, winking playfully as he said goodbye to the blushing supervisor.

The black Harley waited in the shadows, growling softly like a hungry panther. It slipped out onto the main road in pursuit of the Spennimore's van that hurtled through the gates, leaning heavily on two wheels, oblivious to the dark stalker behind. Staying out of sight the bike followed the vehicle to the roundabout. Oliver checked the rear-view mirrors and then pulled into the traffic.

Tracking his prey at a distance the Eyeball tailed the van to the other side of town. Swiftly passing through the streets and skirting around the main shopping area, they eventually arrived at Lily Valley Estate; a grey area of Wolfinger that most would avoid given the chance. Oliver parked close to the block of flats, swerving neatly into an off-road space. An electric cooker looked out from the front garden, nestling in the long grass with its oven door hanging loosely like a broken limb. The first drop was to a man living in a ground-floor apartment. Climbing down from the cab, Oliver unloaded three shopping totes and approached a window at the side of the property. Placing them on the floor he tapped on the glass and waited for the casement to swing open.

"Hi Mr Lawler, how are you today?" he asked.

"Bin better," grunted the man. An extremely large person, Mr Lawler's head was envied by most bulldogs, complete with drooping jowls and sharp yellow teeth. "I'll be happy if you tell me you've not substituted me chicken breasts this week." Hissing and spitting from the corners of his mouth as he spoke, the man sprayed the window with small spots of saliva. "They gave me legs last time; I don't like legs."

That wasn't a surprise. Oliver had delivered to the address several times before without ever catching a glimpse of the lower half of Mr Lawler. His torso could be mounted on a pedestal at the window for all he knew. Passing the bags through the opening at arm's length to avoid being showered with drool, he reassured the customer that only one item had been replaced with an alternative brand.

The next drop was due in half an hour. There was time to get a newspaper and park in the lay-by for a quick review of the sporting news. It was drizzling; the clear sky had given way to a damp blanket of cloud. Squeaking rhythmically, the rubber wipers laboured over the glass; intermittently removing the tiny droplets of rain and smearing a semi-circle of dust across the screen while he read. The Eyeball kept a close watch on the vehicle, partly obscured by a bus-shelter. After quarter of an hour the engine started again. Discarding the paper onto the passenger seat Oliver eased forward into the traffic until a woman in a Mini was forced to let him interrupt the queue. Raising one magnanimous hand out of the window, he grinned cheekily at her via the wing-mirror. She waved back, smiling. Delivering in the rain was a nuisance but gaining flirtatious advantage over a female helped to improve his mood.

Spencer Road was a turning on the right. Close to the town centre, it was a long narrow street lined with terraced houses and parked cars. On market day it was almost impossible to find a space. Oliver followed a green parcel-lorry that gingerly squeezed between the tightly packed rows of vehicles and pulled into the last available slot close to his delivery address. Number 74 was at the bottom of the hill just as the road curved to the right. After circumnavigating the area twice, hoping the courier would depart, there was no option but to block the road. Mrs Bright was expecting six totes of shopping, stacked to the brim, and if he was delayed any longer they would be late. Flipping on the hazard lights to alert his inconvenient presence to other road users, he double-parked and jumped out of the cab. It wouldn't take long, and although the flow of traffic was restricted for anything larger than a bicycle there was no-one trying to get through at that moment. The Harley that followed him around the block must have turned off somewhere else.

Mrs Bright was a breezy woman. Receiving her shopping with delight she thanked Oliver for the firmness of her fruit and offered him a drink.

"I won't today, thanks," he said, pointing over his shoulder with an outstretched thumb, "causing a bit of an obstruction, I better get a move on before there's a queue." Turning back for the last three totes he waved in acknowledgement to the driver of a red car that pulled up behind the van.

"Sorry mate, won't be a minute," he called out, knowing he'd be several. Handing bags of food to his customer, Oliver stacked the totes and got ready to leave.

"Hang on, there's no eggs here. I should have eggs." Checking off items on the receipt with one chubby finger the woman searched the bags like a mother hen looking for chicks. "I paid for them but they're not here. That's no good," she remonstrated, "I've gotta make birthday cake this afternoon and I can't go out, I've got the plumber coming. Bit of an inconvenience really."

Rubbing his stubble-chin with one hand, Ollie nodded politely as the woman explained about the broken toilet and the bucket. She should try being out in a van all day, it wasn't as if he had an en suite; he could tell her a few things about conveniences.

"Don't worry," he intervened when Mrs Bright finally took a breath. "I'll ring the store and get someone to pop over. Must've been one of the new shoppers, sorry about that."

Unless of course they were the eggs that scrambled themselves to death in the back of his van. The town centre roundabouts often proved too much for fragile items of shopping. Especially eggs, they regularly developed a suicidal tendency. It wasn't the first time they leapt out of a tote en route, but most customers didn't notice their loss until he was long gone. The Eyeball parked a short distance away, hidden by the courier lorry. Scribbling on a small pad with a silver pen, he noted the registration number of the yellow car travelling down the hill to join the blockade. Pulling up at the rear of the red vehicle it tooted twice on the horn.

"I'll get that sorted for you, no worries," said Oliver walking back to the van. Holding up his right hand to the retinue like an Emperor halting the troops he unlocked the door and climbed into the cab. There was a problem; an unexpected enemy joined the battle. Entering from the other end of Spencer Road a soft-top convertible advanced along the ranks of parked cars and stopped just metres away. Oliver stared at the couple in the sports car. Someone was going to have to reverse or no-one was going anywhere. Peering back at the delivery driver, the man tapped on the steering-wheel with his tobacco-stained fingers. He spoke to a female

passenger, nostrils flaring and lips curling, like a wild boar being poked with a French-stick.
It was getting ugly. Defiantly folding his powerful arms, Ollie fleetingly searched the sky as if proof of his right of way might be confirmed in the clouds; and then he fixed his gaze belligerently on the man. There was a long blast of Mercedes horn. Piercing the air like a mighty sword, the roar of the silver dragon shuddered on the windscreen and reverberated around the houses.
Oliver pushed irritably on the steering-wheel with both hands, swearing under his breath. He was a part-time delivery driver; an occasional knight of the road - not a highwayman. Why did so many people want to challenge him to a duel? Road-rage wasn't the 'done' thing in a Spennimore's van. Glancing in the wing-mirror he surveyed the small entourage forming behind him; no chance of retreat. There was nothing apart from the stubborn man with a bald head preventing the sports car from reversing. He was probably a short thug with a chip on his shoulder; someone of limited intelligence who had been cuckolded by a delivery driver, no doubt. Nothing else to do but shrug boldly with an open gesture and both palms facing the man in insubordinate capitulation. Unsuccessfully trying not to look too smug, Oliver grinned at the female passenger. Breakpoint; leaping out of the Mercedes and slamming the door, the man strode up to the van with clenched fists.

"You better back up; you're blocking the road," he ejaculated.

"Yeah, sorry about that," Cooke replied glibly, "but actually I was here first, so technically you're blocking the road. You better back up."

Shaking with frustration the man rapped his hand sharply on the side of the van.

"Not me. I never back up," he yelled. "Delivery drivers are a bloody nuisance; think you can stop anywhere. The law doesn't apply to you, does it? Hazards on - job done – park where ya like. Well I got news for you. You're in the wrong - and I ain't moving."

Extending a muscly tattooed arm, the man gesticulated angrily at the van. A blue vein throbbed on the side of his hairless head as he spoke, pulsating rapidly like an emergency beacon.

Calmly alighting from the cab Ollie squared up to the man, folding his arms and leaning back slightly.

"I'm sorry you feel like that." He avoided conflict whenever possible but it was difficult to stop the adrenalin rising when he was confronted by idiots. "I had six totes to unload and there was nowhere else to pull over. Believe me mate, if I could throw shopping through the window without stopping, I would," he barked. "But I haven't found it possible so far. So I suggest you get back in your car and push off; then we can all get on with our lives." He jerked his head backwards, with a sideways eye movement, referring to the developing procession of cars,.

"Yeah, you do, do ya? Well I'm not your mate, I'm your hostile stranger, and if anyone's gonna start pushing it'll be me." The man prodded the delivery driver in the shoulder with a stiff finger.

Clenching his fists without unfolding his arms Oliver glared at the man; he hated being poked. It was tempting to give him a good shove. Lay the stocky twat out on the bonnet of his own car and pummel his face until his nose was flat. That wouldn't go down well at Spennimore's though; punching wasn't considered to be an excellent customer journey. And a record of assault didn't look good on a job application; it would ruin any chance of training to be a teacher. Brushing his shoulder demonstratively with one hand as if removing cretin dust from his person he took a deep breath and leaned against the van. Another vehicle joined the queue. Catching a glimpse of the building traffic in the wing-mirror Ollie gave a wry grin and exhaled.

"Let's be reasonable about this; I'm not in a hurry, got a couple of hours before me next drop," he lied. "Got a pile of *Only the Best*, slow-roasted honeyed ham and pickle sandwiches and a flask of Columbian coffee to keep me busy. If you want to hang around - be my guest – knock yourself out." Looking down at the ground, he pushed his fingers through his thick, dark hair and gently kicked the front tyre. "However, if I was you I'd seriously think about revising your plans before one of these other geezers gets the 'ump." Peering from under his brow at the bulging eyes of the Mercedes driver he cocked his head on one side like a dog expecting a biscuit.

An engine roared into life from across the road. The courier finally departed, leaving the Eyeball exposed straddling his motorbike. He punched the air as if sparring with an invisible foe. Hurriedly, he crouched low enough to be out of sight but still able to view the altercation through the windscreen of an adjacent vehicle. Cooke was in for a thrashing and he didn't want to miss anything; it was probably the disaffected husband of one of his lovers.

Summer drizzle settled on the disgruntled man's head; glistening in the soft down covering his bald dome, resembling dew on a spider's web. Rocking on his feet from side to side like an impatient toddler, the man slapped his right fist into the palm of his left hand. Without flinching, Oliver blinked his steely grey eyes. Leaning forward slightly he re-angled the rear-view mirror with an outstretched hand. The driver of the last vehicle in the queue thundered down the road to join the argument.

"What's going on? Is it an accident?" bellowed the man. He was as tall and wide as a bear.

Glancing back at the woman sitting in the car, the Mercedes driver stepped to one side. Quickly folding his arms he shuffled uncomfortably, his eyes flitting between the large man and Oliver.

"Not an accident," he said defensively. "This idiot's deliberately blocking the road and says he's gonna eat his sandwiches now. No-one can get past, it's a disgrace, bloody delivery drivers - think they own the road."

Ollie observed the new arrival without saying a word; he was a giant with no visible neck, just a small face on an enormous round head, topped with blond curls. The man stared back blankly at Mr Cooke and then turned his attention to the other driver.

"I like getting my shopping delivered. You got a problem with that?" Towering over the bald man his eyes narrowed menacingly.

“I'm not sure he likes you,” said Oliver, shaking his head slowly, and feigning a grimace.

The Mercedes driver puffed out his chest, snorting as he backed away.

"You're with him, aren't ya." There was a nervous realisation in his voice. "I'm armed y'know; you don't scare me. I got a bat in the car and I'm not afraid to use it." He patted the front wing.

"She's no oil paintin', I'll give yer that, but she ain't much of a weapon," said the giant, grinning and scratching his groin with one hand. He stepped towards the silver car and gawked at the woman in the passenger seat.

"You're...you're lucky," stammered the man looking around, "there's a space now, so I'm goin' to pull in and let you through. But I 'ope you learned a lesson. You can't go jammin' up the traffic and thinkin' you can get away with it. It's people like me what pays your wages, and I'll be speaking to Spennimore's." He wagged a finger at Oliver.

The giant growled causing the driver to recoil. Feeling his way along the bonnet the bald man side-stepped to the door and quickly got into the convertible. Ollie waved as the sports car backed up; whining in reverse and narrowly missing parked cars and the squinting Eyeball as it slipped into the gap left by the courier.

Victory for the delivery driver, assisted by the cavalry in the shape of a human tank. Rubbing his enormous hands together the large man turned to face the van.

"You covering my round?" he asked.

"Yep, wish I wasn't now. How's the hernia?"

"Bloody agony, if that bastard had started I'd have run off like a neutered kitten." The man screwed up his face and twiddled his right ear-lobe.

"You're not going to have to wear one of those cones are you, when you've had your op - stop you licking your wound?" said Oliver.

"Piss off," smiled Jiffy. "And shift that bloody van before I obstruct you."

There would be time for a break before the next drop. Flashing his headlights as he passed the Mercedes, Ollie led the procession to the end of Spencer Road. A gap in the traffic allowed him to stamp on the accelerator and tear off towards the dual carriageway and the rural communities north of the town. Verdant Green was one of his favourite places; a chocolate-box hamlet complete with ancient cottages, a willowy pond and a well-kept cricket pitch. The perfect spot to eat sandwiches while listening to the radio.

Remaining undetected was more difficult for the Eyeball. It wasn't easy to keep the van in sight along the winding country lanes without raising suspicion. Stopping short of the village green he concealed himself between two rows of houses in the alley that led to the school. He had a clear view of Mr Cooke in the cab. Using binoculars he could virtually count the lashes around his beady eyes; they were a little too close together to be trusted. Mr Ball noted the exact time that Oliver switched off the engine and sent a text before starting his lunch. Watching him eat and swig coke from the plastic bottle wasn't fascinating but the mission was vitally important. Unzipping his pocket, Eyeball took a small picture from his leather jacket and placed it neatly in the centre of his handlebars. Everyone that visited his neighbour's house was photographed, not just Cate; for security purposes of course. Coincidentally, on the day of surveillance it was extremely hot, and she was wearing a tightly fitting black and white leopard print top with a beige corduroy skirt that finished just above the knee. The photo didn't show her calves but they were distinctive enough to remember. She had two fine legs; definitely a bonus to possess a matching pair.

From the house next to the alley a side-door swung open, and a woman with white curly hair appeared on the step. Taking rubbish to the bin she glimpsed the dark stranger in the passageway and hesitated to peer through the bushes. Mr Ball glared back. Startled by the motorcyclist ogling her at close range through binoculars; she scurried into the house, slamming the door behind her.

A large spot of rain splashed on the photo. Brushing it away slowly with his fingers Eyeball stared at the picture and then tucked it into his t-shirt as if he had an inside breast pocket. Cate could rest her head on his chest any time she liked; he was a human umbrella and would protect her bosom from the elements at any cost. The delivery driver was a very lucky man to have her; however, he didn't know he was being followed, and that his good fortune was about to expire. Turning his full attention to Mr Cooke, Eyeball watched closely as he got out of the cab. There was an air of uncertainty in his movement, a sort of nervousness. Was he about to meet someone? Glancing around surreptitiously Oliver made his way to the back of the vehicle and

disappeared inside. Surely his lover was not secreted amongst the perishable goods?
The Harley throbbed into action, edging slowly out of the alley to a suitable vantage point. Parking behind a small bush at the side of the pond Eyeball sprinted on tiptoe to the van, pressing both hands and his right ear against the double doors. It was challenging to hear anything over the pounding of his own heart. Leaning back to observe the ambience he was certain there were low grunts coming from inside, commensurate with the exertion of an illicit fumble in the refrigerated area. Depravity! A delivery beast in florescent sheep's clothing. The photographic evidence would be indisputable; a fait accompli. Flattening his body against the van Eyeball readied the camera and stood poised to release the metal catch. Suddenly a sharp blow to the head sent him sprawling to the ground. Oliver emerged as the door flung open. Jumping from the vehicle he spotted Mr Ball spreadeagled on the tarmac.

"Jees, that wasn't you was it; that bang? You weren't standing behind the door were you?"

"No, no," replied the Eyeball, pulling down the mirrored visor to cover his face. "I was merely looking for a contact lens." Discreetly retrieving his phone from under the vehicle he pretended to feel around.

"Ah…ok." Ollie eyed the motorcyclist suspiciously. "Do you need some help?"

"Nope. I'm good." Rising swiftly to his feet, he nodded and took a large stride backwards.

"Can you see alright without your contact lens?"

"Yes, I have a prescription visor thank you," he called out tapping the reflective screen.

The man walked away, disappearing into an alley. There was something very odd about him. Checking around guardedly Oliver crossed the road to the litter bin, disposing of a knotted Spennimore's bag before returning to the van. He would have to put his foot down to get to the next drop on time; Miss Ardent lived several miles from the village at the end of a single track road. Driving past the pond he glimpsed something surprising in the bush - a motorcycle similar to the one he saw in Spencer Road; rather an odd coincidence. He paused for a second and then accelerated.

Before the speeding vehicle could vanish from sight, Eyeball raced out of the alley, stopping briefly to examine the discarded bag. A gentle squeeze of the carrier revealed the mystery contents to be firm and slightly warm; similar to a sausage roll without pastry. Gritting his teeth and extending one arm he dropped the package and hurried back to the Harley. He despised delivery drivers.

Catching up with Cooke wasn't hard. The difficulty was maintaining an appropriate distance. However, he was familiar with the area, it was part of his old milk-round; and there was only one opportunity to leave the road before the Canchester bypass. There was a good chance he was heading for the big house behind the farm at the end of Butterfly Lane.

The rain got heavier; dripping from the trees in blobs and stretching out across the road in great glassy-eyed puddles. Oliver checked the satellite navigation; he wasn't late. Turning left into the narrow lane that led to the large detached property he eased off the accelerator. There was no tarmac, just a stony path of potholes. Low branches clawed at the side of the van until he reached the end of the track where it opened onto a small roundabout in a clearing. The road continued to the right and a red post-box on a pole stuck out of the long grass in the middle of the circular island. He visited the address once before, several months ago. Pulling up in front of the electric gates Ollie leaned out of his window and pressed the intercom. It was answered almost immediately.

"Hello."

"Hi Miss Ardent, it's Ollie from Spennimore's with your online delivery."

"Hello Ollie, come up to the house, I've been expecting you. There's a key-box to the right of the front door; the code is 1976-hash. Please let yourself in." The voice was exotically beautiful; calm and sultry like a low-pitched lullaby.

Seconds later with an electronic buzz and then a click, the metal gates swept open, scraping and screeching on the gravel. Following instructions Oliver passed through the entrance. Following Oliver, the Eyeball parked his motorcycle and clambered up a tree, hoping to get high enough to see over the wall that obscured the house. By the time he was safely ensconced between two boughs the van was parked at the end of the driveway close to the arched porch. Focusing his binoculars Ball watched intently as the delivery driver let himself into the building, bending down to pick up two totes before entering and then closing the front door behind him.

"Bastard," he whispered, "you've got a key."

The big gates hummed and clanked shut. Almost falling out of the tree Eyeball slid to the ground and leapt onto his Harley. There was no way he could see Cooke from the current position but he could spy on him from the field at the back of the house. Tearing down the lane to the roundabout, he mounted the island, narrowly missing the post-box before taking the exit on the right. It was the path that led to the farm. Skidding to a halt next to a gap in the hedge he abandoned the bike, heaved open the wooden gate and entered the field on foot. Quickly sprinting across the meadow he pushed his face into a bush; it was several metres from the house and Oliver was standing with his back to the kitchen window. The driver was still wearing his reflective jacket but the woman beside him was either on her knees or extremely short. Highly suspicious; the top of her head was bobbing and swaying. Cooke stretched out an arm, for a moment it looked as though he would stroke the blonde woman's hair but instead he leaned on the draining-board.

Fumbling in a pocket Eyeball pulled out his phone. The screen was shattered; smashed to pieces when the idiot whacked him with the door. All the touch functions were dead, including the camera. How irritating. Peering through the waxy leaves he scrutinized the couple. Oliver looked down at the woman; he was speaking to her. Then suddenly without getting up she backed out of sight. The driver bent forward. Was she showing him something on the kitchen floor? Trampling further into the hedge Ball grappled with the branches, standing on tiptoe and straining to get a better view. Just as he was about to topple onto the lawn Cooke stood up, hauling the empty totes and heading for the door.

Eyeball staggered from the shrubbery, snapping twigs and bending boughs as he struggled backwards through the wet foliage. Racing across the meadow to the open gate he came to an abrupt halt before reaching the road. There was a Land Rover on the grass verge and someone waiting by the Harley; a tall man wearing baggy trousers and a red checked shirt rolled up at the sleeves. Ball noted the chunky bracelet hanging from one thick wrist and the grey wellingtons turned over at the top. The man had a crooked nose and a miserable down-turned mouth. But it was the wooden-handled shotgun that concerned him the most.

"Got yer," said the man.

"Excuse me? Is there some sort of problem here? I wasn't intending to trespass. I'm very sorry – is this your land?" Grovelling earnestly the Eyeball stood with palms raised against his chest in a low form of surrender. "I'm sure we can just forget about this. I mean, I didn't mean to cause you any inconvenience. I just stopped for a leak."

"You bin pissin' in my field!"

"No, of course not...I mean my *motorcycle* had a leak - and so I fixed it and was just admiring the view. But I don't want to keep you, if you stopped because you thought I'd broken down, I'm sure you're very busy – milking and shearing and stuff. And I'll be on my way."

"You let my bull out."

"Bull? What bull?" He looked guiltily at the gate. "Ah, no, actually it was open when I arrived. If there was a bull, it left before I got here."

"And I suppose you didn't let my sheep out last week either?"

"Absolutely not. Trust me, I would never contravene the Country Code. I was indeed brought up on a farm and I'm extremely careful not to trample on any...er...crops...or er...leave gates ajar. I had a pet bull myself once; I know how you must feel." Showing his teeth, Eyeball feebly attempted a smile.

There was no glimmer of reciprocation. Gripping the barrel of the gun, the man stood white-knuckled and stern-faced. A mobile phone rang.

"Are you going to answer that?" asked the Eyeball. "Could be important; it might be your bull."

The farmer's face twisted angrily.

"I mean, it might be *about* your bull," added Eyeball, cautiously eyeing the twitching trigger-finger. Staring intently at the leather-clad stranger, the man let go of the gun with one hand and answered the phone.

"Allo," he growled. There was a pause while he listened. "You sure it's Boris? Yeah, that's 'im. 'Owd 'e get up there? Alright, I'll be there as soon as I can."
Pushing the mobile into his pocket he stepped towards the Land Rover.

"Seems ya luck's in. Bin spotted 'eddin' for the bypass; randy little bastard. More like a bloody race'orse than a bull."
Hurriedly getting into the vehicle, he started the engine and then leaned out of the window.

"But I'm warning you, if you let my bloody bull out again you'll have to replace 'im."
The car sped away.

"I'm not sure that's possible," said the Eyeball under his breath, rushing to the Harley, "and it's certainly not legal."
He tore off at a pace, pulling a wheelie for the first hundred metres. It was another devastating blow; Cooke would be long gone. Not only did he have a throbbing head and a smashed phone, he had to explain to Cate how he lost Oliver before the dastardly distributor made his final delivery. Mission unsuccessful; Operation Bloodhound rendered toothless and put down without a bite.

Just the job

CANCHESTER CENTRAL WAS BUSTLING with people as usual. Peering out anxiously on to the platform Cate shuddered as the train slid into the station, injecting itself into the city. Drab faces flicked past the window; she waited for the squeal of the brakes and the final stagger of the standing passengers before getting up. Mike Pick was already on his feet. He made an involuntary lunge towards her as they ground to a halt. Why were people always so unprepared for the last jolt? Perhaps the train was purely incidental and they were actually carried forward by the inescapable inertia of wanting to be somewhere else.

"Sorry," said Pick, gripping the seat and interrupting her daydream. "My taxi's still waiting, he's just text me. We'll make it. Don't worry."

Hopping out of the cab after a hasty jaunt across the city Cate paused before the revolving doors to squint up at the red brick building; Network House. The bold façade reached into the clouds, causing her to tilt backwards to see the top. This was what it was all about, the giddy heights of fame. She was at the bottom now but at least she was going in at the front entrance; and with no time to spare, it was half past one.

"You go ahead," said Pick, paying the driver, "catch up with you later. Good luck; you'll be brilliant."

Yes, that was obvious; she was completely focused. A little nervous, but a tot of adrenalin never did any harm. Inhaling confidently she turned off her phone. No further messages from Mr Eyeball; and no news was probably good news. Ollie didn't say much – he was an occasional flirt but philandering wasn't his style. He was more likely to run off on a cricket tour than with another woman.

The receptionist at Network House had pink hair and an unconvincing smile. Regrettably, there was no opportunity for self-inspection or an apprehensive wee; an eager member of staff was waiting to whisk her away from the desk. A black marble wall provided enough reflection for a quick preen.

Flicking her hair and pulling her suit straight Mrs Cooke followed the pointy-faced female into the lift. It opened on the second floor, revealing a carpeted corridor and a row of frosted glass doors. A smell of leather seats and polished wood mingled with the sweet aroma of fresh pastries and strong coffee as they made their way along the passage.

The assistant ushered her into a large room; there were chairs at one end, and a table laid with food at the other. Standing next to the buffet a young woman was silhouetted by the light streaming in from a Georgian-style window. She was gazing out onto the ground-floor courtyard where two friendly cars huddled together in the shade. The vehicles were partially obscured by elegant boughs reaching out towards the building from a tiny square of common on an adjacent plot. Extending blatantly over the retaining wall in a bid for freedom the trees wept sap and shed leaves on the windscreens below. A branch tapped feebly on the window, unsuccessfully trying to capture the attention of the girl staring out. Ignoring the plea, she turned her interest to the table, brushing one hand along the crisp white linen as if she was stroking silk rather than touching cloth. There was something vague about her, as though she was experiencing the world in a different dimension; certainly one that most people would be unfamiliar with.

Unfortunately, scanning the room for alternative signs of hospitality proved disappointing; the woman might be the best bet after all. The other four candidates were engrossed in conversation. A tall man with shiny black hair was delivering an anecdote so amazing that his popularity was virtually developing into a visible presence. Sniffing a breath she approached the table.

"Hi. Looks good," said Cate gesturing towards the food. "Anything you recommend?"

"I'm afraid I don't know," replied the girl, appearing slightly scared. She looked slim and pretty in her short navy skirt-suit, like a life-size fashion doll. Oozing the distinctive air of weather-reporter her long blonde hair was tucked neatly behind one ear. "Too dangerous," she added, poking at a mini quiche with the polished nail of one index finger.

Glancing sideways at the woman Cate frowned. Cheese flans weren't particularly hazardous to her knowledge; she must be referring to the calorific content.

"Yeah I know what you mean, don't suppose it will hurt though," she said scoffing one, and then picking up the plate and offering a tartlet.

"Not for me," snapped the girl, recoiling. "I suffered a pizza-related injury last year and I'm not fully recovered." Backing away from the table she shook her head and glared at the food. "I'm sorry; I just wish people would let me forget."

It was an unexpected reaction. Chewing on one finger Cate tried not to smirk. Had Miss Perfect experienced a snack-attack? Perhaps she should cordon off her freezer; not worth risking a *pizza-related* injury. She scrutinized the bite-sized buffet - completely innocuous to an unsuspecting diner. However, she never considered the consequence of an unprovoked assault by a malicious hors d'oeuvre. The woman was clearly two slices short of a deep-pan; but it meant that - irrespective of her big blue eyes and cute little turned-up nose - she was unlikely to be serious competition for the job.

The young assistant, resembling a rodent in a grey suit, appeared in the doorway again.

"Cate Cooke," she whispered through her large teeth.

"Is it okay if I nip to the loo on the way through?" asked Cate, removing shortcrust debris from her gums with a sweep of her tongue.

"Fraid not, you were a bit late, so I was asked to bring you straight in." Shuffling anxiously and wringing her hands the girl backed along the corridor.

The interview suite was diagonally opposite the entrance to the buffet room. Cate followed the assistant into the passageway, shrugging her shoulders and forcing a smile. No-one wished her luck. Unexpectedly turning to stone, the other candidates stood silent and petrified. Only their eyes seemed to move, tracking her progress across the red nylon carpet as though they spied through peepholes in an ancient portrait. All of a sudden she was standing at the foot of a glacier. An enormous frosted glass door materialized from nowhere, unexpectedly making her shrink to the height of a small child. Perhaps oversized people lingered on the other side, sitting around a huge table on giant wooden chairs. Looking away from the door she glimpsed a familiar face, and a boost to her wavering confidence; the reporter had shown up at last.

"Pastry-researchers unveiled an unexpected discovery today, hailed as an exciting advance in height management. The innovation was detected following the rapid ingestion of a mini quiche by a middle-aged woman, labelled by onlookers as the ''Hungry-bird'. Following consumption of the bite-sized morsel the woman diminished to less than half her normal stature within seconds. The phenomenon is described as 'shrinking tart syndrome'.

Scientists, however, refute the claim that a single hors d'oeuvre can produce such an effect, describing the idea as half-baked. They say it's more likely to be an egg-induced hallucination and that the woman is short on self-belief rather than lacking height.

Stay with us for more news and an exclusive exposé on the hidden dangers of the sausage roll. This is Catherine Bartlett reporting for Newsline."

After regaining her full height and composure Cate pushed open the glass door to see two people waiting to greet her with gentle handshakes and false smiles. A woman in her mid-twenties wearing a thin sweater and thick-rimmed spectacles introduced herself as Lizzie Penrose. Her companion was a tall man of a similar age with skinny limbs. One of his shirt sleeves was buttoned at the wrist; the other was rolled up, revealing a network of bulbous veins extending down his arm like white roots.

"Richard Glee. Pleased to meet you, I'm the Programme Director," he said sweeping his curly hair behind one ear. "Do take a seat."

In the middle of the room there was a polished table and three leather chairs. Glee poured water from a jug while Lizzie launched the preamble and then began the questioning. Handling the interrogation was easier than expected, largely due to the hours spent researching and preparing earlier in the week. Regurgitating stunning examples from her studies and placements Cate demonstrated how she would slide smoothly into the role. No more nerves; she was calm, poised and completely charming.

"Fascinating," said Glee doodling on his notepad towards the end of the interview. "And are you able to explain to us a time when things didn't go well? We're really interested to know how you coped and what you learned."
It was a test of character, as predicted. An opportunity to admit that she could make a mistake and find a way to recover, that she was resourceful even when faced with adversity. Questions like this were designed to explore strengths, not weaknesses.

"Well there was one instance that was rather unfortunate," she confessed. "We filmed a Member of Parliament visiting our university. It was pretty exciting at the time, he was rather famous. We put a sheet of paper on the floor with an 'x' on it and lined him up next to the stand. I asked him some questions and the other student operated the camera."

"And how did that go wrong?"

"He was taller than expected. When we played the footage back he was obscuring the 'L' on the slogan behind him, so it read 'Graduate Poo'. We had to dump the film and run the sound over the cutaways; pity really but we learned the importance of framing the subject."

"Yes, thank you for sharing that experience," agreed Glee, scratching his head. "Anything you want to add Liz?"

"Just one final point," she answered, staring at Cate. "Personal appearance is extremely important to Newsnetwork; have you looked in a mirror today?"

"Of course," she replied. If only she checked her make-up instead of stuffing her face at the buffet. "But there was an awful delay on the train and I didn't get chance to nip into the ladies before meeting you. A cow passed away on the track and I was stuck in a tunnel for nearly an hour while they scooped it up. I was with one of your correspondents actually - Mike Pick."

"Oh dear, that's hideous," said Lizzie, without giving any hint as to what upset her more, the dead cow or having to spend time with Pick. Pointing a finger at her own nose she frowned. "Well I suggest you attend to…before you do your screen test. I'm afraid you're a bit of a mess."
How embarrassing; limply shaking hands with her inquisitors Cate escaped from the room and headed for the loo. Under the

bright bulbs of the washroom she could see what Lizzie meant. Not that the skinny bitch had any right to criticize; she was hardly front-page news herself. However, she looked a fright. Her carefully applied foundation, glowing neatly on her chin and cheeks, was missing from the middle of her face. It was pink and bare, showing tiny thread veins to one side of her nose, as if someone wiped a hole in a masterpiece, revealing the canvas underneath. Bloody Mike Pick. The bastard must have removed her make-up with his handkerchief; what a clot. And she was an idiot for snaffling pastries and forgetting to monitor her own output again. A pizza-related injury didn't seem so ridiculous after suffering a quiche-related error.

Sorting through her handbag, she pulled out several cosmetic items to repair the damage. The washroom door sprang open. Sweeping past with her blonde head in the air, the pizza-girl disappeared into a cubicle, banging the door and clanking the bolt shut.

"How did it go? Have you had your interview yet?" asked Cate, applying mascara and pulling faces in the mirror.

"No, I just had the screen test," replied the girl. There was a rumbling of toilet roll unravelling, and then a flush. Emerging from the loo she approached the basin area. "It was totally superb; I'm scripting next. You better get a move on, the cameraman's a bear." She washed her hands and left.

More pressure. Scooping up lipsticks and eyeliners, Cate dashed into a cubicle.

"Mrs Cooke, are you in the lavatory?" It was the whispering assistant.

"Yes, I'm here."

"Sorry but we're on a tight schedule and you're wanted in room nine immediately, it's next to the lift. I have to organise the next scripting session. Please hurry up or you'll miss your slot."

"I don't suppose you could pass some toilet roll under the door, could you?" She listened for an answer. "It's run out." There was no reply. Fumbling for a tissue amongst the medley of items in her bag Cate eventually gave up, deciding to shake and drip-dry. She was harassed and uncomfortable. Scurrying out of the washroom she stepped briskly towards the lift, taking deep breaths as she walked.

Room nine was dimly lit but as she entered there was a blaze of light focused on a large screen in the corner.

"Can you get into place please? Quickly, and look towards me."

Squinting and shielding her eyes from the dazzle with one hand, she could just make out the outline of a man standing behind a tripod and camera.

"Hi, I'm Cate Cooke, I'm here to do a screen test," she grinned, dipping in an unintentional curtsey.

The man wasn't impressed.

"Say your name to camera," he groaned. Explaining what would happen he mumbled directions and signalled with one arm as though he was removing an amorous dog from his leg. Cate nodded intently, pretending she understood. Keeping one eye on the monitor, she pointed at the weather chart and read from the autocue. Coordinating was more difficult than it ought to be, and she tripped over her words several times. It didn't help that the dark shape interrupted at intervals, relaying secondhand orders received via his headset. Her heart was beating like an electric food-mixer. At any minute two metal whisks might punch out of her chest and fly across the studio. If the grumpy cameraman lost an eye she couldn't be held responsible; his brusque tone was making her nervous. There was a great deal to concentrate on and he wasn't making it any easier. Turning adjacent to the camera she took a deep breath and focused on the screen with renewed calm. Part of the problem was aiming gestures at a blank weather chart. She had to look at the monitor to see where she was pointing, and at times it all seemed back to front.

Continuing at a measured pace, she ignored the loud pulsing in her ears. If they didn't break soon, her head may explode. And her mouth was getting drier. Straining to deliver the last few sentences, her voice stretched to a high-pitched whine, like a kettle boiling under the spotlights. But before she could run out of verbal steam the man raised his arm and stepped away from his equipment.

"Thank you," he said, waving with one hand while cupping a headphone with the other. "They've seen enough now."

A small audience monitored her performance from behind a wide glass window at the back of the room.

"Was it okay?" asked Cate, walking towards the man with her hands clasped anxiously together. Moving from the glare she could see he was a trendy-looking forty-something with wavy hair and a smooth face. He looked kinder than he sounded.

"You did fine. Just one thing before you leave." Leaning towards her he lowered his voice to a whisper. "Your clothes are caught up at the back."

"No," she shrieked, freeing one side of her skirt from a knicker leg. "Why didn't you tell me?"

"Sorry, I tried to indicate when you came in. I pointed, but I couldn't really shout it out; didn't want to embarrass you. It only notices when you turn sideways."

Covering her mouth with one hand she stood in shock. Why did they put splits in the back of skirts? At least it was only tucked in at the bottom of her underwear, she hadn't flashed her spotty pants, had she?

"Could you see my…leg?" she hesitated.

"Hardly at all," the man shrugged. "See a bit of thigh when you turned towards the screen but not when you were facing camera. I wouldn't worry; just thought I'd mention it."

Excellent! What a good time to bring it up, when the screen test was over. Fool, she wasn't embarrassed, she was mortified. Skulking back to the buffet room Cate saw the blonde candidate standing outside the door snivelling into a tissue.

"You alright?" she said. "That pizza still bothering you?" It was a vaguely flippant remark but seeing the little princess crying cheered her up.

"My script session. Lizzie said it was completely amazing and I just feel so utterly drained and emotional." Wiping fingers across her tear-stained cheeks the girl looked up to the ceiling with an enormous grin. She was remarkably pretty even with smeared make-up and wet eyelashes. "If I don't get this position, it's still been the best experience of my life. How was your screen test?" The girl sighed. "Bernard is such a grouchy bunny, isn't he?"

Yes, either that or a belligerent troll, Cate was undecided. Clearly, the blonde made a better connection with '*Bernard'* than she established herself; how irritating. And it was unlikely she broadcast her bum in the process.

"I'd say it was a poignant episode," she replied, gripping the door-frame and attempting to look dramatic and mysterious. Sweeping into the room with an enigmatic grin she seated herself away from the buffet, and waited to be collected for the final part of the assessment.

The scripting session went well. Miss Penrose was complimentary, confirming Mrs Cooke as the best and most articulate writer of the day. Stick that in your screenplay, Blondie.

Travelling back to Wolfinger and contemplating her performance, Cate considered each component in isolation before declaring the overall result a success. The content delivered was sound, even though there were minor mistakes. It was more important to demonstrate she could recover from an incident than to be perfect. There was a trembling sensation in her gut that implied she left an impression and they were still talking about her – hopefully, in a good way.

Suddenly darting into a tunnel, the train made her ears pop. Resting against the window she spied her reflection out the corner of one eye. An echo of a former self, trapped behind the cold, black glass. The bank employee, the student and the wife all faded to a shadow as they emerged from darkness into the daylight. It was symbolic. Her media career was about to move from shade to shine. She earned it, without a doubt. Richard Glee was particularly impressed with her First Class degree; she was the only applicant to achieve one, and he had the final say on who got hired. Candidates would receive a phonecall by the end of next week.

Reaching into her handbag she pulled out her mobile and switched it on. There were two texts; Eve and Jemima both wished her a happy birthday, but there was no message from Mr Eyeball. Even if there was nothing to report, surely he would let her know. She sent a message to her sister, and then stared at her phone for several minutes before sending another text.

'Hi Iain, how was operation bloodhound? Kind regards, Cate'

There was no immediate reply. Cate watched the world slide past as the express hollered through the countryside. It was a mistake to get the weird Mr Ball involved. He probably followed the wrong person. By the time the train arrived at the station the sky was overcast and streaks of rain pressed on the windows. Trailing behind a small procession of travellers Cate passed a row of parked cars on her way to the taxi rank. It was difficult to tell with her jacket covering her head but she had the distinct impression that one of the vehicles pulled out from the line and was pursuing her across the car park. Clutching both lapels she quickened her pace but couldn't resist a fleeting 180 degree turn. She was right; she was being tailed by a milk float. Seeing an opportunity, the driver surged ahead to draw level with her.

"Cate, quick, hop in," beckoned the man. It was the Eyeball, wearing a peaked cap and a white anorak over a long navy and white striped apron. Despite the ginger beard and awful wig she recognised him straight away.

"Actually I was just going to ring you, did you get my text?" she said, peering at him through a gap in her makeshift headwear.

"I hoped I'd catch you here. I've got some news about Oliver. Hop on, I'll give you a lift to the end of your road and debrief you on the way."

Shaking the rain from her jacket she glanced around the car park and slipped in reluctantly next to Mr Ball. What horrid secret was he about to reveal? Her insides knotted. No, not now! She was flushing again; the hot water-bottle was back. In this weather she would be giving off steam at any minute. Puffing out a breath and waving one hand in front of her face, she slumped in the seat.

"What did you find out?" she asked.

"I tracked him all over town," he replied, trundling along behind a queue of cars. "You may not like this, but…are you okay? You look uncomfortable."

"I'm fine," she huffed. "Just a little embarrassed at getting a lift on a milk float. You didn't follow him in this did you?"

"My dear Cate, I used the Harley."

He was staring into her soul again with his spine-tingling brown eyes. Tugging her skirt over her knees she looked away, and then chewed on her lip.

"What is it that I won't like?" Gazing at the floor she continued. "Did Oliver meet someone?"

"There were several."

"What??" She was almost sick. Several? A sharp pain seared under her left breast, and her stomach churned.

"Just deliveries," he added. "What I mean is - you may not like it because I lost him after he left the short woman with a big kitchen. I was attacked by a farmer and I'm afraid your husband got away."

Cate frowned.

"So he didn't meet anyone, or do anything strange?"

"Well, there was definitely something peculiar going on at the last house. I tried to get photographic evidence but there was an incident with my phone. I'm sorry; I'll put together a full written report, of course. And I can continue surveillance after twelve hundred hours tomorrow. I just have to wait in for a replacement handset."

They came to a halt at the corner of Rushmore Drive. Resting her chin on one hand she thanked the Eyeball for his efforts, and then heaved a confused sigh.

"I don't think there's any point in following him again."

A passing car tooted its horn.

"I'm a milkman," he shouted, shaking his fist at the driver. "I can stop where I like."

Clutching her handbag and jacket Cate stepped down from the vehicle.

"Why are you a milkman?" she asked. "I thought you gave that up."

"I did," he smiled, tapping his nose with one finger. "But I've got friends in high places. Doll, if you want to be invisible, wear something loud and drive something obvious."

Party time

SLOWLY PUSHING THE DOOR ajar, Cate peered into the dining room. On the table a pale pink envelope with her name scrawled across it was propped against the crystal vase. There was also a small pile of cards and a present in a white cardboard sleeve. The package was flat and square-shaped; the type that contained jewellery. Smiling broadly she opened the box, revealing a silver bracelet with a tiny sparkling heart hanging from one of the round links.

"Where are you? Ollie?"

His car was on the drive, so he wasn't far away. The largest birthday card was from him. Luke's was the smallest; but at least it was shop-bought this time, not handmade like last year's desperate attempt. Standing a row of cards along the mantelpiece, she admired all five and then went upstairs.

Oliver was completely motionless, lying face down on the bed with his arms outstretched like he dropped from the ceiling and suffered a bad landing. His shirt was damp, and his hair stuck together in clumps at the back, resembling the glossy black fur of a wet Labrador. Cate flopped onto the quilt. Lifting his head from the duvet, her husband turned to look at her resting next to him.

"You're back," he said. "Shoulda phoned me, I'd have picked you up from the station. Howd'it go?"

"Okay, I think. Some of the others were pretty good but I got this funny feeling that they saw what they were looking for in me." Leaning forward she kissed him on the cheek. "I like my bracelet, thank you," she said holding her wrist up and showing it off.

"It's not from me," he lied, "I didn't know it was your birthday."

She poked him in the side with one finger. Reaching out Oliver wrapped his arms around her, and pressed his lips against her forehead.

"And now that you do know, I suppose you want to perform sexual favours on me," she said, gazing into his eyes.

"You'll be lucky, I'm knackered. Anyway I'm not sure I can have sex with a fifty year old," he teased, screwing up his nose.

Shoving him with both hands she pulled free and sat up straight. He placed one hand on her breast, squeezing gently and caressing the nipple with his thumb.

"Could manage a blow-job though; you did say you like the bracelet."

Shuffling off the bed and unbuttoning her blouse, she slapped his thigh playfully.

"I do," she said heading for the bathroom, "pity you told me it's not from you."

Getting ready was such a chore. If only she could step into a cupboard, experience a flash of light, and then emerge perfectly groomed. The preparation process grew longer as she got older. It was as though a time penalty was added with each birthday. She would have to get up a whole day earlier soon, just to go out. And was there any point? Would Ollie say how lovely she looked in her smooth, black, bodycon dress? No, but he might swoon if he knew how much it cost.

The whole family was gorgeous by the time Sam arrived; even Luke. With neatly-combed hair, striped shirt and tailored trousers he could easily pass for an estate agent, or even a business analyst, rather than a ladderless window-cleaner. Sam commented on the transition, tousling his blonde curls and rubbing his shoulder affectionately.

"Could this really be the same boy that used to sit on my lap, wiggling loose teeth and burping out the alphabet?" she asked.

Wearing a silky red outfit that hugged her figure, she was slim and confident, as always.

"Wasn't me, must've been James. I seem to remember farting out the National Anthem once though," he replied, carefully avoiding her cleavage by staring resolutely into her sparkling green eyes.

The ten minute drive to the restaurant was suitably prolonged by half an hour in order to take advantage of the champagne detour in a stretched limousine. Sipping drinks and singing loudly, the jubilant quartet circled the town twice on the dual-carriageway before elegantly arriving at the Tun o' Rice. Tipped off by text, the rest of the guests waited outside to cheer the approach. Surprisingly, they were waving small Union Jacks; the sort usually seen sticking out of sandcastles.

"Why do I get the feeling this has something to do with you?" said Cate, looking accusingly at her son. Luke shrugged.

Inside the Tun there was a long table set for eleven. Most of the decorations, including the helium balloons and shiny confetti, were in the shape of a number '50'. After a short kerfuffle everyone was seated. Placing herself strategically between Sam and Oliver, Cate was delighted to find that she was directly opposite James, and too far away from Grace to effect meaningful conversation. Not that it was easy to discuss anything with anybody in the first twenty minutes with waiters bobbing about and everyone talking at once. Some of the guests had not seen each other for quite a while.

"Must be at least five or six years," said Eve, fiddling with her necklace. "The twins were there, but they were quite small. Do you remember? They were arguing about whether daddy had gone to Devon or Heaven. And then one of them - was it Florence - ran away from the dog and fell into the paddling pool."

"Florence? No, I think you mean Nightingale," laughed Jemima. "It's Moon and Nightingale. Yes I remember the party but it was much longer ago than five or six years. The girls are thirteen now. Henry's been gone for eleven, and I think it was shortly after he passed."

"I'm sure it was only about five," pondered Eve.

Her husband interjected.

"She just said the twins are thirteen. Why don't you listen woman? It was obviously longer than you think." Raising his eyebrows and smiling, he turned to face Jemima. "I reckon it's the menopause, she gets battier every day; thought she saw her sister riding around on a milk float earlier."

"I did. Cats, Catty," called Eve, desperately trying to attract the attention of her sibling. "Tell Paul, I did see you on a milk float this afternoon, didn't I?"

"A milk float?" repeated Oliver, before his wife could contemplate a suitable lie. Luckily, although he didn't actually dislike his sister-in-law, he often found it difficult to consider himself on the same intellectual page. It was too tempting not to ridicule her.

"And why would she be delivering milk?" he added, gesticulating. "I mean, I guess it's not impossible but it seems highly unlikely, especially as she was at an interview in Canchester."

"Did I say *delivering* milk?"

"You didn't," interrupted Luke. "It might've been eggs or bread, or could've been potatoes. Ollie doesn't have an expanded mind like you Aunt Evie."

Ignoring her nephew she continued unperturbed.

"I was driving past on the way to pick up George. It was you, wasn't it Cat? I bibbed the horn," she persisted.

Hiding behind a menu Ollie pulled faces and wagged his head. Poor Eve, she was always so kind and accommodating; it seemed cruel to avoid confessing that she was right, and not a complete loon. Pretending to be confused, Cate adopted her most convincing expression and looked to her best friend for backup.

"I'm sorry, but you're wrong Eve," Sam intervened, drawing the attention of the diners. "It might've appeared to be a milk float, but it's a Z4," she added, rescuing her conspirator and annoying Ollie in the same breath. Everyone giggled, knowing how conceited he was with regard to his BMW.

"Bitch," he mouthed, shooting her a scathing glance.

The waiters hovered. Flitting from person to person, they collected orders and gathered menus like happy black and white bees harvesting nectar. Mr Ping opened two bottles of champagne and congratulated Cate - one of his most valued and indeed frequent customers - on the anniversary of her birth. The aged restaurateur was a short man, substantially less than five feet tall; his demeanour not improved by a tendency to stoop. But despite his diminishing height, he was a giant in other ways. Taking an active part in raising money for charity, hosting events and chairing local minority groups ensured his place as a well-known figure in the community. Respect and popularity was earned over a number of decades. However, one point that baffled many was whether 'Mr Ping' was in fact his real name. If common folklore was to be believed it was a nickname established shortly after his arrival in the UK, sometime during the 1970s. It had all changed now, but apparently the moniker related to a suspicious practice of serving scraps to late-night drunks desperate for takeaways. When the restaurant closed for the evening, leftovers were allegedly scooped into a large dish, and reheated to order in the microwave; hence the creation of the vehemently denied, but greatly revered, Special-noodle - 'Ping'. Nobody knew for sure but it was just the sort of cheeky crime that he would be involved in.

"I know this your dad," he said, pouring a glass of champagne for George. "And…er, this lady your mum?" Baring his even, yellow teeth in a wide grin, he nodded at Grace.

It wasn't always easy to determine whether Mr Ping was serious. Cate estimated him to be about one hundred and fifty years old and his eyesight wasn't the best; he occasionally spoke to the coat-stand and often shouted at his own reflection in the mirror behind the bar. He was a constant source of amusement to diners. With his odd way of shuffling around as though his shoes were tied together and his peculiar habit of hollering at himself, some thought him to be trundling happily towards gaga-land. However, he could smell a dodgy credit card from the other side of the room and add up numbers in his head quicker than any calculator. Antediluvian he may be, but he was an astute businessman and harder to read than the strange fortune cookies that appeared on the table at the end of the meal; the authentic Chinese ones that contained Irish jokes.

"We're not related," admitted Cate in her politest voice.

"Who knows? Maybe she's my daughter one day," said Grace, gently touching Mr Ping's arm, and then letting loose a vigorous burst of laughter.

James exchanged glances with his wife; safely ensconced between him and his aunt, the lovely Anya fluttered her extended eyelashes.

"We'll probably shoot off before pudding, Mum," he said, squeezing Anya's hand under the table. They were obviously planning something more substantial for dessert. It was just over a year since the handsome lovers married in what James described as more like a tornado than a whirlwind romance. Captivated by her amazingly long, black curls and her warm hazel eyes he proposed shortly after their first tangled encounter at the indoor snow-slope. In the following months they skied, raced, dived and skated their way to wedded bliss. And ever since the nuptials the active couple had been coupling actively in the hope of enlarging their family. Unfortunately, despite not taking precautions on every conceivable occasion there was no pregnancy yet.

"You can't leave early," said Jemima, leaning forward. "It's a special occasion."

"Yep, that's why we're not staying," said James, looking fleetingly at his wife. Tapping his watch and nodding, he signalled to his mother that it was 'time'. She got the drift of the conversation without him having to extrapolate; he disclosed the purchase of ovulation testing equipment earlier in the month. However, she didn't acknowledge straight away, causing him to point to his wife, and then gesture the shape of a pregnant stomach with both hands. Wincing, Cate confirmed her understanding. It wasn't something she wanted to consider in any detail. She was perfectly aware that her son had to perform a sexual act in order to make babies but the whole idea was quite abhorrent. There was probably only one thing worse - imagining George and Grace together. That was definitely taboo. Ollie occasionally made reference to what her step-father might get up to with his concubine, just to annoy her. The thought that he could be involved with Mrs Braithwaite in the same sort of explicit things that she took part in herself triggered an inner revulsion; usually making her cover her ears and run off chanting a 'la-la' noise.

"Yes, yes, I don't need all the graphic stuff thank you," she said, reaching for a prawn cracker. Luckily she was rescued from reflecting on the matter any further by the appearance of several waiters carrying plates of steaming food to the table. Delivering a veritable banquet, the attendants swept discreetly around the diners. The aroma of spicy meats and sweet vegetables filled the air, exciting bellies and whetting appetites. Consequently, much of the ensuing conversation was prompted by the tasty cuisine laid out before them, and the consumption of several bottles of wine. Eventually the dishes were emptied and one by one the guests stopped scoffing viands and leaned back on their chairs.

Placing his napkin next to the plate Ollie spoke softly to Cate, and then stood up and made his way across the restaurant. Watching him weave through the tables Samantha leaned close to her friend.

"I've been dying to ask, where did he go?"

"He's gone to the loo."

"No, not now," she said, moving closer and touching Cate's hand. "What happened when the Eyeball man followed him?"

"Oh, nothing unexpected. He made deliveries."

"Really? That's odd, considering he avoided taking you to the interview. And he stayed with him the whole time?"

Sam stared. Looking away Cate nonchalantly smoothed her napkin.

"More or less. He lost him before the last drop," she confessed.

Her friend paused, as if in frustration, bowing her head

"We can still catch him out," she said. "The dating site, he's pretty keen to meet up. Or rather *Ancien Reg* is."

"It's not Ollie," said Cate, glancing across the room towards the toilets. "So what have you lured poor old Reggie with?" she sniggered.

"I merely hinted at how slim and sporty you are. And I might have casually mentioned how much you like to dress up as a French empress."

"Yeah, thanks for that. You're completely off your rocker, you know. I'm not going to meet up with some barmy old lecher who thinks he's Napoleon."

"You don't have to," whispered Sam. "We just have to arrange a date, hide, and see who turns up. If it's not your husband, there's nothing to worry about."

A phone beeped. Both women glared at the jacket hanging over the back of Oliver's chair.

"Quick, before he comes back. See who just text him," hissed Sam.

Shaking her head and biting her lip Cate gazed around at the others. They were all engaged in conversation.

"No-one's looking, get his phone," urged her friend.

"I can't. It's a complete invasion of privacy; and it doesn't feel right. I think I should just forget all this. There's no proof he's up to anything. How can you have a relationship if you don't trust each other? He'd be devastated if he thought I was spying on him." Her eyes never left his jacket.

"Well - you are. And for good reason; what about the text?"

"We don't even know who it's from, could be his mum."

"I mean the first text; for goodness sake - the one he sent to *Babe*."

"Actually, he sent it to me."

"By accident," scoffed her friend.

Cate glared at Sam. She couldn't do it. Her heart raced, and there was that trembling sensation in her stomach again. Resting with one elbow on the back of Ollie's chair, she assessed the movements of her guests. It was as though she was about to commit a heinous crime, and she was ashamed of losing faith in his fidelity. They took vows, promises to each other, a long while ago maybe, but nothing had changed. She had more than one opportunity over the years to spoil their contract; the wild parties at the bank, the incident on holiday in New Zealand. Actually, that was something she preferred to forget. However, as she was confronted by temptation in the past, was it naïve to think that her husband never experienced the same? Sliding her arm down the back of the seat she reached into his jacket and gripped the phone in her hand. What if an unscrupulous floozy bullied him into submission? Removing his mobile slowly, she stopped and then released it back into the pocket. He would resist, she was sure of it; Ollie was 45, not a teenager, it would be completely pointless to risk everything for a quick shag.

"Hurry up," begged Sam.

"This is ridiculous. He wouldn't have left his phone unguarded if he had anything to hide. I know you can't understand this but there's something special between me and Ollie. I can't explain it and I'm not going to try; I don't need to check up on him."

Getting up from the chair Cate walked over to Jemima, who was grinning inanely and beckoning with one finger. She wore a pink cotton dress and an item that resembled a woollen tea cosy on her head. It would have seemed unusual on anyone else.

"So, how is the magazine piece coming along?" asked Jem.

"Needs a little more research but it's good thanks."

"Super, you got your night of passion, then. And are you going to include all the sexy bits? Men can't resist frilly knickers and a good spanking, can they? Did he enjoy it?"

"Loved it," she nodded, hoping she wouldn't have to fabricate the details.

"Fabulous; can't wait to read the article."

"The Editor wants me to put something together on monogamy next," she said, looking in Sam's direction; her friend hovered around Oliver's jacket. Suddenly she got up from the table.

"Hi Jemima, how are you?" said Samantha, walking over and discretely pressing a phone into Cate's hand. "You're looking really well, been up to anything exciting lately?" She took over the conversation, pretending to be captivated by the latest design and results of the Farthing-Thomas patent badger-scarer.

Cate's stomach churned, she had to read the text now. It was likely that the mobile clenched in her fist contained the evidence that might clear or condemn her husband; she couldn't ignore the truth forever.

"Back in a sec," she mumbled. Marching across the restaurant she gazed blankly at the phone. If only she could be left alone to age peacefully, like a piece of cheese. Pausing at the doorway, she leaned forward and looked along the corridor. There was no sign of Oliver and only one of the two toilets was in use; the other was marked 'out of order'. She was about to make a dash for the vacant loo when she heard her husband's voice. Appearing from a doorway to one side of the restrooms he headed straight for her. There wasn't enough scope to hide a SIM card in her dress, let alone a whole mobile. Fidgeting with it in her hands she made a swift exit before he could turn the corner. He'd be angry if he knew what she was up to. Rushing back to the table, Cate disposed of the phone along the way, slipping it into a tall oriental pot containing an attractive flowering plant.

"What's going on?" whispered Sam, seeing her friend returning hurriedly to her seat. "Who sent the text?"

"Don't know, he's right behind me, I didn't get chance." Picking up a glass of wine from the table she took a large gulp.

"So where's the phone?"

"Shoved it in the vase before he saw me."

"Bloody hell, you're completely useless, what if it rings?"

Oliver appeared. Resuming his place next to Cate he noticed the women seemed agitated.

"Had to hang on for ages; there's only one toilet working," he said,

"Yeah, I've been waiting for you to come back," said Samantha, getting up.

Smoothing her silky dress with both hands she strolled across the restaurant. There were four indoor plants en route. Sniffing at the blooms and pretending to admire the foliage Sam examined each of the pots in turn. The first was disappointingly devoid of mobile telephony equipment and so was the second, but the third contained what she was looking for. Glancing back at the table she slipped the phone into the neckline of her dress, concealing it in her bra, and squashing it against her left bosom. Mr Ping stood in the gangway, smiling and bowing his head like a nodding dog.

"Very nice, thank you," he said, watching her assault the plants.

"I think they need watering."

Feeling obliged to poke at the fourth leafy shrub as she passed, Sam turned the corner and disappeared from view. She would have to hurry, the party was starting to break up.

Most of the guests were wobbling around stuffed with food. Ollie was conversing with Paul; James and Anya had already sneaked away, leaving a pile of money under a glass. Grace was trying on Jemima's hat at one end of the table, while George and Luke sat slightly apart from the others, deep in conversation. Moving closer, Cate overheard the last few words, "…but don't let your mother know."

They were plotting something. It was either an exotic birthday surprise - more Union Jacks and other tasteful artifacts left over from the Queen's Jubilee - or they were discussing an air rifle. Probably the latter.

"Don't let me know what?" she interrupted.

"Nothing," said Luke, smirking at his grandfather.

"Never said a dicky bird," added George, shaking his head.

"It's the poor little dicky birds I'm worried about; I've got my eye on you two," said Cate. Luke backed away, scratching his head, and looking guilty as usual.

"Talking of which," said her step-father, "how did Ollie perform?"

"What?"

"Being observed? Are you getting that free food?"

"Free food?" she said, suddenly remembering the story she told a couple of days before. "Yes. No. Ollie did quite well apparently but we don't know the full result yet. Some sort of argument over…a pork pie I think; and it could count against him."

"Be a surprise to me if he wins," huffed George. Staring into her pretty eyes he searched for any indication that she was hiding something. He was fully aware that 'pork pie' was rhyming slang for an untruth but not completely sure if she was pulling his leg about the competition.

"Did it have egg in it?" he asked, hoping she would give herself away if he probed deeper.

"I'll try and find out," she lied with a smirk.

Samantha was about to make a discovery of her own. Squeezing past the door and into the toilet cubicle she slipped the bolt across, and turned to face the loo. There was an unholy stench. Emanating from an enormous terd protruding like a whale tail above the water, it made her stomach gag and her eyes stream at the same time. Oliver! He was the last one to return from the lavatory; disgusting pig, he hadn't even bothered to put the lid down. Cupping one hand over her nose she leaned forward and pushed hard on the handle. Water gushed from the cistern. Flooding the bowl, it removed the offending faecal matter in a flash. Unfortunately, the exerted effort used in flushing, simultaneously dislodged the secret stash in her bra. Sam watched helplessly as the phone suddenly became upwardly mobile, leaping out of her dress in a perfect dive for freedom. Flapping her hands but unable to force them into the rapids she gasped as the cellular equipment chased the poo around the pan before being sucked noisily around the bend.

"Oh shit," she said gazing pitifully into the mirror above a tiny hand-basin. Unlocking the door she sneaked into the corridor and made her way back to the dinner party. Her best friend was chewing on one finger, and staring at the menu. It was a look she recognised. Maybe not obvious to the rest of the world but Sam could see sadness seeping from her like steam rising. Hovering apprehensively, she waited until Cate noticed her arrival before sitting down.

"Go on, tell me. You got the phone, didn't you? Was it one of his friends, or his mum?"

Grimacing, Sam glanced up at the ceiling. It was difficult to find the right words. She wanted to say that everything was okay and there was nothing to worry about; but somehow instead of taking away the pain, she was about to add to it. Irritatingly, Oliver was laughing and chatting with the others in the background, oblivious to his wife's mood, and totally unrepentant with regard to the evil torpedo.

"Um, I didn't get to find out. There was an incident." Sam paused, looking sideways at her friend. "Not completely my fault by the way. I took it into the loo, no wonder he came skulking back, you should've seen what he left in there. It was some form of toxic waste. I had to flush; I was nearly sick."

"So you didn't get chance to look at the text. Is that what you're saying? You're not trying to tell me that you dropped Ollie's phone down the bloody bog, are you?"

"I didn't drop it; it jumped out my bra and disappeared 'round the bend. I'm really sorry. I was only trying to help."

"Fuck; couldn't you get it back?" hissed Cate. "What am I going to tell him?" Leaning back on the chair she breathed out with a huff.

"Don't be daft; he doesn't know we took it." Pouring wine for them both, Sam pushed a glass into her friend's hand. "Look, you're the one being deceived here; you don't have to be so honest all the time. You should never underestimate the power of denial, you know."

An interesting concept, honesty. Cate wrinkled her nose. It was funny how the words of her dear mother flooded back every birthday. As well as the adage about her falling into a bucket of poo and coming out smelling of roses, there were two other things the late Mrs Bennett was particularly fond of recalling. The first was her most diabolical delivery; how she pushed her daughter out into the world, resulting in so many stitches that her bottom resembled a patchwork quilt. Not an ideal image; as a child Cate envisaged it to be pieced together with scraps of chintz and blanket-stitch. Of course the doctor had a wide choice of yarn, and a thimble. If only he put in a zip she might have a half-sister, too.

The other favourite remark was that her daughter wouldn't know truth if it bit her on the bum. It was a misconception; she was never dishonest, just imaginative. However, the whole thing with Oliver seemed strangely ironic. If she was searching for the truth, why did she find herself telling so many lies? Sam was busy with her mobile phone. Gazing around the restaurant Cate noticed a familiar figure reporting next to one of the plants.

> *"Organisers of the annual 'Most lies in a day' competition are delighted by the response from this year's entrants. With a record number of fictioneers recorded in both the 'Self-defence' and the 'Protecting the innocent' categories, the contest looks certain to push previous boundaries to a new anecdotal limit.*
>
> *A recently emerged classification - the 'Hour of deceit' - draws the greatest interest this year, with one competitor tipped for stardom following a stunning restaurant performance. Over a sixty minute period the bold contender pulls together a combination of untruths eventually culminating in one dubious fib. The crucial question is - could the contestant really be dishing out dishonesty in order to discover the truth? It's been hailed as the ultimate act of self-deception – the most perfect lie achievable. This is Catherine Bartlett reporting for Newsline. Stay with us for more as the story unfolds, but now it's back to the studio."*

Slinking back to the table and reaching for a bottle of wine Oliver topped up glasses as he weaved around the guests.

"You have some revolting habits," said Sam. "I hope you washed your hands."

"Sorry I'll wear gloves next time," he smiled, pouring a drink. "But nobody else is complaining."

"You know exactly what I'm talking about; the toilet was disgusting."

"Wasn't me," he retorted, walking away.

Staring after him Cate chewed her bottom lip.

"I've just remembered," she whispered. "He hadn't been to the toilet; he came from the direction of the bar."

Sam scoffed.

"Doesn't mean it wasn't him; but if he wasn't in the loo, what was he up to?"

Suddenly the lights dimmed and Mr Ping appeared carrying a small inferno cunningly disguised as a cake. In addition to being adorned with fifty blazing candles it was elaborately decorated with marzipan figures in a television studio. The main character, complete with camera and microphone, bore a striking resemblance to Cate.

"Surprise!" announced Oliver, raising his glass.

Hi-viz

OPENING ONE EYE AT A time and squinting into the daylight Cate could see the world had not entirely stopped shaking. The cake must have been laced with something; everything was a complete blur after she blew out the candles. Perhaps that was it; maybe it took so much breath to extinguish the two score and ten that she passed out and everyone went home. If only. The details were fuzzy; her articulate brain had been replaced with a ball of wool but there were tiny flashbacks knitting together into an embarrassing cardigan. She hadn't made a birthday wish at the time, and if she could have one now it would involve a gag. There was definitely a moment when she requested the entire restaurant should stop eating, and listen to her important message. Something to do with world peace and Chinese food. And how trust and honesty were the most important things in a relationship; the exact content was hazy.

Then there was a gap in her antics, but following on from that she could see the faint imprint of two round breasts on the bedroom window, where she pressed her naked upper body against the glass. It seemed like a good idea at the time, after throwing her bra out onto the lawn. Whatever happened subsequently she was pretty certain it didn't result in sex because she still had her knickers on. How disappointing; maybe Oliver really couldn't be bothered to part the cheeks of a fifty-year-old. He mumbled something to her before he went to work but it was about his missing phone, rather than her absent foundation garment.

Rising slowly from the bed, Cate peered at the pale, dishevelled woman in the mirror. Strange because from the inside, looking out at the world, nothing changed much over the years. But the reflection told a different story. Her body was thicker than that of a young girl, her skin less firm and her face more lined. She was officially a pentagenarian, if there was such a thing, with a first class degree and an errant husband. What did it all mean? Was there a purpose to her current dilemma, and why was her tongue so furry?

She needed tea, and possibly toast. Slipping into a silky black dressing-gown she made her way downstairs. Unfortunately, the kitchen was wired to an amplifier, with spoons jangling like a set of giant tubular bells, and the kettle roaring and cracking with the force of a jet taking off. Making breakfast turned out to be a delicate operation, followed by gradual consumption of warm, buttery bread, and lengthy periods of vacant staring into the garden.

Eventually it was an enjoyable experience, sitting in the dining room, watching wasps, and absorbing the sweet scent of summer while her internal organs rebooted. Then the peace was shattered. Swinging open with a clatter the front door bounced off the wall, announcing the arrival of her son and his dim-witted disciple. Luke appeared at the doorway.

"You look rough, Mum. Good job you're not fifty every year," he smirked.

"Thank you for that valuable appraisal, I'll bear that in mind next time you want me to invest my hard-earned cash in one of your highly-commendable schemes. Anyway, it's unusual for you to be up so early, isn't it? Or are you returning home late from last night?"

"Actually, we've been out doing the four-letter word thing. You know that 'work' stuff you're so keen on. Uncle Pat commissioned us to carry out remedial maintenance on his property portfolio. Stick the kettle on Monk," said Luke, brushing back his curly mop of hair with one hand.

"And that means what exactly?" said Cate.

"Means I'm making the tea, Mrs C. Would you like me to get you one?"

"No thank you Mr Monk," she snapped. "I think I know what happens when water is boiled, and quite frankly I wouldn't trust you to operate the tap. However, I wasn't addressing you; I was asking my son to elucidate."

"I'll just get out the way, sorry about the kettle," whispered Monky backing into the kitchen.

Cate glared at Luke.

"What?" he protested. "What have I done now?"

"I don't know. But if it's to do with him, it can't be anything good." She looked towards the kitchen.

"You're suspicion is misplaced, mother dear," said Luke, folding his arms and leaning against the doorpost like a contented sleuth. "I secured a window-cleaning contract on Fruitfarm Estate, and I have been carrying out my duties, for which I will get paid later this month."

"Well, I feel as if I should be impressed," she said viewing her son apprehensively. "But where does the Monky's uncle fit into all this?"

"Uncle Pat owns the flats. He lets them out to students, so not only do we get the job, we get to do the whole peeping-tom bit, and it's all legit," he smiled.

"How reassuringly despicable," she sighed. "And did you spot anything of particular interest?"

"Interesting – no. Surprising – *yes*." Inspecting the fingernails of one hand he waited for his mother to investigate further.

She didn't take the bait. There was nothing more to be gained from an interrogation about the voyeuristic habits of her son and his half-witted Monky. Securing her dressing-gown Cate ambled across the front room. It was one rung closer to having a job though, and small steps were better than nothing. Spying was unethical under any circumstances; but snooping on unsuspecting females brought a whole new meaning to the definition of 'self-employment' – one she wasn't keen to dwell on.

"I'm going to get dressed. Don't scoff all the biscuits," she said without turning around.

"We're only doing the ground floor at the moment, of course, but I foresee my career scaling to great heights - as soon as we get some ladders. Pity we couldn't borrow Ollie's really. Oh yeah - Ollie – I nearly forgot, that was the thing that surprised me."

"I wouldn't be too shocked; he's not in the habit of lending anything," she replied.

"Yeah, well he must've loaned someone his jacket. It was hanging on the back of a chair in one of the flats."

That stopped her, like a harpoon through the heart. Searing her chest, the pain took her breath away momentarily.

"What jacket?" she asked, spinning around to face her son.

"His blue and yellow Spennimore's one," replied Luke. "I know it was Ollie's; the pocket was torn and I could see the tooth-marks on the sleeve where that dog bit him. It was definitely his. Strange, cos I didn't see his van. Does he deliver to Fruitfarm?"

"I don't think so, as you said - it's more likely he lent it to one of the other drivers," she said dismissively, turning and continuing her journey upstairs. "Did you see the occupant?"

"Nope, must've been out. But judging from the underwear lying around, I'd say she was pretty fit." He sloped off into the kitchen, suppressing a grin.

Fruitfarm Estate was not in their catchment area. It belonged to the larger Spennimore's in the next town. Oliver hated anyone using his jacket and he certainly wouldn't have given it to a driver from another store. It was serious. What possible excuse could there be for leaving a hi-viz somewhere he wasn't even supposed to be? When he left for work yesterday he definitely picked it up. However, when she discovered him lying on the bed later his clothes were damp, and she didn't recall seeing his jacket in the closet. There was probably a reasonable explanation but she was going to have to start looking much harder. Dashing upstairs she burst into the bedroom and flung open the wardrobe doors. The butterflies were back, irritating her stomach and making it churn. He would be home soon. Sweeping her dresses to one side Cate paused to look at Ollie's black denim pants hanging limply from the rail. Suddenly she grabbed at the garment and stuffed her hands into the pockets. Feeling around with her fingers she explored every inch and then moved on to the next item. Shirts, trousers, jackets and jeans; she made her way methodically through his entire wardrobe before progressing to the drawers. Pulling out tissues and inspecting receipts, her heart pounded each time there was something worth scrutinising; but eventually it wasn't possible to convict him of anything more heinous than serial snacking. How could he eat so much chocolate? By rights he should be half-man, half-biscuit. She flopped onto the bed and closed her eyes. The familiar voice in the background gradually increased in volume, like a radio being turned up.

"Police say a man found slumped in the doorway of sweet-shop amidst a pile of empty wrappers broke down under questioning and admitted to eating between meals. The 45-year –old delivery driver confessed to consuming more than the suggested daily intake of sugary snacks without gaining weight.

After further interrogation he owned up to being an unlicensed chocoholic telling officials that his obsession was out of control. He said he was ashamed of what he'd become, but his addiction pushed him to the limits.

A police spokesperson said, 'It's a sad case. The man tried to suppress his passion for the sweeter things in life but eventually temptation got the better of him. He believed replacing his genitals with 75% cocoa solids may offer a cure. But after a botched operation he discovered his chocolate wanger was too short and he couldn't reach to eat it. Confronting the backstreet confectioner who performed the procedure he was told that he should have selected the dark chocolate version if he wanted a bigger one.'

The man was later released without charge, and advised to keep out of the sun. This is Catherine Bartlett, reporting for Newsline. Stay with us for more on this story later, and now back to the studio."

Dressing slowly, she considered the alleged crime and the substantial lack of evidence. Her hair was curly, and her face all puffy. No wonder Ollie was losing interest; she looked like a hamster in a nest of wood-shavings. Ignoring the mirror Cate opened the bedroom window and gazed down at the street. Bob was outside cleaning his car. Hamish was close by, sprawled across the pavement, licking the inside of his back leg. Spennimore's drivers were always getting bitten by something. One was chased by an angry chicken last month. In fact, it was highly likely that there were several torn jackets in circulation.

It was time to find out; the open-top Z4 growled onto the drive with Oliver at the wheel. He retrieved the bra from the front lawn before entering the house. So where was his hi-viz? Could he have gone skiing off piste after the Eyeball lost him?

The possible sighting of a dog-chewed garment on the Fruitfarm Estate was circumstantial – unless of course, the genuine article couldn't be produced.

She developed a sudden and unexplained bout of hiccups. Pragmatism was called for. Sitting at the dressing-table she applied a light layer of foundation and a heavy slick of mascara, intermittently hindered by involuntary spasms of the diaphragm.

"Hallo," she called out, running straighteners down the length of her hair. "You alright?"

"Yep."

Kicking off his shoes Oliver padded into the kitchen to examine the aftermath of the small tsunami that left puddles of tea, milk, and broken biscuit debris on the work-surfaces. The occupants had already abandoned the area but he recognised the tell-tale signs of his step-son. Muttering under his breath he filled the kettle and was considering whether to clear up the mess when the doorbell rang.

"Someone at the door," shouted Cate. Making final adjustments to her make-up she walked over to the window and looked out. There was a blue car parked on the road outside the house. Her husband was talking to someone downstairs. It was a woman. Running onto the landing she heard part of the conversation.

"I text you loads of times, but when there was no reply I thought I better bring it over, in case you needed it," said the female voice.

"Yeah, I lost my bloody phone somewhere. Thanks. I'm getting a replacement delivered this afternoon."

Peering over the bannister Cate descended the stairs slowly. There was a shuffling sound and then the blonde girl came into view, standing next to Ollie. They both looked up as she appeared.

"Lucy popped over with um - that Ripper research I was after. You've met before, haven't you?" said Oliver, pushing something into the closet.

"Hi," smiled Lucy, holding up the book. "Can't stop, got to get to uni before the library closes. Congratulations by the way."

"Thanks," replied Cate, gripping the newel post from which her generously cupped undergarment was dangling. "I was just going to make coffee if you fancy one."

Her heart thudded. Something devious was occurring. Now that she could see them together - handsome, rugged Oliver with the slim and beautiful Miss Watts, it was obvious they shared a secret. She sensed the tension. A good-looking man, fit and charming might seem like a challenge to a strong-minded girl with a clear complexion, baby-blue eyes and bouncy tits. And being unobtainable, on the surface of it, could make him even more desirable. As for Ollie, he was a typical male; an hour-glass figure and an innocent smile was enough to turn his head, despite the fact he must be almost twice her age. He could never resist the flattery. Men; simple to please and easy to lead. A bit like dogs; not much either species wouldn't do for a kind word and a flash of tail. And the glossy-coated Lucy was really good at wagging it – bitch.

Suddenly they were all looking at each other, suffocated by the silence and throwing glances like a game of pass-the-parcel. When the invisible music stopped someone would have to speak. Cate's tongue was tied in a knot, attached to the one in her stomach. Luckily Miss Watts replied to her question before she choked to death.

"No, I better get off," she said smiling, and gazing sideways at her friend.

Swallowing hard on the lump in her throat, Cate forced a grin.

"It's good of you to drive all this way to just deliver Jack the Ripper, I'm sure Ollie could have picked him up. Whereabouts do you live?" she asked.

"Not far really - just the other side of town."

"I'll have a coffee," interjected Oliver.

"Oh, over by the Fruitfarm Estate?" enquired Cate.

"Yes, do you know it?"

"I know there's some student flats over there," she replied, glaring at her husband.

"Well, thanks for bringing this over," interrupted Oliver. "You better get moving or the library will be shut," he said, taking the book and gesturing towards the door.

Miss Watts nodded coyly, like a naughty schoolgirl being ushered into the playground. Swaying her dainty hips she passed the stairs, perfectly balanced on shiny black stilettos as if she was a model strolling down the catwalk. Oliver followed behind her, stepping forward at the last moment to open the door.

"Let me get that for you," he murmured.

How gallant! Cate stifled a scowl on the way to the kitchen. What a gentleman her husband could be at times; she must remember to mop the floor before he drowned in his own drool. The couple drifted outside and stood next to the Z4. Ollie was describing something, talking and gesticulating with his arms, as he always did. The kitchen door was ajar allowing her to peep along the hallway to see him outside, laughing and leaning towards the girl. Then they took a step closer to the car and the view was lost.

Tapping her lips with an index finger she paused to consider the situation. Would the stunning Miss Watts really be so bold as to show her face if they were having an affair? Perhaps they hadn't actually got around to shagging yet; or maybe she was letting her imagination get the better of her. She could disrupt their tête-à-tête by taking some rubbish out to the bin; but what would they be getting up to on the drive? The sensible action was to calm down and make tea. A Jaffa cake might unlock her cognitive insight.

It was disturbing that she never noticed how immaculate the incredible Lucy was until now. With her firm bottom and slender thighs, and her azure eyes and long lashes, and her silky hair and soft pink mouth – she was an alluring figure by any man's standards. Flicking the switch on the kettle Cate reviewed her chipped nail-polish. She hadn't observed Miss Watts' fingernails; the little temptress. Would they match the scratches on Ollie's back perchance?

Her internal inferno resumed, welling up in her belly and spreading through her body. That sudden sensation of being put in the oven; now she knew what it was like to be a turkey. The heat was impossible to get away from, like someone had turned up a radiator in her chest. Flapping her hand helplessly without causing a draft she puffed out her cheeks and exhaled in despair. She had no time for hot flushes. Walking past the breakfast table she flung open the door and marched out onto the patio. It was warm and bright outside but the air was fresher, and after a few deep breaths the thermal episode subsided.

"Yes, we'll go to the swings after we've been shopping."
Cate looked towards the fence. She couldn't see her, but a young woman pushed a toddler in a buggy on her way to the supermarket. A tiny voice replied but the words were indiscernible. The house was a corner plot and the road ran parallel to the back garden. At the front a tall hedge of cherry laurel obscured the view of passers-by. If only she could take a little peek at Oliver saying goodbye to his friend she would get a much better idea of how close they were. She might even be privy to their parting conversation, which could be particularly revealing if they didn't know she was listening.
Without giving the matter further consideration she hopped across the grass, jumped up onto the compost bin, and clambered up the wooden fence. Peering down at the pavement it was clearly too high to leap from the top. She would be risking serious injury, compounded by the fact she wasn't wearing shoes. The only option was to turn around and go down backwards. Clinging to the post she swung one leg over, and then the other, gripped the edge of the fence and dangled with arms extended for a few seconds before dropping to the ground. Landing in the gravel, she grazed her knees on the wooden boards on the way down. Leggings would have been a better choice of attire than a short skirt but she hadn't anticipated tackling an assault course. Brushing small stones from the soles of her feet she scurried along the path, bending low as if she was about to storm an embassy.
The hedge provided adequate cover. Sweeping branches aside Cate pushed her face into the leaves and peeked through the foliage. They were still on the drive – the happy couple. Oliver was smiling and talking, performing an unintentional mating ritual as he rocked from one foot to another, while the attentive Lucy gazed up at him, nodding and grinning. It wasn't looking good from a fidelity prospect, but judging from the conversation he was delivering a captivating rendition of trying to find a phone, not conducting a wooing ceremony.
Rubbing an injured knee she watched intently for signs that the exchange was about to come to a close. Principally she wanted to observe the actual departure, whenever that might finally occur. Much could be established from the way they said goodbye; a quick friendly peck or something displaying a

little more chemistry? Like a sensual brushing of lips on the cheek.

"That was quite a manoeuvre."

The voice took her by surprise, resulting in an involuntary jerk that knocked her off balance. Floundering in the bush she grabbed at the branches to regain her poise.

"What?" she hissed, turning to face her aggressor.

"Steady on," smirked Bob. "I was going to award you a 9.9 for your vault over the fence, but I don't think much of the dismount."

Clutching her elbow Bob gently pulled her from the shrubbery. That was all she needed, intervention from her crazy neighbour; trust him to sabotage her surveillance. Resisting her first instinct to punch him on the nose she put one finger to her lips.

"Shh," she whispered, dragging him to one side so they were hidden by the house. "There's something nesting in my bush."

"What, something unusual?"

"Yes, I think it's one of those little cappuccino monkeys."

"A capuchin? I doubt you'll find any of those around here," he protested. "Where would that've come from?"

"South America, I think," said Cate, trying to look earnest. "Anyway, you're probably right, I must've been mistaken. I better scoot." Lucy couldn't spend all day gawping at Oliver; she would drive past at any second. Just one minor problem, there was nowhere to dash off to.

"Before you go – can I ask if you've seen Teddy? We've misplaced him and Hamish is worried."

The giant dog peered up at her with sad brown eyes. Dropping a small rubber dumbbell at her feet he slumped into a sitting position, and then stared at the toy. It made a sweet jangling noise as it bounced gently off the pavement and onto her bare toes, spraying them with slobber.

"You're honoured," added Bob. "He doesn't give up his bone for everyone."

Looking down at the Great Dane Cate could see he was experiencing the misery and sadness of loss. Had an avaricious Poodle stolen Teddy away, right from under his leathery black nose? Perhaps he failed to pay the bear enough attention and it was enticed into the jaws of another. A car door slammed in the distance, and an engine started. Whatever the predicament, a canine dilemma really didn't compare with her own, and it was about to get much worse if she couldn't get back into the garden imminently.

"I'm sorry Hamish," she said, wringing her hands and backing away, "I haven't seen Teddy for a while but I'm sure he'll turn up…unless you've buried him somewhere."

Edging towards the fence she chewed her lip, contemplating how she could make the return journey without a ladder.

"Would you mind just giving me a leg up?" she asked. "I think I left something in the oven."

"Okay," said Bob, making a stirrup with both hands. "Wouldn't it be easier to use the door, though?"

"No, I smell burning," she replied, hoisting herself up. Scaling the fence she managed to swing one leg over and lie along the top of the panel, panting. But before she could recover her breath the blue car tore up the road with Lucy at the wheel, waving and tooting the horn. Cate raised one hand in acknowledgement, unsure how she might explain why she was balancing on the boundary with a neighbour crouching in the gravel, looking up her skirt.

However, it wasn't important as long as she got inside before Oliver saw her. Shimmying down the wooden slats she bounced off the compost bin and landed safely in the grass. Bob watched in amazement as she disappeared from view; staring first at the fence, and then at his dog.

"I told you she wouldn't have him. You shouldn't leave your stuff lying around. And pick your toy up; do you want people to think you're bone idle." Marching off, he sniggered to himself. "*Bone* idle," he repeated sticking out his pointed chin.

Looking around nervously, Cate strode into the kitchen. Oliver was changing out of his work clothes; she could hear him stomping around upstairs.

"Do you want a Jaffa cake?" she called.

"Yeah, put five out for me," he replied. "It's a good job you had your party yesterday. I just passed the Tun and there's water pouring out the front door. The drain people are there and Ping's jumping around on the pavement waving a plunger."

"Really?" She tiptoed to the downstairs loo. "Let's hope they don't dredge up a phone," she whispered to the reflection in the mirror. Pulling a twig from her hair, she sneaked back along the passageway, passing the cupboard under the stairs. The door was slightly ajar. Pushing it fully open with one hand she peered inside. A Spennimore's jacket hung on the hook. Luke was wrong; he couldn't have seen Ollie's hi-viz earlier. It was obviously hanging in the closet all the time – he definitely wasn't wearing it when he got home. Reaching out and touching the sleeve with a sigh, she brushed the raised welts caused by the dog-bite. She ought to be relieved, but it wasn't a satisfactory conclusion somehow. Could it have appeared in the last few minutes; delivered by a blonde? If only she saw the coquette arrive she could be sure. And if only she saw her depart - she might feel more relaxed.

The Honeypot

WHOEVER OBSERVED THAT *'silence is golden'* certainly wasn't waiting for news about a job.
Blinking only occasionally, to prevent her eyeballs from drying up, Cate stared purposefully at the mobile phone for a full twenty minutes. It wasn't intimidated. Gazing back vacantly, it remained uncommunicative. Even picking it up and waving it around didn't produce a result. There was definitely a signal; so what possible reason could there be for it not to ring? It was several days since the interview; they must have come to a decision by now. The curious tingling in her belly indicated that something was about to occur - imminently. Some sort of visceral omen. Hopefully it indicated the manifestation of a job offer rather than a bout of diarrhoea; although the squits might be easier to contract than employment. There was certainly something in the offing; her stomach never lied.

Of course it could be nervous apprehension regarding the blind date she managed to rope herself into. Unlikely; the whole thing was ridiculous. Ollie might be acting rather odd but the chances that he was an internet stalker were extremely remote. And despite being a teensy bit curious, the idea of a clandestine encounter with a Napoleonic nutter wasn't compelling. However, it really was the only way to appease Samantha. While she had a wasp in her onesie there would be no peace until an exorcism had been performed.

Nothing difficult; all she had to do was to turn up at The Honeypot and prove to her friend that her husband wasn't a philandering saddo. One fleeting photo of ancient Reggie outside the pub, ensconced between the roses would suffice. Everything was arranged via the Dates2Remember website; Sam made out the respondent was about to find the girl of his dreams – a slim, sporty student with an insatiable lust for history. Old Reg was gagging to meet her, apparently. The poor sap had no idea he was being set up. It was a shame really but she couldn't help sniggering to herself. In a way it would be even funnier if it did turn out to be Oliver - for at least sixty seconds until she tore off his genitals with her bare hands, and fed them to the nearest herd of pigs. Luckily, that was an improbable outcome; and there wasn't a farm around for miles.

Cate stared out of the window. The sun streamed down from a stunning blue sky, and everything was warm and vibrant like a freshly baked muffin. Shopping for bread and cakes all morning embedded the aroma of sweet pastries and crunchy crusts in her nostrils. How much longer would she have to work at Spennimore's? Yawning, she checked her phone. Still nothing, but it was five to eleven; the snacking hour. Her stomach let out a low groan of delight. Time to dunk digestives and collect cookies; she hadn't read her emails yet. As usual, she was greeted by a plethora of exciting offers designed to meet individual needs according to her internet browsing habits. Within a few clicks she could revamp her wardrobe, take tea at a stately home, and arrange for the ironing lady to pick up the chores while she smoothed out wrinkles at the spa. None of this was of particular interest. Employment agency emails deserved a little more attention but there was nothing on offer that warranted more than a breathless sigh or a raised eyebrow.

Suddenly she spotted it, tucked between the unlimited train travel and an invitation to adopt a zebra. Burgeoning with excitement, her heart pummelled on her ribs. Cate froze, caught in the executioner's spotlight like a hedgehog confused by the appearance of headlamps. Just a glimpse of the sender was enough to arrest her elevenses, mid-dunk. She wasn't expecting a written message. And then, flopping like a digestive landslide, the biscuit leaned over and splashed into her coffee mug in perfect synchronization with her jaw dropping. This was it; an email from Newsnetwork. The awaited communication. She was promised a phone call. Reading aloud the words in the preview pane she paused at the missing text.

"Thank you for applying for the position of Weather Present…"

The rest of the sentence wasn't visible. Chewing her lip, she wiggled the mouse, forcing the cursor to scurry around the page in a frenzy. Just one click could be a life-changing event. Bearing down on the plastic rodent with one powerful digit would reveal her future; her finger of fate. Was she ready for this? With a flotilla of Red Admirals fluttering in her belly and a racehorse galloping in her chest she highlighted the title and opened the message.

> *Dear Cate, thank you for applying, blah, blah blah, exceptionally high standard, blah, blah, we regret to inform you...blah – blah – blah.*

Oh. That wasn't supposed to happen; she was the best candidate. A lump ballooned in her throat, pressing on the back of her tongue like a ping-pong ball. Swallowing hard she dislodged the obstruction, forcing a bolus of tears into her stomach to drown the butterflies. The racehorse was down too; a faller at the first fence. Still twitching, but at least it was out of its misery. Her agony was just beginning. What now? Someone else had her job - unless they made a mistake and emailed the wrong person.

Flopping onto the swivel chair with her head tilted backwards Cate pouted, and then sighed. Actually there was no great overwhelming sense of failure. It was more of a short, sharp shock than a sustained electrocution. The worst thing was staying on at Spennimore's. She was worth much more, and the thought of shopping until the end of time far outweighed the initial feeling of rejection. And what did that tell her? Absolutely nothing; there would be other opportunities. One minor setback didn't mean she should give up at the first hurdle, like her stupid inner-horse. There was no anger, just sadness; and a sort of void she didn't understand or quite know how to fill. Scrutinizing the ceiling she rocked back in the chair, causing the leather to emit an empathetic creak. She was at the bottom of a steep-sided pit, surrounded by darkness, staring up at the warm light above. Squinting into the charming glow of the blue sky she could see the other world clearly – a brighter life – just out of reach. So, what next? Should she climb out of the hole and carry on as if nothing happened? Her phone beeped; a text from the Eyeball. What impeccable timing; just what she needed. It wasn't enough to be stranded in an abyss; he had to come and shovel dirt on her head.

Poking her phone with one finger revealed a message and an internet link. A black screen loaded as she typed the web address into her computer. Flashing in the middle of the page a small yellow box invited her to sign in with user id and password, which would follow separately according to the text. Cate nibbled her thumbnail waiting for further instructions. When nothing arrived after several minutes she sent a text and then tossed the phone onto the desk. It rang almost before it landed.

"You didn't get it? What, the job? You didn't get the job?" demanded Sam's voice from the mobile.

"I didn't get the job," confirmed Cate.

"Oh no; bastards. I'm so sorry. Who got it? Do you know?"

"Probably the blonde – the one who's afraid of food. Wish I was scared of pizza, I might not look so much like a stuffed crust."

"Don't be ridiculous. Anyway it's only your first interview, there'll be others."

"How many?" whined Cate. Suddenly it all came bubbling out, without warning. "How many times can I plan and prepare and take all the stress just to be told someone else got the job, when I know I've got the best qualifications? What was I thinking? Taking three years out to study at my age; it doesn't matter if I've got a First. I could have a PhD and I'd still lose out to some snackaphobic bimbo less than half my age. It's all been for nothing, what a bloody waste."

"That's crazy," whispered Sam. "You can't expect to get the first job that comes along just because you've got a degree. It's a fantastic achievement but you can't seriously tell me that the only value to all that study was a piece of paper that says you can do it. Come on. I know better than anyone that the destination is important; no point in driving a train without one. But it's the journey that counts; what happens along the way. That's the part that changes your life - if you let it. Shit - I can't believe I'm hearing this from you. Is there something else? Is this to do with Ollie?"

"No. Well maybe; I got the full report from Mr Ball today," said Cate.

"And? What does it say?"

"I don't know. I'm still waiting for my secure logon. It should arrive any minute."

"Right, I'm coming straight over. Don't do anything until I get there."

The text message appeared ten minutes before Samantha. Pausing for at least thirty seconds Cate typed the user ID and password into the flashing box, and entered the site. By the time her friend arrived she had read the full report. And one thing was for certain – he *was* wearing a dog-bitten, yellow jacket that morning. The document gave a detailed account of her husband's every move from the moment he appeared in Spennimore's yard right up to the second he vanished from surveillance; somewhere after delivering to the short woman with a bobbing head. What on earth was that about? Exactly what was Eyeball suggesting? No photographic evidence. Even if there was, a customer performing sexual favours on Oliver in her kitchen was hard to swallow. However, there was no shortage of pictures from earlier that day. Flicking though the images Cate shuddered; it was so wrong. A vulgar peek into the activities of an unwitting man. The more she looked, the greater her exposure, like some sort of reverse voyeurism. Peering at him through a window in time, he seemed perfect in his innocence; stacking totes, delivering goods and driving with naïve beauty. Spying on him at work made her shiver. She was the one conducting something creepy. It was a violation; and she couldn't go through with it any more. Closing everything down, she stared blankly at the empty screen for several seconds before the reporter faded in.

> *"A woman who scaled the tallest mountain in the world recalled her experiences today at a news conference. Reaching the summit a few weeks ago, after a three-year climb, the middle-aged mountaineer talked candidly to local news teams.*
>
> *Feasting openly on digestives and latte, she described surviving for many months on grubs and melted snow. However, she admitted the biggest shock came after conquering the final ascent. 'The most amazing thing,' said the 49-year-old explorer, 'was that from the ground, looking up, I could see the mountain had a sharp and very distinct apex; it's what I aimed for. But when I reached the top, after all that effort, I found there was absolutely no point*

at all. It was flatter than yeti spoor and far less rewarding. I won't be doing that again in a hurry.'

The woman has since announced her next quest as finding the end of a rainbow.

And we'll be reporting on that story and more later; you're watching Newsline with Catherine Bartlett."

The doorbell rang. Pressing her nose against the frosted glass, Sam waited on the step.

"Are you okay? Shame you didn't get the job," she said smiling sympathetically as she followed her friend upstairs. "You can't give up though. I know you'll make it. Did you get the logon details for the Eyeball report?"

"Yes, it's awful. I can't go through with this. I'm not going to the pub," replied Cate.

"What? What's he been up to? I knew it; let me have a look."

"There's nothing to see. He didn't get up to anything, apart from doing his job and being threatened by a bald man." Logging back in Cate reloaded the website. "I'll make tea," she said, leaving her friend to browse the documents.

After ten minutes Samantha joined her in the kitchen; with her blonde hair tucked behind her ears, she looked calm and professional in her sleek, dark uniform.

"I'm sorry," she said quietly, "your calendar just fell off the wall in the office. I think the hook's broken; I didn't really touch it." Sipping her drink she continued, "I see what you mean about the stuff from the Eyeball though. It's inconclusive, which is why you need to go and see who turns up at The Honeypot."

"He's not going to be at the pub, it's not unproven – it's inconceivable."

There was silence. The women eyed each other as though both had something to say but neither could get their mouth open. Finally Sam spoke.

"I know you don't want to believe Ollie's cheating on you, but what about the text he sent to Babe? He's up to something."

"Circumstantial," snapped Cate.

"Okay, so where is he now?" Sam's beautiful green eyes filled with compassion, and then dropping her chin to her chest, she looked towards her friend.

Turning to stare out the window Cate avoided the question. Ollie was definitely out delivering when she left Spennimore's earlier; but it was fair to say that she hadn't a clue where he was at that moment. Perhaps she should trundle along to the pub as a final measure to prove he wasn't involved with the ridiculous Dates2Remember ad. Then she could forget all about it, concentrate on her graduation, and find a decent job.

"Okay, I'll go," she said folding her arms. "But only because I've got to go out anyway."

Sam smiled.

"George's pulled a muscle and he can't iron his shirt," said Cate with a defiant smirk. "It's old people bingo this afternoon, otherwise I wouldn't bother. I'll call in at the pub on the way and take a picture of ancient Reggie, and then that's the end of it. This nonsense stops after today; I've got more important things to get on with."

"Cool," said Sam. "I'll get off to work – text me later."

There was time to slip into a clingy red dress. Decorated with large blue and white flowers, and hanging modestly above the knee, it was one of her favourite summer items. She finished off her outfit with sandals and her tiny white leather bag slung diagonally across her body. A final glance in the mirror before leaving the house confirmed her attire was perfect for the occasion. Looking appealingly elegant Cate set off for the pub. There was no possibility that Ollie would be at The Honeypot; but where was he exactly? Pulling the mobile from her bag she dialled his number; the phone was switched off, diverting her call to message.

"Hello, it's only me. I'm on my way to George's, so I'll see you later – bye."

How irritating; he never seemed to be around when she needed him these days. She hadn't even told him about not getting the job. Newsnetwork was such an ideal opportunity; why couldn't they give her a chance? It wasn't as if she did anything wrong at the interview; nothing that mattered. The make-up incident was Pick's fault, and the knicker flashing was an unfortunate result of being rushed about. Both events were completely out of her control. Unless she didn't really want the job and the failure to check her appearance was a subliminal but deliberate attempt at self-sabotage. Unlikely. But maybe she was more reckless with her career at times than she cared to admit. There was no point dwelling on it. Life had something exciting in store for her; it was a foregone conclusion. Once she found a path out of the maze, a suitable opportunity would be right around the corner, waiting to present itself. Falling head first into a bucket of manure was an inconvenience but the roses of success were bound to bloom.

It was a ten-minute walk to the pub. Conveniently opposite the university and set back from the road, The Honeypot nestled at the bottom of a tree-lined slope. Standing at the top of the path Cate squinted, trying desperately to see past the leafy boughs obscuring the tables and benches on the patio. It was no use, she would have to get closer. Tip-toeing apprehensively towards the outside seating area she scoured the tables for singletons. Then she spotted him. Sitting alone, away from the beer-drinkers, a portly man with brown hair and a thick moustache waited under the arbour; the suggested rendezvous point. Smiling broadly Cate peered through the foliage; it definitely wasn't Oliver. There was more a sense of exhilaration than relief; though it was no surprise. She was silly to have even bothered.

The man looked at his watch. Surrounded by overhanging roses, and wearing a wrinkled white t-shirt stretched over his paunch it was no wonder he used the internet to date. Ancient Reggie, he may be – but he was no Corsican Emperor, not by a long stretch of the imagination. Conspicuously his right wrist was pinned to his chest, by means of a pink foam cuff attached to a crepe bandage sling. How pathetic. That was Nelson, wasn't it? Not Napoleon. The man was clearly an idiot and deserved to be hoodwinked. She should probably report him to the university. It was disgusting; a fat old vulture hanging around for an unsuspecting student to arrive so he could whip out his bicorne and steal a French kiss. Fumbling for her phone she made ready to snap a photo.

"Excuse me, you couldn't tell me the time could you?"

Grinning hopefully a thin man with a protruding Adam's apple looked enquiringly at Cate from his seated position at a wooden table to her right.

"Sorry?" she replied, taking her eyes off the other man and glancing in the direction of the voice. A handsome face stared up at her; a smooth-skinned ginger lad of twenty-something years. Wearing a pale-blue double-breasted bomber jacket and carrying a large bouquet of bright flowers, he was noticeably upright, as if there was a rod fixed to his spine.

"I just wondered if you could tell me the time. I left my phone on the bar – and when I went back in, someone had already picked it up," he said gloomily. "I'm supposed to be meeting someone 'round about now, but that large man over there took my seat. I'm not having a very good day."

"*You're* waiting for someone," said Cate, conscious of her cheeks reddening. "But you haven't got smoky blue eyes; or dark hair."

The man frowned.

"*My* Josephine?"

"Certainly not," she replied, spotting a large woman wobbling towards the arbour carrying two drinks. It was all beginning to make horrible sense, and she was in trouble. "I'm - Josephine's friend," she lied confidently.

"That's a relief," he said, rather too quickly. "I mean - it's lucky we found each other. I obviously guessed that you weren't her. You don't look the sporty student type." Smiling anxiously, he waited without success for an acknowledgement to his comment. "Where is Josephine?"

"She couldn't make it," said Cate, shaking her head dismissively.

"I knew it wouldn't work out," said the man, pulling the head from a flower and tossing it onto the grass. "I'm never that lucky."

"Perhaps you'd be more fortunate if you weren't pretending to be someone else," she scoffed, aware of the irony, and disappointed not to be considered as a contender for the blind date.

Covering his face with his hands the man bowed his head.

"Sorry," he said. "Please tell Josephine I didn't mean to mislead her. Actually it wasn't me; it was a friend of mine.

She thinks I can't get a girl so she set me up with a Dates account – made it all up; y'know. Well, I do like history, but I told her no-one would ever want to go out with me. I'm afraid I've always been boring old Ancien Reg; so she reinvented me as Sexy Napoleon. As if! Suddenly I had shedloads of interest, mainly peculiar suggestions I have to say - and then came the glorious reply. She sounded so sweet and genuine I couldn't resist giving it a bash. I should've known she'd take one look at me and run in the opposite direction." Another bloom lost its head.

Chewing slowly on her bottom lip Cate considered a suitable untruth to ease the man's suffering. Like her, he was merely an unfortunate pawn caught up in someone else's deceitful game.

"I wouldn't be too despondent," she said grimacing. "Josephine really wanted to meet you but she's been unavoidably detained. It's a bit hush-hush and I can't go into detail. But you shouldn't give up; you know what they say – there's plenty more spiders in the web."

Holding out a freckled arm to shake her hand the man looked up and smiled.

"Archie Hibbert," he nodded. "Pleased to meet you."

Glancing around fleetingly for inspiration Cate introduced herself as Rose Bottle. She had no intention of engaging in extended conversation, whoever he was, but somehow it was hard to drag herself away. His attentive innocence was captivating, like a young Labrador frolicking with a toilet roll. Exuding an appealing aura the brown-eyed Mr Hibbert commanded her attention for more than thirty minutes, during which he bought drinks and recalled the worst parts of his life in a series of amusing anecdotes. Finally, after draining her glass, Cate announced her departure.

"Shame about Josephine," said Archie, cocking his head to one side. "But actually, I'm glad it was you, and not the person I was expecting after all."

"Yes, I could say the same about you."

"Really? I think that's some sort of compliment," he grinned. Leaning forward he held her shoulders gently and kissed her firmly on the cheek. "Miss Bottle, it's been a pleasure."

Smiling, she walked away from the pub towards the slope that led to the road. George would be flapping about his un-ironed shirt. Arriving at bingo unpressed would be an unprecedented misdemeanour. Another hangover from National Service; those 24 months shaped his whole life. He couldn't get out the door unless he could slice a tomato with the crease in his sleeve, let alone show his face at a prestigious number-calling event.

Something attracted her attention ahead, just before she reached the top of the incline. A momentary glimpse; but it was enough to identify the crimson comet - Oliver's Z4. Flashing past with the top down and music blaring, it was highly likely that he would turn right at the roundabout and enter the university campus. Hurrying to the road to peek through the bushes she observed her husband execute the manoeuvre as anticipated. The unexpected factor was the passenger. Seen from the back - but it was Miss Watts alright; her blonde hair streaming in the breeze like a film star on her way to the Oscars. Crossing the street quickly Cate took the gravel path leading to the university; if luscious Lucy was about to perform, she wanted a seat in the front row this time.

The darkest hour

GLEAMING THROUGH THE HEAT HAZE, the Z4 wasn't hard to spot. Few students ventured onto campus during the summer months and the car park was virtually empty. Only the School of Health and the most tenacious undergraduates bothered to visit university out of session - and Oliver. In retrospect, he didn't fit into either category comfortably; and despite his hard-on for Jack the Ripper he was spending a suspicious number of hours studying. Unless of course, his investigations concerned someone a little less gruesome. Whatever he was doing he obviously wouldn't choose a public place for sex. But it could be a good location to have an intimate conversation without raising suspicion. Westside Campus was home to the main grounds. Sprawling over 70 acres of parkland it was much bigger than the sister site that Cate attended, two miles away; plenty of space to get lost in. Even so, her husband shouldn't be too difficult to find; much of his academic life revolved around the library. Either he was an outstanding researcher or he was crafting out a career as a bookend. The second floor was crammed with history journals and littered with cosy study booths; the perfect place to hide without being concealed.

Cutting across the sports pitch to save time she marched to the main building. Hurriedly turning the corner she came face to face with the mighty glass-fronted library. Towering before her, and dazzling in the sunlight, it caused her to squint as she approached the revolving door. Hesitating at the electronic barrier she peered into the lobby hoping to recognise someone. Without a student card she would have to blag her way in. Rattling the gate deliberately she leaned over to inspect the empty reception desk. Perhaps she could squeeze under the metal railing; or maybe not. Pressing the red button on the intercom several times in quick succession she scanned around impatiently for assistance.

"Yes." A face appeared on the ceiling-mounted monitor in the foyer; a grey-haired woman wearing large glasses and an officious glare. With pinched cheeks and an aquiline nose, she was one of the evil band of cyber-space librarians sent to impede the path to education. Often less helpful than a spaghetti hoop, they were the result of an ill-fated genetic experiment by the Vice Chancellor, according to rumour.

"Hello, I've left my student card at home and I need to check something urgently, please," smiled Cate.

"Why did you leave your card at home?"

"I didn't mean to." She stared at the tiny camera on top of the screen. "It's really important; I can give you my student number."

"You need your card to gain access, and if it was that important you wouldn't have forgotten it. You'll have to return later." The woman glowered without blinking for several seconds like a bird of prey.

Closing her eyes, and then opening them one at a time Cate exhaled with a sigh. As if she didn't have enough to deal with. Her husband was so easily led. The blonde might be pouting across pages at him, or bending over behind bookshelves; one provocative pose in the tomes could end up with them both being caught in the classics. English Lit shared the same floor and it was only a short passage from History to Romance. Ollie wouldn't hear the warning; he'd just follow the siren. It was a perilous path. He might resist at first but with Miss Watts in orbit like a personal satellite, it'd be one small step for man, followed by one giant leap across the perineum. Somehow she had to circumvent the frilly-blouse vulture posing as a librarian, find out what was going on, and perform an eclipse. Rubbing her cheeks with both hands she peered up at the face.

"I'm sorry – but who are you? I'm a student here at this university and I'm entitled to go anywhere I like – so if you wouldn't mind letting me in?"

"Anyone can pretend to be studying here. It's my job to stop people like you getting in; and prevent terrorism. You could be concealing something hazardous." said the woman.

"*Terrorism*," protested Cate. "Are you insane? Do I look dangerous? I can't conceal anything larger than a felt tip in this dress. What am I going to do – highlight with intent?" Gazing up at the stern attendant in despair, she bit her lip and considered deploying an alternative tactic. "Actually, you're right to be vigilant; but I'm pretty certain I saw the man that stole my husband's wallet enter the library with his accomplice. They may be running amok amongst the hardbacks. You know – folding back corners, scribbling subtext; all that sort of stuff. Hardly bears thinking about what they might be getting up to in the margins. Perhaps if you checked to see if Oliver Cooke's student card has been swiped in, it would be beneficial for both of us?"

"That's out of the question; accessory to a breach of data protection. I wasn't born yesterday," snapped the face.

"Yes, I can see that," said Cate, losing her patience. "You fossilized fascist; I thought you were supposed to offer virtual assistance rather than actual obstruction."

Leaning into camera the woman scowled down the lens.

"If you don't go away I'll call Security. Now push off." The screen went black.

Inflexible individual. Shoving the gate half-heartedly with both hands Cate stuck out her tongue at the blank TV and then turned away, kicking back at the metal panel in a final protest. There was no other way to get inside. She might as well give up. Probably over-reacting, anyway. He was perusing the dusty annals, not making history in the archives. Studying with a friend was perfectly reasonable, even if she was an attractive bimbo. And there were other pressing things on her mind; George's shirt for one thing. Any other wrinkles could be ironed out at a later time. Crossing the courtyard slowly she walked towards the cafeteria, passing the reporter standing by the flower-bed.

> *"Potential disaster was averted today after a librarian stopped a suspected terrorist from carrying out an attack. A middle-aged woman, purporting to be a student, attempted an unprovoked assault on a university library, but was prevented from entering the facility by an alert assistant. After failing to provide identity the intruder became aggressive. The librarian said she was certain the assailant had come equipped to cause malicious damage to chronicles, but she was uncertain as to where the weapon was concealed. Police have warned members of the public to be on the lookout, and as a precaution, not*

to approach anyone wearing sandals until the villain has been apprehended.

Stay with us for more on this story later. This is Catherine Bartlett reporting for Newsline."

Continuing her path to the restaurant Cate pulled the door open, and slipped inside the building. She would never make it to George's without a pee after the large glass of wine she guzzled at the pub. A few students were spattered around the coffee bar but no-one she recognised. No sign of Oliver.

The ladies loo consisted of two cubicles. Cate opted for the one on the left after noticing the other was out of paper. Shortly after locking the door another visitor arrived at the facility. Heels clicking sharply across the tiles, it was someone in a hurry. The door of the right-hand cubicle banged shut; and then there was a triple knock on the adjoining wall.

"Scuse me," chirped a voice, "if there's any paper in that toilet would you mind passing the roll under; there's none in here."

Staring in surprise at the grey partition Cate slapped her hand over her mouth. Lucy Watts! The cheeky concubine was in the next bog. Grasping a handful of paper she pushed it through, making use of the gap between the panel and the floor.

"Here, I share toilet *sheet* with you," she said, attempting an eastern European accent.

"Thanks hun, you're an angel."

"No problemmo." Grimacing silently, it was difficult not to snigger. Dressing and flushing at the same time, she waited behind the door until Lucy had left. Then she made a dash for the exit, surreptitiously following Miss Watts through the food hall, and back to her seat in a secluded booth opposite the coffee bar. The brazen hussy was wearing a tight, white, low-cut, off-the-shoulder top, barely big enough to blow her nose on. Batting her lashes and smiling coyly at Oliver, she fiddled with her hair, scooping it to one side, so as to cover one breast and expose the other.

Scowling, Cate sunk behind the ornamental indoor palms, hidden from view but still within easy spitting distance from the couple. Oliver had his back to her; Lucy was facing him. Cross-legged in a tiny lycra skirt, one slim, tanned thigh was visible almost up to her knickers. It was virtually obscene. Of course Ollie didn't need to go onto the internet to fish for women. Miss Watts was practically hooking herself up to his rod. He was only human, after all. How was she supposed to compete with this woman? Lucy was less than half her age, with shinier teeth and bouncier boobs. Her heart pounded in desperation. Watching her husband laughing and talking to the pretty girl it was obvious that her marriage was officially in crisis. Nightmare; it couldn't get much worse - screening right under her nose - a rom-com crossed with live sport.

Staring through the thin leaves without blinking she chewed on her lip. The strumpet was offering something rather insistently, and Ollie was playfully pushing her hand away and shaking his head. They should experience pain. Like kittens pawing at a ball of string they toyed with each other; blissfully unaware they were about to be neutered without anaesthetic. She wanted to cry and scream, stamp and wail, burst out and shy away all at the same time. Obviously she wasn't emotionally extinct after all. How surprising to discover her sensitivity was only dormant, and that at any moment the magma churning in her belly was going to erupt and blow her head off. Time for her inner lion to stand up and roar; almost.

But still a tiny voice at the back of her brain fought to be heard over all the lava spewing, and animal snarling. If she confronted them, emerged from the palms screeching and flailing like a banshee, would it do any good to expose him? Or would she just look like a fool and risk ruining the rest of her comfortable life? Quelling a volcano might be difficult, but it was easier than trying to mop up the devastation after a pyroclastic flow. If she could flick off a little ash and stand the earthquaking it could all stay plugged. No-one would be any the wiser. She could think things over, put events into perspective, and challenge him later.

At least the recreational sparring had stopped. Smiling smugly Miss Watts adjusted her top and wriggled her bottom. Then without warning Ollie lunged forward and ruffled the girl's hair, causing her to shriek mischievously and lean back to avoid him. Turning away crushed, Cate sat on the cold floor leaning against the planter. A tear glazing one eye brimmed over and slid down her cheek. Tasting the saltiness and brushing it away with one hand, she bowed her head as a droplet fell from the other eye. Ollie used to tease her like that; messing up her hair after she spent half an hour straightening and grooming. This couldn't go on any more. Sniffing hard and wiping her face with the palm of one hand Cate stood up. Arms folded and feet apart she glared at the couple from behind the plant. Seething silently, she watched as they sipped coffee. Seconds passed. Was she invisible; why hadn't they noticed? Her condition worsened the longer she waited. Drawing a breath to speak, she opened her mouth but the words stalled. Like a car holding up commuters at green traffic lights she was exposed and embarrassed. They weren't doing anything wrong now; just drinking cappuccino in a public place. Suddenly her phone rang. Startled by the noise she ducked behind the palms and rejected the call. Luke; what did he want in the middle of the day? Flicking her mobile onto mute she crouched low and held her breath, hoping no-one would hear her heart doing the rumba in her chest. She had to get away. Staying close to the ground Cate crawled through the chairs, ignoring surprised onlookers as she headed towards the exit opposite the main door. Vibrating in her purse the phone went off again. Her son wasn't giving up but she waited until safely outside before answering.

"Hello, y'alright?" she said, staring up at the sky in defeat.

"Mum. Where are you?"

"Um, nowhere. Why?" Cate replied, detecting anguish in his tone. Hopefully he hadn't been arrested for illicit window-cleaning.

"Are you with Ollie? His phone's switched off."

"No. What's wrong?"

"Where are you then?" Luke persisted.

"I'm at Grandad's," she lied. "What's the matter?"

"You're at Grandad's now; actually in his house?" His voice was strained and unusual.

"I'm on the *way* to Grandad's. Just tell me what's wrong."

"Mum - it's Grandad – he's dead."

The world went quiet. Shaking her head slowly, Cate desperately tried to make sense of the conversation and absorb the meaning.

"Mum?"

"Whose grandad?" she asked.

"Mum - my grandad – Grandad George, he's died. I'm sorry. You need to come home. Where are you, we're coming to pick you up."

"I'm um, I'm um - at the university," she stammered, struggling to comprehend the situation. "But how do you - how do you know Grandad's dead? He was alright when I spoke to him."

"Mr Eyeball's here, Mum. Grace got him to use his spare key when she saw Grandad through the window, slumped in his chair. I think he had a heart attack..." Luke's voice trailed to a whisper as if it was too painful to speak any louder.

"Cate, it's Iain here, wait by the gate and I'll pick you up. I'm so sorry."

"Okay," she murmured, hanging up the call and pushing the phone into her bag. Eyes bulging and lip trembling she re-entered the restaurant and searched for signs of Oliver. Two empty cups on the table; her husband had gone.

Ambling across campus the unironed shirt made her cry. Hanging on the back of the chair; patiently waiting for her never to arrive. Too late now, it was far too late. Cold, and empty, and creased forever; the blue checked cotton shirt with short sleeves would never play bingo again. Perhaps it was a mistake; he wouldn't die without warning, surely. It wasn't like him; he couldn't even go to toilet without announcing it to all and sundry. Maybe one of his friends had popped in and expired. George was upstairs asleep, almost certainly. Actually, his brother looked very like him and was eighteen months older; it was quite possible that Uncle Jack had been confused for her step-father. Churning around in her stomach half a dozen giant butterflies flapped so hard her whole body shook. By the time she reached the road in front of the university she was convinced that Mr Ball would leap out, head in hands, screeching apology. But he didn't. Leaning against the white Audi with his head tilted to one side, she could see his handsome face filled with compassion. Facing up to truth was never high on her list of priorities, but this time it was unavoidable. Without warning all the energy drained from her body like a receding tide causing her to stumble across the pavement and flounder into his arms.

"Did you see George?" she said, looking up into his huge brown eyes.

"Yes, I saw him. He looked very peaceful," he lied, not wanting to torture her with details of his neighbour's ashen complexion and distorted features. "There was nothing you could do."

Pressing his lips against her soft hair he cradled her quivering body, rocking gently until she regained enough strength to clamber into the car.

Nothing was too much trouble over the next ten days; Mr Ball offered comforting conversation, kept an eye on her father's house, and helped to sort through documents and possessions. Even Mrs Braithwaite turned out to be useful occasionally. She whimpered often, which was to be expected, but she knew exactly where George stashed his will, and a sealed letter with instructions for the funeral directors.

"Such a good-looking man," said Grace, staring at a picture tucked into the frame of a wooden clock. It was a photo of George in the garden, resting on a shovel. His hair was wild and white; he wore a crumpled shirt, wellington boots, and a pair of baggy canvas trousers. "I think he knew he was going to die."

Anticipating an adverse reaction, Eve glanced sideways at her sister. The three ladies were in Mr Bennett's sitting room boxing up piles of ancient model aircraft magazines.

"No," frowned Cate, "he would have told me if he was ill." She glanced up from under her brow gently wobbling her head in admonishment.

"Did he tell you he had a pain in his arm?" asked Grace, pointing to her shoulder. "How many times did he say we find him dead in his chair one day? He knew alright. He said; but sometimes people have cloth ears," she wailed, puffing out her double-chin like a bull-frog.

Biting her lip, Cate held back a tear threatening to wreck her self-composure, and stared at a square patch of carpet next to the fireplace. Brighter and less worn than the rest of the flooring, it was a reminder that George's armchair had occupied the space until recently. Iain moved it upstairs to spare them the distress of having to gawp at the old man's final resting place every time they entered the room.

"That's ridiculous Mrs B," said Eve, reaching out and touching her sister's arm. "George never suffered in silence, and he certainly wasn't daft enough to sit around and wait to die. He would have called the doctor if he wasn't feeling well; if he had time that is." She eyed Grace musingly. "I hope your Collin's alright on his own. I've heard dogs are sensitive to loss; more sensitive that some humans." Kneeling on the floor she rocked back on her heels, and then sucked in her cheeks in a sort of irritated peacock expression. Cate got up and went into the kitchen. She leaned against the draining board and was gazing out of the window when her sister arrived.

"Are there any biscuits left?"

"Nope, they've all gone," answered Cate, without mentioning she finished off the last chocolate digestive two days ago. Turning and flinging her arms around her sister she sobbed quietly. "I didn't realise I'd miss him so much; silly old bugger. Why did he have to die?"

"I know."

"If I'd've been here I could've called the doctor."

"I don't think they would've been able to save him."

"Maybe not, but at least he wouldn't have died alone."

Rubbing her forehead reassuringly against her sister's Eve smiled.

"He never expected you to be here all the time; he knew you had other things to do. Anyway, you were on the way here. There was nothing more you could do."

A light knocking interrupted their conversation. Cate wiped her face on the tea-towel and went to answer the front door, seizing the opportunity to avoid discussing what actually delayed her on the day George died.

"Hi," said Iain, looking sympathetically handsome. "I noticed your sister's car out front earlier, and saw you had Mrs Braithwaite with you. I've got to go over that side of town at some point today, so if she would like a lift home I can save you the trouble. Oliver's gone back to work now, hasn't he?"

Cate nodded. There was no time to worry about Ollie. He made all the right sounds and gestures but was best suited to being normal in the background while everyone malfunctioned around him.

"Thank you," said Grace, appearing in the hallway. "That would be a great help; I have to get home for Collin." Clenching her large handbag she wobbled up the passage. "Don't mind me Catherine. Sometimes my mouth just talk all by itself. I'm sorry I upset you; Gawdy was fortunate to have such a caring daughter. And your sister too; he loved you both very much." Pushing her wiry hair into shape she left with Mr Ball.

The funeral was planned for the following Thursday, in the afternoon. Waking earlier than usual that morning, Cate stared at the ceiling for several minutes without moving. Only the gentle rise and fall of her chest and the occasional blink of her pale blue eyes showed that she was still alive. It was an enigma - the difference between life and death. Everything working one second, heart beating, blood pumping; and then nothing, like a mortal switch being flicked. When it came to it, there were no half-measures, it just wasn't possible to be almost alive, or partially dead; complete brilliance or absolute darkness. Unlike mornings - they continued to be a gradual process of illumination. Dawn was already sliding back under its comfortable duvet, giving way to the day. Assuming it would be raining she was surprised to see a single shaft of sunlight forcing its way through the gap in the blinds like an angel's arm reaching into her bedroom; a bright, triangular sleeve shimmering with dust particles. She watched as the tiny specks chased and avoided each other in divine amusement. The birds tweeted loudly; calling out to one another in their mockingly melodic manner. Smiling, she pushed back the quilt, got out of bed and stood by the window. If her step-father had reached his heavenly destination he would be grumbling about the noise and searching for his holy catapult by now. A strange sort of excitement bubbled inside her, as if he would be waiting to greet her at the funeral. It was a peculiar sensation but it gave her the strength to get ready for the ordeal ahead. The last few days were particularly vapid, and she missed him nodding his old grey head, and complaining.

She chose her outfit especially for the occasion, he liked her to be smart; a white silk shirt with pearl buttons and three-quarter length sleeves, and a black pencil-skirt. Simple but effective; the crisp sheen of the blouse reflected light onto her complexion, enhancing the last remnants of her holiday tan. Waiting inside George's house for the cars to arrive was awful. It was too quiet, and far too tidy; much of his clutter had been removed or packed away, and the familiar scent of embrocation and mints was absent. Luke and James spoke softly in the corner of the room, while Eve and her husband stood by the fireplace, whispering and pulling faces. Cate couldn't hear the discussion, and wasn't interested in joining a conversation. Then the hearse came into view, rising up the hill like a mighty raven with its great, glassy eyes and shiny black plumage; carrying her dead step-father on its back. She glimpsed at the flowers and bowed her head, unable to look. Stepping forward, Oliver took her hand, and led the mourners outside.

Blooms Lane was almost always busy, but the traffic adopted a respectful pause as the skinny funeral director walked in front of the cars until they reached the main road. Staring sadly from behind their wooden gates several neighbours watched as the procession passed. Cate was surprised to see Mrs Turney made it up the garden path. Leaning on two sticks the old woman stood sedately as George floated by on his final journey. She used to come out with cakes and sweets for all the children forty years ago, and she was practically dead then. Kids used to play out in the street in those days and although Mrs T offered irresistible treats she also owned a black cat and a noisy parrot. Naturally this fact, coupled with her thin face, qualified her as a witch in the mid-sixties, necessitating reasonable caution at all times. Mr Turney looked fierce every day. He worked shifts as a security guard at the car factory, and couldn't smile because he was under a spell, apparently.

George never met the mesmerized spouse; Mr T expired way before he arrived on the scene, leaving his poor wife alone ever since. Gazing at Oliver, sitting opposite her in the car, Cate was only partially glad that he was there. He looked striking in his silk tie and dark suit. She was desperate to know the truth but too afraid to find out right at this moment; torn between blissful ignorance and what might be agonizing disclosure. If Ollie was betraying her, having an affair with the pouting temptress, what did it mean? Divorce? Selling up all their goods and chattels, maybe? And then there was George's house. At some point she would share an inheritance with Evie – could she be forced to give half of it away to set up her husband's love-nest? Even scarier, would she ever find anyone as beautiful as Ollie to share her life with? Mrs Turney never managed it; all her subsequent soulmates had either four legs or a beak. There was always Iain – the attentive Eyeball. Actually, he was such a darling; far more reassuring and helpful than *anyone* else. It was pretty obvious that he didn't need much encouragement to step into Ollie's shoes, or fill his pants probably. However, for all his polite consolation and obliging assistance there was definitely something peculiar about a man that watched films with artificial friends and kept his dead wife's plastic leg under the bed - or wherever it was. Attractive maybe - weird undeniably.

The car stopped in the middle of the road. Still following the hearse it pulled into a parking space in front of St Luke's Church. Placing one hand on her knee, Oliver grinned comfortingly. Cate stared into his eyes, possessing neither the power nor inclination to respond. A tear trickled down one cheek. Then the funeral director appeared at the window and made her jump. Opening the door of the limousine the skinny spectre bowed his head and waited. Eve was the first to move, grabbing her sister's hand she gently heaved her out of the vehicle.

This was it; no escape. With adrenalin pumping and head swimming, Cate walked slowly towards the church. Pausing at the door gave Oliver the chance to slip his arm into hers, while Eve linked up on the other side. Together the trio made an entrance into the nave to be met by the most magnificent sight. Glorious rays of summer sun criss-crossed the congregation like search-lights from the blitz. George would be ecstatic, if only he wasn't so dead. Every guest clutched a tall red chrysanthemum, issued upon entry, as per his explicit instructions to the funeral directors. Seemingly, the whole town turned out to bid farewell to Mr Bennett. Friends and acquaintances from near and far, Wonky Warner and the Fifty-fifty fold, Mrs Grace Braithwaite - of course, Iain Ball and several ancient family members, many of whom Cate hardly knew; although she recognised Uncle Jack, he looked much like her step-father. Dressed in his grey suit, that might have fitted fifteen years ago but now hung from his bony frame like a tweed tent, he leaned against a silver walking-frame. He was unmistakably despondent but overall the atmosphere was relatively upbeat; rather like a wedding after the bride and groom have departed for the honeymoon. Glancing around the church it was clear that people had come to celebrate George's life, as well as mourn for his passing. Some smiling wistfully, others speaking quietly and nodding in mutual agreement, exchanging stories and anecdotes about the deceased. After all, he was a bit of a character, which concerned Cate slightly; she wasn't privy to all the arrangements, and somehow it had the elements of a surprise party brewing. There was an unusual buzz in the air, not associated with a funeral. Everything was organised in accordance with his sealed note to Watson Funeral Service. Her step-father liked precision, and his last wishes should be carried out to the letter – but what exactly did he put in the letter?

Assuming her place in the front pew she squeezed her sister's hand, and waited for the pall-bearers to arrive. There was a hush; and then the music started. Softly at first, like an orchestra playing in another room, gradually getting louder until a familiar tune was ringing in everyone's ears – the Dambuster's March. Taking a deep breath Cate stared at the vicar. He looked back kindly without altering his expression as George's coffin appeared, pushed on a trolley, and draped with brown and green camouflage cloth. Turning slowly on the front a black propeller complemented the balsa wings and protruding tailplane. After seventy-seven years as God's ground-crew he finally got to fly his own plane. An aviator extraordinaire; Mr Bennett controlled and captivated his audience from the other side of life. The congregation was both shocked and delighted, and although it didn't seem fitting to laugh aloud, stifled emotions trickled out. Had he meant to cause hilarity or should they be howling with sadness; no-one could decide for sure. Instead there was sniggering and joyful weeping, for the man they loved and missed already. Smirking, Cate allowed the music to lift her spirit while tears cascaded in rivulets down her pink cheeks. Whatever his aim, her step-father would be remembered for his unique passage into the clouds.

When the trumpets finished Reverend Collier addressed the mourners with his velvet voice, opening the service and leading the singing with clerical confidence. Mrs Cooke couldn't manage more than a few squeaks, although she mouthed the words and considered their optimism. Thankfully she was not required to speak, Charlie Warner delivered the eulogy. Knowing George since he was boy, and being reunited with him after the death of her mother, qualified Mr Warner as one of his closest friends. Gracefully walking to the lectern, after being poked and pointed in the right direction, he gave an eloquent speech, despite not being able to hear it himself. His kind contribution reverberated against the cold stone walls and resonated with his audience. Dressed in his best black suit and tie he recalled stories from the past, raising grunts of agreement and respectful mirth from the other guests. Finally before resuming his place in the gathering he looked towards the coffin, removing his spectacles and pushing them firmly into a top pocket.

"Well Gawdy," he said taking a deep breath, "farewell ole friend. Chocks away, you're all clear for take-off lad. I have to say I was shocked and saddened to hear about you passing. Sad to lose yet another member of the Pommel Street gang; and bloomin' shocked to find out that after all these years your name's George. 'Ave a good flight ole chum, it won't be the same down 'ere without ya."

He wasn't wrong; everything would be different. Apart from Ollie; that situation hadn't changed. Cate lowered her head and thought about Charlie Warner's wonky ears to take her mind off the subject. Graduation was only one week away; it was a shame George wouldn't be there to see her dressed in a mortar board and gown. He would complain about it being a waste of money – but enjoy it all the same. It was supposed to be a family event. However, there was a distinct dearth of relations queueing up for the occasion. Evie was flying out to Canada for her mother-in-law's birthday, James was busy at work, and Luke would be bored to oblivion way before they reached the marquee. Asking her youngest son to voluntarily attend an educational institution was bound to be traumatic.

She would have to consider electing an ambassador, or leaving the seat empty. Mrs Braithwaite was on next, after a short prayer. Wobbling her way up a small staircase she took position in an alcove, standing upright and virtuous behind a low ornate wooden panel. Lit from the back by the sun streaming through a round stained-glass window, her heavenly glow cast a broad shadow across the aisle. Wearing a brown pencil-skirt with a black belt, cream blouse and an orange jacket she could easily pass for an over-sized liquorice allsort. Cate huffed; she was in enough pain, the last thing she needed was Mrs B warbling for the next five minutes. Nervously touching the black and orange fascinator growing out of her wiry hair the old woman waited for the whispering to stop.

"Hallo everybody," said Mrs Braithwaite clasping her plump hands together, "I know Gawdy Bennett for many years and I'm sorry to say goodbye to him today, but a long time ago he made me promise that I sing this at his funeral, so he could hear his favourite song one more time. This is for you my love," she said gazing over at the Spitfire. There was a brief pause and then she launched into the sweetest a cappella version of Amazing Grace ever sung. Her splendid voice, rich with tone and perfect pitch, floated high up into the eaves and then rained down onto the mourners in a harmonious shower of sound.

Flowing gently through the church, a cool breeze caused Cate to shiver, brushing over her skin and raising hairs on the back of her neck.

"Bye," she said quietly.

Outside she watched silently as the aircraft wings were folded, and the propeller removed and laid on top of the coffin before it was lowered into the ground. Aunt Celia tugged at her sleeve.

"I bet you're glad that's all over with. Are you alright duck?" asked her shrivelled aunt.

"Yes, thanks. How are you? I haven't seen you for a while. Is Uncle Ernie okay?"

"Well he's better than nothing," groaned the woman. "Was that 'is idea to 'ave wings and a propeller?" she nodded towards the grave with her little grey head.

"I believe so. He loved planes," said Cate.

"Damn stupid if you ask me; long flowers and all that caterwaulin'. Always was one for makin' a drama. I'm not sure what our Betty saw in 'im." Lowering her voice to a whisper, "an' who's that black woman?"

Frowning, Cate looked down at her; she was frail but robust with stupidity. No wonder Eve referred to her as Aunt Silly.

"George's *friend*," she replied faintly, deliberately mirroring her aunt's hushed tone.

"His who?"

"His lover."

"Never. At 'is age? Dirty beggar, no wonder he pegged out. And 'im bein' laid to rest with our Betty. You must be glad 'e weren't your real dad."

"My real dad? Are you implying that George was artificial in some way? A cardboard cut-out perhaps – a stand-in father, while the 'real' one was too occupied to bother with his paternal duties. You don't have to be blood-related to care about someone. He might not be perfect but he was more of a dad to me than the one that buggered off. Now, do join us for tea Auntie Cill, and excuse me while I go check the rest of the family for authenticity." Grinning inanely, she backed away.

"Barmy. Just like 'er father," muttered the old woman.

Standing alone under the shade of a tree Mrs Braithwaite sobbed into a spotted silk handkerchief. Amazing Grace, yes she was quite amazing, and although George was married to her mother for nearly fifteen years, he was friends with Mrs B for a decade longer.

"Thank you for singing," said Cate. "It was beautiful. He would've really loved it." Grace nodded. "And – and I hope you don't mind too much that he's buried with my mum. He never mentioned changing his mind or anything, so I guess that's where…" Pausing, she glanced at the hole in the ground.

"Don't you worry about that. He's right here in my heart," said Grace patting her chest. "I'm not so concerned with where his feet are. And who knows, I might jump in there with him when I go."

It wasn't quite what she had in mind, but smiling politely Cate tossed her red chrysanthemum into the grave.

Spitfire pilot - his great dream; organised so he achieved in death what he most wanted in life. A poignant moment, but gazing up at the sky for several minutes didn't help pinpoint her utmost desire. After years of being certain where she was going it was a difficult task. She stared at Oliver. The things previously important were no longer urgent. But no matter how awful the truth was to bear, it was time to face up to reality, and stop hiding behind her dreams. A showdown was imminent; unavoidable. Time to stop faffing about and finally take control.

Before dawn

IT WAS EASIER SAID than done. Despite several opportunities to speak with Oliver, something wasn't right. He was on edge since George's funeral, and kept looking at her as if there was something he wanted to say - but nothing emerged. She was tense and uncomfortable; what could he possibly be desperate to discuss? If anything was to be said, she wanted the upper hand to catch him unawares. One of them needed to pluck up the courage to clear the air – but neither was prepared to make the first move. Instead they danced around each other all week like a pair of anxious boxers.

Peering out the bedroom window for signs of the Z4 Cate noticed Hamish in the garden across the road. Typical male; rolling on his back with his slim brown legs in the air, shamelessly displaying his genitals. Turning away, and then flopping onto the bed, she shook a bottle of nail varnish in one hand before applying it to her toenails. A sudden bark of mobile phone made her jump, causing Blushing Bronze to streak across her skin.

"Hallo, how are you?" asked Samantha. "Looking forward to tomorrow?"

"I'm alright; you okay?" said Cate, wiggling her varnished toes and striped foot.

"I don't suppose you've had it out with Ollie."

"Not exactly. I wanted to but he's been a bit odd. He keeps staring at me, but then he looks away, as though he's apprehensive about something."

"Is he there now?" enquired Sam, lowering her voice.

"No, he's out getting petrol; and why are you whispering?" said Cate mimicking her friend.

There was a pause.

"You're so naive. How long's he been?"

"Don't know. Hour maybe," she replied quietly.

"An hour? Where's he bloody gone for it, Kuwait?"

"Perhaps he's getting me a present."

"You need to get this sorted out; you can't go on living in deceit like this. I knew you wouldn't have said anything. Does he even know about George's ticket yet? Oh shit."

"I'll tell him when he gets back. Oh shit what? What have you done?"

"Got Kittychunks up my arse now."

"Different, I suppose. What flavour?" she quipped, taking the opportunity to veer off at a tangent.

"Never mind that, I've just sat in Rocky's bowl. I better go; had an argument with the washing machine earlier and everything's off the floor. I was only checking to see if there's any last minute instructions for tomorrow."

"Not really - well, only one."

The front door slammed. Hobbling out onto the landing Cate peeked over the bannister.

"Wash the cat-food out your bum," she sniggered before hanging up.

Puzzled, Monky looked up from the hallway.

"Luke's parking the equipment," he said gingerly. Then gazing down at the floor he kicked the skirting-board gently with his grubby trainers. "I'm sorry about your dad."

"Thank you Monky," she said with half a smile. "It's good of you to say. However, to be honest it would be better if you didn't mention it every time we see each other; and perhaps you wouldn't mind scuffing the paintwork."

"Sorry," he replied. "I didn't mean to, well y'know, it's just that I am - sorry about your dad; y'know – that he snuffed it. I mean died and everythin'. Ell really liked 'im too; he'll have nobody to buy glue for now. Speck you'll both miss 'im." With one finger jammed into his ear, he stared at her with his small eyes, like a chimpanzee hoping for a banana. The front door opened again. Glancing at his best friend, he continued with a slight bow. "May he rest in one piece, Mrs C."

Luke winced. Shoving Monky sharply in the shoulder he managed to silence the babbling, and move him in the direction of the kitchen at the same time.

"Haven't you made that tea yet?" he asked with a diplomatic grin.

"Doin' it now Ell." Pointing overtly towards the door with a raised arm and extended finger, he shuffled down the hall. "Sorry about your dad, though," he added while simultaneously sniffing and inspecting his finger.

Smiling apologetically, Luke climbed the stairs.

"I thought he was going to eat what came out of his ear for a moment," said Cate.

Plodding towards her, her son pushed blonde curls from his handsome face.

"He can't help being a prat, he doesn't mean any harm," he said.

"I know. I just wish you wouldn't waste your life on him. You could be doing so much better for yourself than window-washing with a half-wit."

"Yeah maybe, but it's not all to do with the party at the end, is it? Grandad said it's more about the fun you have getting to know who you're gonna invite. I know Monky's as sharp as a cushion - but we have a laugh, and he'd gnaw his own leg off rather than let me down. He might not be the star, mother, but he's gotta be on the guest list." Walking into the bedroom, he pulled off his t-shirt and continued to talk. "And he's completely honest. He wanted to give refunds after he found out about the calendars; took me ages to explain what caveat emptor is."

Frowning, Cate sighed and went back to her room. She was engrossed in applying a second coat of varnish to her toes when Luke appeared at the door.

"Mum," he said, fiddling with the buttons on his shirt. "You know I wasn't meaning Grandad when I said that some of the people who bought calendars might not make it to July."

"Course I do," she said pausing her paint-job to look up at him. There was sadness in his eyes. He was close to his grandfather, and even though Luke was a man, they were both boys at heart. It wasn't unusual to find them pawing over plastic aircraft components, talking and laughing like a couple of kids planning to trick the teacher. "I never even gave it a second thought." Actually it occurred to her, but George would understand; he ought to, the number of times she arrived at his door purporting to be the Grim Reaper, or a ghost from Christmas Past.

"Good. Um, there's something I have to give you for graduation – but I don't want it to upset you," he said pulling a small box from his trouser pocket.

"Oh, what is it?" How unexpected.

Entering the room, he sat on the edge of the bed and held out the package.

"It's not from me," he said, staring into her pale blue eyes. "It's from Grandad."

An emotional jolt poked her in the chest. George bought something special for her but didn't get chance to present it. He must have been really looking forward to the graduation; and the moment was stolen from him. How proud he would be. She could see him now, in the front row, smiling and clapping as she walked through the crowd in slow motion, with her gown flowing and mortar board tassel dancing in the air. And then rapturous applause as she accepted the certificate.

"Mum?" asked Luke. "You okay?"

"What? Yes, yes of course." Screwing the top onto the nail varnish, she tossed the bottle aside and received the gift with both hands. "How did you get it?" she asked smiling. "Grandad must have given it to you ages ago."

"Well, sort of, yeah. He ordered it from me at your birthday party; you thought we were talking about air rifles. But we weren't, see. It came a couple of weeks ago - Grandad wanted to surprise you. Go on then, open it."

How exciting, even though it was sad at the same time; it had to be jewellery. Gently lifting the lid revealed a sparkling silver letter on a curb chain. It stood out against the blue velvet cloth interior. Brushing an index finger thoughtfully over the pendant Cate squinted at her son.

"It's very pretty," she said. "But why is it a letter D? Are you sure it was meant for me?"

"Oh yeah," reassured Luke. "It's 'D' for daughter."

"Ah, I see. That's a little unusual." Removing the necklace from the box and holding it in the palm of one hand she eyed her son for signs of skullduggery. He was scratching the back of his head while admiring the ceiling. There was definitely something more.

"Sooo," she said slowly. "Grandad asked you to get him a letter D from the outset, did he? D for daughter?"

Covering his top lip with the bottom one, Luke half closed his eyes and scrutinized her suspicion. She was unlikely to let it rest.

"Um, I suppose he did want a letter C; *initially*," he said, tapping one index finger on his chin, and adding cheekily, "no pun intended. However, when it arrived, it was a D and I never really noticed until Grandad pointed it out. Which probably means that no-one else will clock it either, so there's nothing to worry about. Iffy doesn't do refunds, so we were a bit stuffed, until Grandad thought of the D for daughter idea. Like he said, it's more personal – everyone calls you Cate, but he's the only one that calls you daughter."

Not any more, she was an orphan. Rubbing her eye to conceal a tear she shuffled off the bed and stood by the window. Completely typical of them both; often frugal and slightly criminally minded but thoughtful to a T, a C, or a D, or whatever fitted the occasion. The gesture was the important thing. She couldn't argue with the logic; it was her step-father's way of letting her know she was unique, and that he was proud of her.

"It's lovely."

Luke got up from the bed and walked to the door, grinning happily.

"I better go see what Monk's up to, before he scoffs all the biscuits."

Opening the window, Cate rested her elbows on the sill and leaned out into the sunshine. Across the road Hamish chewed on a toy in the shade while Bob pulled weeds from the drive.

"Morning Cate, not working today?" he called.

Astute as ever.

"On holiday," she replied. "Graduation tomorrow."

"Superb, that's come 'round quick. You'll be pleased to know we found Teddy." He glanced over at his enormous dog. "In next-door's bin. Luckily Sandra noticed when she put the rubbish out, and the poor thing was rescued."

"That's a relief," she smiled, enjoying the warm sun on her cheeks. Although likely to have been a shock to the unfortunate neighbour that discovered the bald, slimy bear staring up at her from the bin. No prizes for guessing who tried to dispose of Teddy. Oliver had run over him more times than a zebra crossing. The Z4 growled around the corner, right on cue.

"Here comes your ole man; better get on, no point in putting it off any longer I suppose," said Bob, stooping to tug at a dandelion.

"Yeah, you're right," she said closing the window, and biting her lip. It was time to clear her own path; procrastination over. The front door slammed. She would have it out with Ollie, right there and then. No more excuses, she had to know; was he having an affair or not? Footsteps on the stairs. The moment of truth - confront him with the evidence, face to face, and finally find out for sure. It had to be done. Ollie appeared in the doorway. Maybe - straight after graduation - it could wait 'til then, but not a day longer.

"You were ages; where've you been?" she smiled.

"Nowhere really, but I did stop off to get you this." Pulling a single red rose from behind his back he presented it to her together with a kiss on the cheek.

"Oh thank you. Two presents in one day. Aren't I popular all of a sudden," she said showing off the necklace. "It's from George."

"It's a D."

"I know – he wanted it to say daughter, but they were out of stock."

"That's a pity, he must've ordered it weeks ago."
Cate nodded.

"What about George's ticket for tomorrow? Can James make it?" he asked.

"Ah no, he's too busy, and you know Luke hyperventilates at the thought of education – so, I invited Iain."

"Iain?"

"Yes, Mr Ball, he's been so good about everything that I felt awkward not offering it to him, and he was delighted to be asked."

"Oh, I bet he was," said Oliver folding his arms. "You invited the freak to your graduation? Professor Oddball?"

"He's been very kind to me," she replied, brushing wrinkles off the quilt cover.

"Kind to you," he snapped. "What are you a kitten? What's going on between you two?"

"There's nothing going on between me and Iain," she sighed.

"*Me and Iain*," he mocked. "So tell me, when did he stop being 'the Eyeball', exactly? Was it after he kissed you at The Honeypot? Or maybe he kissed you 'on' the honeypot?"

"Don't be ridiculous. That was someone else."

"Someone else? Someone else!" he remonstrated. Leaning over the bed he poked the air with a pointed finger. "I knew you'd been acting weird. I've been trying not to say it, but that's where you were when George died, wasn't it? That's why everything was so mysterious; you were at The Honeypot when you should've been calling an ambulance."

"No, no!" she shrieked, shaking her head and almost collapsing onto the bed.

"Your own step-father. I didn't think it was the moron from next-door you sneaked off with. So who was it?"

"Archie, his name is Archie - something," she sobbed, "I don't even know him."

"Even better. George is having a bloody heart attack and you're snogging a stranger."

"It wasn't like that," she hissed. "It was a peck on the cheek, and I was at the pub making sure it wasn't you. I told Sam you wouldn't be there."

"You're damn right I wouldn't be there, and I might've known she'd be involved somewhere."

Smudging a tear away with the palm of her hand Cate walked around the bed and stood facing her husband.

"Well, she wasn't completely wrong, was she? And the real reason I wasn't at George's was because when I came out of The Honeypot I saw you go sailing past in the car, so I followed you. So don't even say that; I would've been there if it wasn't for you."

Taking a step back, Ollie swept a lock of dark hair from his forehead, momentarily allowing his hand to linger at the crown. His grey eyes narrowed to a slit, piercing her pomposity.

"You've been spying on me? How dare you."

"Why do you care if you haven't got anything to hide?" she snapped.

Sweeping past he walked over to the en suite.

"Don't try and blame me for something that's your responsibility. I'm not the one feeling guilty, and I don't appreciate you snooping around. I don't violate your privacy," he said.

The door slammed. Perhaps she was wrong; he was hurt and indignant. Now really wasn't the time to accuse him of having an affair with a bimbo. More to the point, if she hadn't been so occupied with her own predicament, maybe she could have saved her step-father? Poor George, it was all her fault. Sloping away downstairs, she switched on the television and stared at an old film, without seeing or hearing a word of what was going on. Life was often a black and white movie, all drama, and shrieking, and wringing of hands. Closing her eyes, Cate leaned back into the cushions, allowing the reporter to take over.

> *"An extremely rare copy of the 1930s black and white classic, Reasonable Doubt, has been discovered intact at a disused cinema in Upperfinger. The film, previously thought to have been lost forever, will be restored and shown at the Wolfinger Festival of Art, later this year.*
>
> *Pundits say the famous scene of Alice murdering her father and then rushing to her husband's side, only to discover him with another woman, is an Oscar-winning performance likely to trigger a modern remake.*
>
> *This is Catherine Bartlett, outside Moviedrome, reporting for Newsline. Stay with us for more later, and now back to the studio."*

The next time Cate opened her eyes two brightly coloured shapes danced across the television screen. Enthusiastically regaling her with the joy of angles adding up to 180 degrees, a red, furry triangle leaped around, circling with apparent glee, a sad looking square. She must have nodded off; unless wartime Britain had been mysteriously invaded by singing polygons.

Emanating from the kitchen, a chopping sound prompted her to investigate. Ollie was making one of his multi-layered sandwiches. Folding her arms and leaning on the work surface Cate watched her husband cutting and slicing. It was vaguely disturbing that his snack construction could manifest into a sensual experience; but she was a little desperate following what seemed like a prolonged abstinence. A consequence of the recent stress and worry. Gently squeezing a tomato, he glanced over at her before puncturing its flesh with a small knife. He had very masculine hands; slightly tanned with pale, broad nails.

"What?" he asked, conscious of her intense observation.

"Nothing," she smiled. Butterflies fluttered in her stomach. "Actually, there is something. I've been thinking - and - I'm sorry."

Dividing the sandwich with a decisive chop, he affected the precision of a man splitting the atom. Then he pushed away the two halves, like a biblical parting. One piece at each end of the bread board, as though he was expecting a great procession of vegetables to march through the gap in his honour. Staring at the scores in the wood, he brushed away the crumbs and then turned to face her with a smug grin.

"What were you expecting to see?" he asked.

Avoiding his gaze, Cate fixed her eyes on the sandwich.

"When I followed you – I don't know. It was all getting a bit mixed up. I wasn't really expecting to *see* anything; it was more about trying to prove there was nothing *to* see."

Raising his eyebrows and blinking as if he had witnessed something remarkable Oliver looked up to the ceiling, and then turned back to his snack. Carefully picking up one half he took a large bite.

"Sorry," she said sheepishly. "It was the stupid text that started it. I should've deleted it. But you've got to admit, it was a bit odd."

His avid mastication slowed to a furtive chomp.

"Text? What text? Not that bloody Eyeball."

"No – it was from you," replied Cate. "Referring to someone called - Babe." Her heartbeat quickened, and her face flushed. This was it; the moment had arrived, and now at last she could find out the truth and move on. Babe – she finally said it; she received a text meant for Babe.

"I don't know what you're talking about."

"It was a few weeks ago now." Moving into the dining room, she retrieved her phone, flicking through the saved texts as she returned to the kitchen. Presenting the offending message, she stood, tensely waiting for an answer. A calm exterior concealed her racing pulse and jangling organs, functioning discordantly like metal wind chimes in a stiff breeze.

Squinting at the screen, Oliver read the text and frowned in bafflement.

"It's not from me." He looked at Cate; she stared back blankly. "Oh yeah, I did send it. I remember - but I'm not sure why you got it. It was about your birthday cake. Lucy made it. I asked her to look for something to do with journalism and she text me when she found a recipe for a TV studio. I must've sent it back to you, but it was meant for her; it was a surprise obviously, that's why it says about not suspecting anything, that's all."

"I thought you said it was made by a master baker."

"She's professional; she sells them on the internet. You liked it, didn't you?"

"Yes," she said, holding out one hand for the return of her mobile. ""'And she's a Babe, then, is she?"

Laughing, he extended his arm so the phone was out of her reach.

"I'm deleting this. You're bloody crazy," he said.

"You've never called me Babe," she sulked.

"It's a joke - Babe." He erased the message, and then leaning forward, attempted to kiss her on the cheek. Cate swerved the embrace. "You tried to follow me because of this? You're obsessed woman."

"Well, you've been acting suspiciously for quite a while." She leaned back, resting on the work surface.

"I have not." Scooping up the remaining sandwich he shovelled it into his mouth. "Like what?" he said with a mouthful of food.

She recognised the tone; he may have delivered the words casually enough, but it was a direct challenge. He was goading her into revealing whether there was any further evidence. If there wasn't, he was home-free. Sam could be right after all; he may actually be guilty.

"Ok, what was so really important that you couldn't take me to the interview at Newsnetwork?"

"What? On your birthday; you know I was working. And I couldn't drive you there because I had to pick up your cake after, and get it to the restaurant. There was no-one else to do it. Stop being paranoid."

Plausible, but his last comment was a defence mechanism.

"I might have stood a better chance if you had taken me." Pausing, she folded her arms again and tipped her head to one side. "Anyway, when we were at the Tun, and you said you were going to the toilet, I saw you coming back from the direction of the bar and you went straight past the loo. So where had you been?"

"Goodness knows," he said. "You're not going to grill me about my every movement since I sent that bloody text, are you? How the hell do I know? Actually, I think I do, because Sam had the arse with me for stinking out the bog – and it wasn't me. I went to find Ping, to get him to bring your cake out. Satisfied?"

Possibly, or was it a little too convenient that he had an answer for everything? He could have been rehearsing alibis for weeks. There must be some evidence that was more damning; unless he was innocent after all. So far, the cake had a lot to answer for and Oliver was smelling of roses.

"Is that all?" he asked.

"Not quite. Do you remember the day when you brought me that lovely bouquet of flowers? Let me see now, wasn't it the same day you appeared covered in scratches?"

"I'm not listening to any more of this." Pushing past her he stomped off towards the front room. "This degree's gone to your head. I told you, I tripped over a dog. What's the matter with you?"

But did he? In retrospect, if only she had taken a picture for closer examination.

"I've only got your word for that," she shouted after him. Appearing in the doorway Monky took one look at her and stopped in his tracks.

"Piss off and clean some windows," she yelled, marching into the dining room.

"Sorry. Sorry about your dad," he whispered, backing out of the kitchen with a bowing motion.

Slumped on the settee at the other end of the room, Oliver tapped on the television remote.

"Perhaps you protest a little too much," he said, pausing his rapid-fire channel-hopping to glance up at her. "People who live in glass houses shouldn't chuck bricks. A diversion tactic; I mean, you haven't explained what you were doing at the pub with another man - apart from kissing him. And how do I know this isn't another New Zealand episode?"

"There's no need to bring that up. And as I mentioned," replied Cate, "it was a mistake. Someone pretending to be Napoleon was asking for French kisses on a dating website." Oliver stared in amazement. "I simply met up with him to prove it wasn't you."

"I'm sure that makes sense in some parallel universe," he said, leaning forward, and discarding the remote. "So what is it precisely that you're accusing me of?"

"I'm not accusing you of anything." She feigned a smile. "But maybe some reassurance, since you ask, that you still find me attractive. Last time I gave you a massage you fell asleep. How come you're so tired all the time? You never used to turn down an opportunity. Especially when I go to so much trouble to make it exciting."

She stepped in front of the television.

"You think that getting drunk, interrupting the cricket, and whacking me with a bat is sexually arousing?"

Cate scoffed.

"I don't know what turns you on any more – you online gigolo. I suppose you don't need to bother with sex at home, when you get paid to deliver it with a bag of shopping?"

Oliver grinned. Springing off the settee, he walked over and stood before her. His close proximity was provocatively menacing. Peering down at her through silky lashes he disarmed her with the erotic charm of his smouldering grey eyes. She ached to feel the power of his tanned thighs pressing on her, pumping into her body. Leaning towards her, his muscular arms slipped around her shoulders, drawing her against his firm chest. Instinctively, she moved one hand up for a gentle squeeze of pecs; they twitched with each beat of his heart.

"Is that what's worrying you? You think I'm flirting with naughty housewives; slippin' them an extra sausage." Laughing, he kissed her on the forehead. "Don't be daft. What? You think women come to the front door in their underwear, licking their lips and pouting at me?"

True enough – the Eyeball took quite a few pictures, but there was no concrete evidence to suggest any wrongdoing.

"Yeah but there's some funny people living down Butterfly Lane," she said, smiling coyly.

"I know you've been under a lot of stress lately, but can we just stop all this nonsense and get back to normal." Hugging and rocking her at the same time, she was safe and loved again. "And for goodness sake, don't take any notice of bloody Sam, she's…" Oliver stopped abruptly. "I never said I was in Butterfly Lane, how did you know I delivered there?"

"I didn't. It was just an example." Nestling her head on his chest, she closed her eyes and bit her lip.

Pushing her away, Oliver stepped back.

"You devious bitch. You were following me." His grey eyes filled with hate. "What on earth did you expect to see?"

Dropped herself right in it, might as well go for the jugular now.

"Well I didn't expect to see a midget giving you a blow job. You're disgusting," she sobbed. "I heard what you were up to at the big house, in the kitchen."

Pointing angrily he moved towards her, and poked her shoulder.

"It wasn't you, was it? You weren't actually there. No, because that was the day you were at the interview in Canchester. You had somebody else follow me, didn't you? Don't tell me. It was that idiot Ball, wasn't it? I knew I'd seen that bloody bike before. You got him to spy on me, and he told you I was having sex with a midget. Well, that serves you right, you stupid cow. That woman is disabled; she's uses a wheelchair. You've gone completely off your rocker this time. Anything else I'm guilty of? Come on, let's have it."

"No," said Cate, shaking her head and staring at the carpet. It was all wrong; he had an answer for everything. She should have trusted him, and her own judgement. But there was something niggling at the back of her mind, and she might as well be hung for a sheep.

"Yes, actually – why is your phone always switched off when you have 'coffee' with your 'friend'? Raising her hands she made quotation marks in the air with her index and middle fingers, emphasising the words. The vision of him fooling around with Lucy Watts in the cafeteria was still raw. Sweeping away stray tears with the palm of her hand she glared at her husband. "One more thing; perhaps you could tell me why your hi-viz was hanging on the back of a chair in a flat on the Fruitfarm Estate, the day after my party. When you got home on my birthday you were wet, cos I remember you lying on the bed. And the next day you drove home without your jacket, I saw you. But then miraculously it appears in the cupboard. So don't tell me you've not been making unscheduled deliveries. Cake my arse. You cheating bastard." Running out of breath, it was a struggle to get the last sentence out, but now she had him backed into a corner.

His beautiful grey eyes watered; lips clamped tightly together, he clenched his fists and then exhaled.

"Some detective you are," he snapped. "Of course I was on Fruitfarm; I already told you I picked up your cake and took it to the Tun. And yeah, I committed the crime of going in for a cup of tea and leaving my jacket on the chair. Did you see me do anything else?"

That made sense. Maybe he was telling the truth. Her guts churned; if it wasn't for the last remark she would've believed him.

"Are you having an affair with Lucy Watts?" she demanded.

"Luce? I'm not even going to answer that." Turning away, he walked towards the door.

"Oliver."

A squeak of chamois on glass caught her attention. Rubbing at a colourful streak of bird excrement, Monky grinned at her from the French doors.

"Not *my* windows," she wailed. "Bugger off!"

"Sorry..."

"Don't you dare, don't you dare say sorry about my dad," she interrupted.

Cowering on the patio Monky backed away. He picked up a plastic bucket, spilling the contents onto his feet.

"Handle's loose, sorry about the handle," he said, disappearing from view.

Cate glared after him, and then made a sudden dash into the hallway. Oliver was about to step onto the landing.

"You were emailing someone when we were on holiday; who was it?" she asked. "Oliver, I'm asking you a question. It was her, wasn't it? You were emailing Lucy."

"I'm not answering any more. Is this what happens when you get to fifty? Are you going to fly into a jealous rage every time I talk to someone younger than you?"

"You called her Luce." Her voice wavered.

"What?"

"A minute ago, you called her Luce, and suddenly it all falls into place." Gripping the balustrade she looked up at him wide-eyed. "In Barbados, you were drunk and I thought you said the balcony was loose. But you didn't. You said her name. You were wishing it was her instead of me. I'll ask you one more time Oliver; are you having an affair with Lucy Watts? You might as well tell me."

Glaring down at her, Oliver slapped his hand on the bannister.

"I can't put up with this. I'm through playing games; work it out for yourself." He stormed into the bedroom, reappearing seconds later to hurry past her at the bottom of the stairs.

"Ollie," she said, reaching out to touch his arm.

No acknowledgement; ignoring her he walked away, slamming the front door behind him. The Z4 roared; with a screech of tyre it reared off the drive and galloped into the evening. Stunned, she stood without moving for several minutes. Whatever reaction she expected, that wasn't it. What did he mean, work it out for herself? If she could do that she wouldn't need to ask. Or had she already worked it out, but failed to accept the answer? A searing pain in the chest made her cross one arm in front of her body on the way to the kitchen. For once Jaffa cakes would not heal the suffering. She was experiencing a hideous void and the only thing that could save her from turning to stone was to know one way or the other. Oliver was avoiding the question; he neither denied nor admitted having an affair, which was confusing, even to someone with a First Class degree. Assuming she bothered to collect the certificate; it wasn't worth attending a graduation ceremony without him in the audience. It was all too much really; not knowing what to believe - the fighting and the uncertainty. After ten years of marriage surely her heart would know if he was having an affair, wouldn't it? Despite what her head thought he couldn't be going off with a girl half his age. So where was he? The next few hours of apprehensive waiting did nothing to answer the question. She watched the light fade and the stars appear in the night sky, like tiny sparks of hope in a bleak forecast. But there was no illumination, merely faint optimism.

Arriving home shortly before midnight, Luke was cautiously concerned by the absence of his step-father and the strange calm of his mother.

"What's going on?" he asked. "Why are you still up, and where's Ollie?"

"I want you to do something for me," she replied.

"What? Dispose of his body? You're looking a bit scary, mum. I'm not going to find his blood splattered up the walls am I?"

"Not yet," she said. "Don't ask why – but remember the flat you saw Ollie's jacket in?"

Hunching his shoulders and concentrating with a frown Luke nodded.

"Good because I want you to go 'round there and look in the window."

"Mum - I've already looked in that window, why would I want to go do it again in the middle of the night?"

"Because I'm going to buy you a set of ladders if you do," she said, pushing him out the door. "Ring me when you get there."

It seemed a fair price for a midnight prowl; the offer was accepted. Two minutes later there was a knock at the door. Expecting to see Monky begging for forgiveness she was relieved, although somewhat surprised, to find Iain Ball on the doorstep.

"Cate, thank goodness. I was on the way home, and noticed your son running down the street, and Oliver's car missing. Is everything alright? Are you alone?"

He was in uniform, looking handsome and powerful as always. Sighing, her eyes glazed with tears but she managed to keep them from spilling over.

"Yes, I had a bit of a fight with Ollie," she mumbled. "I've no idea where he's gone. His phone's switched off."

Reaching forward he rubbed her arm sympathetically.

"Your poor honey; and right before your graduation." His big brown eyes stared down at her. "I can't leave you like this."

How sweet of him to care; he was a whole new dimension in community policing. Sipping tea together in the front room helped to put matters into perspective. The worst thing was the dreadful butterflies in her stomach. Although it was impossible to tell whether they were because she was frightened Ollie wouldn't come home, or because Iain looked so dashingly sexy.

"I hope you don't mind if I take this off; I'm not on duty now," he said, removing his jacket.

She had no problem with him revealing his firm torso, rippling beneath a crisp white shirt; it helped to relieve the stress. At least someone found her attractive. Discussing her predicament made it clear that despite everything she was still none the wiser as to whether Ollie was having an affair. The anticipation was immense, like being stuck at the top of a rollercoaster. Mister Ball was not suffering the same confusion.

"Forgive me for saying this Cate, but your husband is a selfish and arrogant fool. I want you to promise me that you'll go to your graduation no matter what. If he doesn't turn up, I'll be there for you; and I'll be the proudest man in the audience. You'll be absolutely stunning." Leaning forward he gathered a tress of hair, that was partly covering her face, and gently tucked it behind one ear. "You always are," he continued.

Cate blushed.

"I'm not sure I can go," she said.

Lifting her hand lightly by the fingers he bowed his head and touched her knuckles with his lips, as though he was greeting a princess.

"You're a very special lady; you're clever, you're beautiful, and I want you to know that I will move heaven and earth to protect you, and make you happy. There's nothing I wouldn't do for you." He kissed her hand again, but this time turning her fingers over and pressing his smooth lips firmly against her palm. Closing his eyes and lingering for a second, he smiled and then looked up at her, his pupils dilating likes spots of black ink on absorbent paper. A shiver pulsed through her body. Starting somewhere in her chest it trembled over her stomach, and shuddered into her bottom. She squirmed in her seat, trying to disregard the sexual pangs, but it was impossible to ignore his attention. His sensuality exuded a virtual presence; like a hungry wolf ready to lick at her flesh and devour her throbbing heart. Even his smell was hypnotic, an intoxicating blend of crisp cologne and earthy masculinity. Drawing closer, as if an invisible thread was pulling her in, she leaned forward until they were only inches apart. For almost a full minute they breathed and stared without saying a word, surrounded by waves crashing on distant beaches and fireworks exploding overhead.

And then her phone rang, shattering the moment and disturbing their exclusive connection. It was her son. For once, doing as he was asked. Fumbling with one hand Cate answered the call.

"Hallo."

"I'm here. What do you want me to do?" asked Luke.

"Can you see anyone?"

"Nope. The curtains are open but the lights are off; I don't think anyone's in. Do you want me to break in?"

"Certainly not. You're sure it's the same flat?"

"Yep, there's no-one around; I can get in if you want, Uncle Pat showed me a little trick with these windows."

"No thank you, you can come home now." Hanging up, she rested the phone against her lips, pensively. No sign of Ollie. A sudden text made her jump. Expecting it to be her husband she swiped the screen and searched for the message, but it was Luke informing her that he was spending the night at Monky's.

Enclosing her hand within his, Iain regained her attention.

"I meant what I said, angel. There's nothing I wouldn't do; I would kill for you."

Smirking, Cate shook her head.

"I don't think that'll be necessary." It was surprising how quickly events moved from subterfuge, to burglary, to assassination.

Moving close to her ear, he whispered.

"No-one would find out; it looks like a heart attack if you know what you're doing. That is, if you want to dispose of someone that is…irritating you."

He was teasing; glancing sideways she laughed and nudged him with her shoulder.

"I'll let you know," she said, grinning mischievously.

No doubt

CATE HARDLY SLEPT A WINK. Her unexpected guest stayed late, sharing a bottle of wine before leaving in the early hours. Secretly she hoped Oliver would come home and catch them getting cosy on the couch; but he didn't. At 2am she finally gave in and went to bed. Peeping intermittently at the clock, waiting for the night to be over; the last time she looked it was ten past five. And then without noticing she slid down the plump helter-skelter into duvet-land, spiralling away from her clumsy wakeful monsters, to land on a fluffy cloud. Soaring over green fields and yellow flowers she flew with the wind in her hair. It was limitless and exhilarating. Clinging to the corners of the cumulonimbus until the front door shuddered, and the clunk of the metal latch brought her back to reality, like a balloon popping. Daylight; her eyes sprang open. Scrabbling to check the time she sat up and listened for movement downstairs. Luke or Oliver? It was hard to tell; pretending to be asleep she snuggled into the quilt and waited. The footsteps were slow and quiet, unlike her son; he invariably trudged up the staircase as if he was bearing the weight of a large donkey on his back. Definitely Ollie; her heart raced. Caring and remorseful, or had he returned to pack a case? She was about to find out.

Entering the room silently, he stood next to the bed. Cate paused, expecting to hear the door push open, and then sensing his presence she looked up with a start.

Her husband stood over her. Steely grey eyes peering through soft dark lashes, he didn't speak for several seconds.

"Sorry," he said, crouching down. Reaching forward with one hand he swept a lock of hair from her face, tucking it gently behind one ear.

He wasn't going to leave; she could breathe again.

"Where've you been? I was worried about you."

Exhaling loudly he got up, kicked off his shoes and then cuddled up next to her on the duvet. Unshaven and untidy he put his arm around her, pulling her head to his chest.

"I went up to the Beacon to think," he said.

"What all night, on your own?"

"Mainly. There were a few odd visitors driving 'round but it was quiet enough; good place to chill. I wanted to sort my head out."

"And did you?"

"It took a while, but yeah. I was watching a couple in an Audi."

"Isn't that doggin'?" she frowned.

"I suppose it might be, but they were arguing, not shagging. At it hammer and tongs, then all of a sudden she jumps out the car, storms across the car park, and chucks her ring in the bushes."

"How do you know it was a ring?"

"I saw her pull it off her finger. Then he gets out the car, shouts at her, and they both get back in and drive off."

Cate scratched her head.

"That's inspirational then, is it?" she said after a pause.

"Maybe not on the surface, but later he comes back and starts searching on his hands and knees through the thorns. He scratched around for about half an hour before he found it, poor bugger."

"I'm failing to see the significance here," she said, craning her neck to stare at her husband. "It's probably on iBuy by now; is there supposed to be a moral to this tale?"

"Yes, and as usual you misinterpret the signs," he said, touching her nose gently with one finger. "It's simple - they had a bust up – maybe she even accused him of seeing someone else." He feigned a grin. "But obviously he worked out there was something worth hanging on to."

Silence; gazing into her blue eyes Ollie waited for a response. Cate blinked twice, slowly; what exactly did he mean about misinterpretation? That she was wrong about the text, the scratches, the lethargy and the balcony incident? Or that she was right – but somehow the car park couple instigated an epiphany? Had the incident prompted a sudden realisation that their relationship was far too valuable to discard like an old sock?

Squeezing her with his arm, Ollie indicated he was expecting a reply. But his muscular embrace implied more than that; it meant he wanted her. However, it didn't answer her burning question.

"What are you saying?" she asked, resisting the temptation to lean forward and kiss his bottom lip.

"You want me to spell it out? I'm saying I sat all night thinking about *us* - new careers, new challenges - completely different directions maybe. Who knows where we'll end up? Tell you one thing - staring at the stars didn't answer much." Shrugging his shoulders he flicked a piece of fluff from the quilt. "I even wondered whether we should go our separate ways."

Mild panic surged through her gut. Glancing down at his wife Oliver continued, "Then the sun came up and it dawned on me – the only thing I'm sure about is that I love you. You've gone a bit crazy lately - I assume it's to do with everything that's being going on, and maybe your age. But you don't need to go nuts over something you heard in the heat of the moment. Or rather - think you heard." He hugged her again. "We're worth more than that, aren't we? Why would I risk spoiling things?"

Why indeed - but he hadn't actually answered the question.

"So you're not having an affair with Lucy Lastic?" she asked.

"How can you even doubt me? I shouldn't have to keep going over and over what you already know. I'm here aren't I? And there's no need to talk about her like that."

"I just want to hear you say it, that's all."

"Don't be daft."

Cate glared.

"Okay, okay, if it makes you happy." Looking up to the ceiling, Ollie held up both hands in surrender. "There's nothing going on; does that satisfy you?" He kissed her on the head. "Better start getting ready or they'll be one student short of a graduation. Forget the last couple of months. I love you; just remember that and stop being stupid."

She let a smug grin slip out. Her husband was telling the truth; 99.9% certain. If he was up to something, he definitely wasn't doing it now. Without doubt it was over - if it ever existed in the first place; she could make plans for the future, and concentrate on becoming a journalist.

The morning spilled into the afternoon with a wave of showering, plucking, shaping and brushing. By the time Cate and Oliver arrived at the university, Samantha was sitting prettily under the shade of a white-blossom tree.

Reflecting off a silver plaque in the grass a beam of sunlight accentuated her pale complexion against the shadow, highlighting her sparkling green eyes and elegant visage.

"Hi," said Cate, embracing her friend, and catching hold of one hand. "You look gorgeous."

"Thank you, so do you," she replied.

Lightly kissing one cheek Oliver glanced at the cleavage on display. Her bosom fitted neatly into the strapless black and vanilla taffeta.

"Very pretty dress," he said smiling mischievously, "lovely fabric."

Sam grinned.

"Yes, it's moral fibre - you wouldn't know much about that."

Seizing the opportunity to intervene, Cate spotted Mr Ball in the crowd investigating the female graduands. He looked striking in a dark suit and pale silk tie, with his strong features and well-groomed stubble. It was sweet of him to come, but sad that George wasn't there to witness her moment of glory.

Leading the party across campus she entered the sports hall with her best friend, leaving the men outside to discuss the hot weather and abundance of short skirts. It took fifteen minutes to arrange and pin a mortar board and gown to perfection; enough time to update Samantha and persuade her that she was wrong about Ollie. He clearly confirmed he was not having an affair.

"I'm really happy for you," said Sam, looking vaguely convinced. "As long as you're sure about everything."

"I am." Cate smiled at the reflection in the mirror. "My bum's not sticking out, is it?"

"Please don't make me stare at your bottom. Talking of which, I wish you hadn't invited Mr Eyeball; he gives me the creeps. There's something very odd about him; and the way he looks at you scares me. I think he's lining you up to be his next victim."

Cate sighed.

"He didn't murder his wife."

"You know what I mean."

"He's just a little eccentric. How boring would it be if we were all the same? Anyway, he's really been there for me since George died; even picking me up from uni, he was amazing. He always pops up at the right moment - especially when Ollie goes missing – he's so sweet."

"Yes," said Sam, straightening the silky gown. "Doesn't that strike you as a bit strange? He must be watching your house."

"Of course not; if he's on duty late at night and sees the car missing, he worries about me. That's all."

"I worry about you; but mainly with regard to your sanity. That - and your blatant inability to avoid villainous men."

Flicking her hair over one shoulder Cate smiled sweetly.

"Why do you always think there's something sinister going on? You're too suspicious."

"You're too trusting. What if he orchestrated the whole thing just to get close to you? Perhaps he saw an opportunity after you asked him to follow Ollie."

Pouting into the mirror, she eyed her companion.

"How could he have done that? He couldn't have known George was going to die."

Staring into the glass she watched the colour drain from her own face.

"You okay?" said Sam. "You look like you've seen a ghost."

"Oh – my – God."

"What? What is it? Have you forgotten something?"

"No," said Cate, covering her cheeks with her hands. "I've remembered something. He said - it looks like a heart attack if you know what you're doing. But I didn't take him serious." Turning to face Sam she lowered her voice. "What if he did kill his wife? He could've done the same thing to George. Oh shit, he wanted to bump Ollie off as well; it's all my fault. I'm an accessory."

The hall was bustling with excited students, some showing an interest in the anxious conversation. Looking around nervously Samantha grasped her elbow, pulling her to one side.

"I told you he wasn't normal. You have to call the police," she said staring wide-eyed.

"I can't, what if…they think I'm involved." Tears bulged on her lower lid.

"Don't be ridiculous."

"But it was me, I gave the murderer a key to the house; and I'm a beneficiary. Supposing they accuse me of having an affair with Iain to get him to do away with George?"

Taking a deep breath Sam forced a smile.

"Calm down," she said squeezing her friend's hand. "We're jumping to conclusions here, and anyway there's no reason they would think that."

Cate chewed her lip.

"No, no; you've got to be kidding me," said Sam. "What the hell? I thought you were trying to save your marriage – not wreck your life. Tell me you are not shagging the psychopath."

"Not exactly. I was upset – and we just had a bit of a cuddle."

Sam stared in astonishment.

"Unbelievable. When?" she said, placing her hands on her hips.

"Last night. Ollie disappeared, and Mr Eyeball happened to be passing. He popped in to make sure I was okay."

"I bet he did. Well you're going to have to go through with your graduation now, and consider the consequences of anything else later." Pulling a tissue from her bag she carefully dabbed a tear from Cate's face, and kissed her on the cheek. "Idiot," she whispered.

"You don't really think..?" said Cate.

Sam shrugged.

"What? That the mysterious Mr Eyeball is a murderer? All things considered, I doubt it; but perhaps you better keep your 'little cuddle' to yourself. Your judgement - or lack of it - is incredible." Linking arms with her friend, she ushered her towards the door. "You're a complete nightmare."

Sam was right; she should push recent events to the back of her mind, where they could reside innocuously with her other dark secrets and skeletons. It was a moment of madness brought about by her recent stress. Actually, there were a few bouts of temporary insanity over the years, since the New Zealand incident; but nothing worth mentioning, and certainly not now. All relationships endured little tests from time to time; no-one could ever replace Ollie. She could focus on the future; there was definitely nothing going on between him and the Watts girl.

The marquee was packed with chairs and proud relations. Next to a large flower arrangement the Cooke party found seats at the end of row H. Although several metres from the small raised dais at the front it was close enough to view of the constant procession of speakers and graduands. Students were seated in a block adjacent to their guests. Cate waved discreetly as the journalists were called forward to line up.

"You must be full of emotion Oliver," said the handsome Mr Ball, nudging his neighbour as he spoke. Ensconced between the two he obscured Sam's view, but it was obvious that Ollie was preoccupied with his mobile phone.

"Full of something," she interjected scathingly. Leaning forward to gain advantage she reiterated. "Do you feel emotional - Oliver?"

"Indubitably - Samantha. I may burst into tears at any moment. Any idea how much longer this is going to take?"

She sighed.

"After your darling wife receives her certificate I believe there's another thirty minutes - according to the programme. Perhaps if you paid more attention to what's going on you would know. Who the hell have you been texting all the way through anyway?"

"I don't believe that's any of your business, and perhaps if you paid *less* attention to what you *think* is going on, we'd all be much happier."

Without turning his head Mr Ball observed them both in turn out the corner of his eye, glimpsing first towards Oliver and then Sam.

"Let's just watch the awards, shall we," he said, smiling diplomatically.

"I'm watching," said Samantha raising her hand and pointing her index and middle fingers at the men like a snake tongue. "I'm watching you both, very carefully."

Shaking hands with the Vice Chancellor Cate paused for the photographer before moving off stage. It was a glorious moment that nothing could spoil. Looking triumphant in her silk gown and mortar board she beamed at her applauding guests, and waited for the signal to join them.

Oliver tapped out a final text before discreetly slipping his phone into his pocket.

'its not over yet babe'

Cate smiled at her husband. She was happy; no-one else mattered. They were the perfect Bellini.

Christie Barton grew up in Bedfordshire, the second daughter of a civil engineer and a lampshade factory worker. She worked in the financial services industry for two decades before swapping employment for study.

After graduating from the University of Northampton Christie worked for a local magazine before joining independent filmmaker, FanaticFilms.

19128593R00133

Printed in Great Britain
by Amazon